ARAN

THE KNIGHTS OF THE BRENIN GUARD

P. L. HANDLEY

For Sarah and Ellis

1

THE STABLEBOY

Aran had never liked horses.

"Brush him, don't prod him, Aran!" barked his Uncle Gwail one morning.

This was a lot easier said than done, for Aran knew full well that the towering monstrosity above his quivering head was no ordinary horse. Named after his uncle's favourite beverage, Meaden was the most valuable steed on the entire farm. With a neck the size of a tree trunk, and more muscles than the boy had freckles, Meaden had been prepared for greatness since the very beginning.

Aran had never forgotten the way that determined newborn first leapt up on its perfectly formed hoofs, stumbling amongst the hay, without a care or worry in the world. Unlike Aran, that foal with the shaking legs and squinting eyes would someday go on to leave this small holding at the foot of the hill. There were adventures ahead of Meaden that he could only dream of.

"That horse's worth more than you are," said Gwail. "And don't you ever forget it!" This was not the first time Gwail had uttered such words, and it would not be the last.

Aran looked up at the horse's elegant mane; it flowed down

the back of his head like a stream of bright silver. The pure thoroughbred glanced back at him with a snort of disapproval. Meaden was a work of art — and the horse knew it.

Aran, on the other hand, was a stableboy. The most *he* could ever hope for on this cold and drizzly morning was not being smashed in the head by one of Meaden's enormous hind legs. His Uncle Gwail's limping walk was living proof of what these animals were capable of (not that it had ever discouraged Gwail).

The farmer scratched away at his hard and ragged chin. An overgrowth of wild, scruffy hair covered most of his face, whilst his eyes were scrunched up into a permanent scowl.

"We haven't got time for being scared," said Gwail.

But Aran *was* scared. He was *terrified*, in fact. The boy flinched as his uncle snatched away the brush and thrashed it hard against Meaden's silky coat. At that very moment, Aran knew exactly where he preferred to be (and it was far away from the backside of some hairy animal).

Gwail Saddler had been breeding horses his entire life. Although he had never taken much pride in his appearance (Aran was doubtful if his uncle had ever even *seen* a razor blade, let alone used one), there was no question that he knew these animals better than anyone.

"The act of bringing a horse into this world is not something to be taken lightly," Gwail had always said.

Although the farm was a modest home, Gwail's natural talent for churning out four-legged beasts had always put food on the table. Patience and discipline was the key. According to Gwail, it took years of strict dedication and expert knowledge to produce a good horse. But a good horse was not enough, not for Gwail. His stallions had to carry some of the finest horsemen in the entire kingdom, and the finest horsemen deserved the finest horses. But it was not the horses that interested Aran; it was the people who would go on to ride them.

Aran had only ever seen a Brenin once in his short life, and it was not a memory that would leave him anytime soon. A Brenin was not merely a mounted swordsman, but an elite protector of the Queen herself. To serve as the Queen's most personal guard required far more than skills with a blade. To become a knight of the Brenin Guard required a brave and noble blood (not the stewed, manure-covered blood of a mere horse servant).

Aran had never been strong, and he had never been quick, but he did possess more than enough imagination to become anything he ever wanted. With enough solitude and inspiration, he could even become a Brenin (or, at least, he could for the afternoon).

Beyond the rooftops of Penarth Farm were the sprawling trees of Skelbrei Forest, and beyond those were a cluster of stone walls. The ruins of Lanbar were the last remaining echoes of a long-forgotten castle, which many centuries ago had towered high above the ever-descending landscape. Aran had spent many of his afternoons amongst these ghostly structures. The temptation to explore their various caverns and beaten-down walls had proven far too much to resist, even for a cautious boy like him. From now on there would be a new king of the castle, and *his* armoury consisted of a carved-up rolling pin and a flimsy wooden stick.

That afternoon, after a couple of hours fending off an entire army of imaginary invaders, Aran had somehow found himself on a rather unexpected foot chase through Skelbrei Forest. Running was yet another activity that Aran had never particularly excelled at. Still, it was surprising how fast a pair of legs would carry someone when they were being hunted down by the likes of Pedrog and Fugris.

The two teenagers from Madoc Farm may have been strong, and they may have been quick, but their sense of balance and agility was soon being tested by the forest's vast array of deep potholes. Weaving around this maze of Morwallian oak had so far proven quite effective, but it was only a matter of time before a twisted ankle and a misjudged slide would change all of that.

After a hard fall — and an even harder landing — Aran's last chances of escape had quickly evaporated. As he lied there, flat on his back against a muddy footpath, his view of the curling branches in the skies above became eclipsed by the emergence of a giant forehead. In Aran's mind, there was nothing more terrifying than the sight of Fugris' pimple-infested face glaring back at him with those beady eyes. That toothy grin and flaring nostrils had often reminded him of one of Gwail's horses. And Aran had never liked horses.

Fugris and Pedrog, however, were very much in their element. The pleasure of seeing their helpless victim squirm around against the beaten-down track only fuelled their passion for cruelty even further. They normally would have settled for the occasional stray cat, or even an injured rabbit, but today they had hit the jackpot.

Aran let out a horrified screech, as the solid heel of Pedrog's great boot trod down against his twisted ankle. His cries for help echoed across the entire forest. It was during this unlikely moment that the young stableboy came across something that would change his small world forever. Even as the brutish force of Fugris' oversized foot came crushing down against his tiny joints, Aran's main focus was on the angelic figure making its way towards them through the rising mist.

Unbeknownst to his captors, the mysterious horseman floated behind them like a wandering spirit, his helmet glistening in the beams of harsh sunlight. Distracted by the mesmerising power of this impressive figure, Aran's pain had all but melted away. That striking emblem on the stranger's chest was an image he would recognise anywhere. It had become quite evident that this stranger was more than just a soldier on the back of a horse. His red-plated armour and fiery helmet could have meant only one thing: this was a knight of the Brenin Guard.

These smartly dressed warriors were not only the highest-ranking horsemen in the entire military, but also some of the greatest fighters in the Kingdom of Morwallia.

The only thing more impressive than a Brenin was the appearance of his humongous sword. This immaculate piece of steel had already found itself hovering beneath the stray hairs of Fugris' chin, and the high-pitched scream that followed was something Aran would cherish for many months to come.

"Do you wish to make *me* your next victim, oh brave one?" asked the Brenin, in a deep, commanding voice.

Both teenagers became weak at the knees. Pedrog whimpered at the sight of the sharp blade against his friend's quivering jaw.

"What brave young men are these who spend their days tormenting small creatures?" he continued. "If you value your tongue boy, I would suggest you use it!"

With his head raised high, and his body shaking, Fugris stammered his way through a response.

"W-w-we, uh — we meant him no harm, Sir!" said the teenager.

His eyes pleaded for mercy, until the Brenin pulled away his sword.

"We were merely trying to help our little friend here," added a blubbering Pedrog, who was now scrambling to help Aran to his feet.

"Exactly!" agreed Fugris. "We would never wish pain on anyone — especially ourselves!"

He dusted off the remaining dirt from the stableboy's clothes.

"I should hope not," said the knight. "For every scratch I find on that boy's body, I shall create *twice* as many on your own, all with the tip of my freshly sharpened sword."

The two farmhands looked down towards Aran's bramble-shredded legs. One look at the myriad of cuts and bruises sent them scrambling towards the nearest bank.

"But why the great haste, my dear boys?" the knight called out. "It will only take but a second!"

Aran struggled to contain his excitement. The soldier turned to face him.

"Do you find the misery of others amusing, boy?"

Aran felt a sudden rush of fear. He immediately shook his head.

"Not at all, Sir!" he cried.

"Good," replied the knight. "Revenge is a serious matter."

The Brenin placed his sword firmly back in its sheath and jerked his horse back towards the path. Aran watched the effort-less grace with which this accomplished rider moved. The stableboy's eyes were still wide open in awe when the man turned back his head to reveal a cheeky grin.

"No matter how much fun it might sometimes be," the Brenin added.

The man slipped him a playful wink before continuing on his way.

Aran turned his focus to the striking emblem on the back of the knight's armour. A red dragon spiralled around with its giant claws, as if reaching out to grab him, before it faded away into the distant mist.

2

THE KINGDOM OF EMLON

The surprising encounter in Skelbrei Forest had left quite an impression on Aran. The chances of seeing a Brenin on the North Island were very slim indeed, especially so far from the capital.

Little did he know that this euphoric feeling would soon to be trampled on by the harsh reality of his neglected chores. Gwail was in no mood to hear about his exciting journey back from the old ruins, nor did he care that much for the sudden appearance of a mysterious horseman. The following day they were due a visitor, and Gwail would be damned if the farm stables weren't in immaculate condition from top to bottom.

Every year, the Earl of Falworth made a special journey to a remote farm on the outskirts of Galamere. It was during these regular visits that the lord was finally reunited with, what he considered to be, his *"finest investment"*.

Lord Falworth and the keeper of Penarth Farm had been friends for many years. But it was the birth of a young foal named Meaden that had really brought these two men together. Falworth had very high hopes for his eldest son, Tarin, who in less than a year would be embarking on his long-awaited journey to become a knight of the Brenin Guard. To succeed in this highly ambitious endeavour, he would first need to participate in an event as old as the Guard itself: the Brenin Tourney. Hosted by the Queen herself, the tournament had long produced some of the greatest knights in all of Morwallia. In order to join such an illustrious list, Tarin would first need a stallion who was as gifted as he was. Fortunately, the proud lord knew *exactly* where to find one.

Word of their latest visit had proven very bad news for Aran, who had gone on to spend the rest of his afternoon shovelling piles of fresh manure with nothing but a small spade and a broken wheelbarrow. Even with the fumes of rotting horse dung burning through his lungs, it was impossible not to be distracted by the haunting memories of that gleaming sword cutting through the air.

The evenings on Penarth Farm were not that much different from the day. There were, at least, fewer menial tasks to be done (which was perfectly fine by Aran).

After the horrors of his uncle's experimental rabbit stew, Aran spent the rest of his time buried in his favourite book. His uncle had quite a measly selection of reading material (most of which consisted of uninspiring farming manuals and neglected cookery books). But there was one book in particular that had always stood out from the rest.

Sir Vangarn and the Kingdom of Emlon was, according to many people, one of the greatest adventures ever written. Although generally dismissed as nothing more than a children's fairy tale, it was a story that had been around for a very long time. With little else to entertain him during those long winter nights, the book had soon become one of Aran's most devoured reads.

A Rider can only be destroyed from within, read the opening line. Named after the impenetrable metal that formed their green body armour, the Riders of Emlon were a group of ruthless assassins from a far, distant land — an ancient kingdom that many had searched for but very few had ever managed to find.

"The Kingdom of Emlon is a myth," Gwail had always said. Still, it was a myth that had proven extremely popular amongst the people of Morwallia, and Aran was no exception.

On most nights he would delve into that bundle of old, tattered pages and lose himself in the greatest story ever told. On *this* particular night, however, the book remained closed. Aran stared at the bedroom ceiling, his mind wandering and his imagination on fire. He couldn't help but wonder what the knight he had encountered in Skelbrei Forest would do if *he* ever came across an Emlon Rider. The idea was far too exciting to even comprehend.

He blew out his candle and turned over to one side. As he lied there in the darkness, another, more important, question scorched his overactive mind: *what would Sir Aran of Penarth Farm do?*

These dreams continued long into the night, and it wasn't until the early arrival of their special guests that Aran was unwillingly pulled back into reality.

"How is my precious Meaden fairing, old friend?" asked Lord Falworth, only moments after his carriage door had swung open. After a brief struggle up the short footpath to Gwail's front door, the overweight man embraced the farmer with a hearty squeeze.

"Far better than we are!" replied Gwail.

His guest let out a booming laugh, as they patted each other on the back. Stood beside this bearded man was a small girl. Almost half the size of her father's great waist, Sarwen was no stranger to this remote farm. Aran watched her from the safety of his bedroom window, her golden hair flowing in the icy breeze.

"Aran!" summoned his uncle. Aran knew exactly what was

coming. Every year, the young stableboy was expected to play host to this spoilt, little rich girl and her winging voice.

Sarwen had always been a reluctant traveller. And yet, despite the frequent protests and exhausting arguments, Falworth was adamant that these annual excursions would do his daughter the world of good. For there was once a time when he too had roamed the earthy soils of Galamere's woodlands as a youth.

"A bit of mud and grass will do you no harm," he told her.

Sarwen had very much begged to differ. She could think of nothing worse than a whole day in that gloomy forest with some worthless stableboy by her side. The fact that her brother was allowed to stay home only aggravated her prickly demeanour even more.

Aran had only ever come across Tarin on a handful of occasions, but he had heard far more about his perfect ways than he cared to remember. From Sarwen's perspective, her brother was a fine example of what every young boy should strive to become: strong, dashing, confident – everything this clueless farm boy was certainly not.

Despite her reluctance, Aran was determined to show his irritable guest that there was far more fun to be had in the middle of nowhere than a person might think. *Surely the ruins of an old castle would impress anyone, wouldn't they?*

"Where are you taking me, horse boy?" Sarwen asked, as they began making their way up a muddy path.

"It's not much further," Aran lied.

Once they were deep amongst the tall oaks of the forest, he could sense that the power had very much shifted in his direction. There was not a chance in the world that Sarwen would ever find her way back to the farm at this stage of the route. Unfortunately for Aran, Sarwen was well aware of this fact.

When the reality of her situation had finally sunk in, her

temper flared up like a burning hot rash. She had now become dependent on the very same person she had chosen to berate for the last hour and a half.

"You little toad!" she cried. "You're doing this on purpose. You wait until my father finds out how you got us both lost. He'll have both you and your smelly, old uncle thrown in a hole!"

Aran ignored her. He knew this forest better than anyone, and the sour look on his companion's face made that fact well worth keeping to himself.

"Answer me, horse boy!" she screamed.

Aran tried to contain his amusement. He hated the name *horse boy*.

Before Sarwen could throw yet another tantrum (one that could quite easily have shaken every last leaf from the branches above their heads), Aran pointed to a small opening up ahead in the distance.

Beyond the last branches of the forest was a great mound. On top of this mound were the bare remains of a great fortress. Having once stood tall on its grassy perch, the solid structure had withered away into nothing more than a scattering of receding walls. The harsh stone, even to this day, was completely out of place in these green and luscious surroundings.

Realising that they had reached their final destination, Sarwen shoved her small guide out of the way and marched straight towards the seclusion of the old ruins.

It wasn't long before they were both sliding down the bank of a surrounding moat. Overgrown and slippery, this dried-out ditch was anything but dry. It also served as a great reminder of Aran's severe lack of natural balance. He slid down the bank with an ever-increasing speed, until he reached the bottom with an inevitable squelch.

With his face planted in a puddle of thick mud, he could hear Sarwen's high-pitched laughter still ringing in his soggy ears. It had also been the first laugh he had drawn from her that entire afternoon.

After another long climb, they had reached the edges of the southern wall. The ruins appeared much larger in person, and behind them was a view that even Sarwen couldn't help but admire. It was like standing on the stage of a rising amphitheatre, with an audience of surrounding valleys that appeared to go on forever. It was no wonder that Aran had spent so much time amongst these old relics. From up here, you could see everything, like a lone kestrel, soaring across the sky.

Sarwen let out a rare smile from her cold, chapped lips. The sight of an orange glow in the middle of the horizon gave her an outbreak of tiny goosebumps. The spires of Gala stuck out like tiny needles in the far distance. On the other side there was Lake Carreg, its still waters glistening with the white reflection of the passing clouds.

"What do you think?" asked Aran with a proud smirk.

Sarwen turned around to face him.

"You call this a castle?" She pointed to a line of crumbled walls and folded up her arms in protest. "There's hardly anything left."

Before Aran could even let out a disappointed sigh, his eyes widened at the sight of an enormous stone heading straight towards them.

"Lookout!" he cried.

Sarwen looked up to see the object go flying past, only inches away from her carefully maintained scalp. They both shuddered in relief as it went crashing down against a nearby wall.

Over in the distance was a familiar pair of local farm boys. They stood there, side by side, grinning in amusement. Clutched in their arms was a rather worrying selection of rocks, which had been gathered specially for their newly discovered sport.

"Where's your knight in shining armour now, little princess?" called Fugris.

"Looks like we have *two* little princesses today!" his brother chimed in.

Aran looked over towards the two siblings. They were already gearing up for their next throw.

"Follow me!" he said, grabbing Sarwen by the arm.

"They almost hit me!" she cried in return. Her horrified face was still distracted by the aftermath of fallen rock.

"Then we'd better not let them have another go."

Aran pulled her around the maze of crumbled walls. He knew these ruins all too well, and he was not going to be outwitted by a pair of mindless teenagers with more firepower than brains.

A bombardment of flying stones soon followed, as the two brothers came charging towards them with flailing arms.

"Let go of me!" cried Sarwen. "You're hurting my arm!"

Her words did not faze Aran in the slightest. He'd squeeze tighter if it meant dodging the next incoming meteor shower. Before she could complain any further, an explosion of rock stopped them dead in their tracks. Sarwen's scream was loud enough to bring down the entire castle.

Clouds of dust swept up from either side of them. Having only narrowly dodged yet another volley of stones, they continued on towards the heart of the old ruin.

When they reached the final corner, a nervous Sarwen began tugging away at her small guide.

"It's a dead end!" she cried. "Those filthy pigs are going to trap us!"

She pointed towards the huge obstruction blocking their path.

Sarwen gasped; two curly-haired heads were now bobbing their way along on the other side of the wall. They could hear the brothers sniggering away, as they followed their prey into a welcomed trap. She turned to Aran, who, to her great surprise, seemed to have a peculiar looking twinkle in his eye.

Fugris' vile breath spilled out into the damp air. He let out an excited grin and turned to his brother. Around the next corner were two helpless victims, and, as luck would have it, there were still plenty of rocks left over to spare. Fugris hushed his eager sibling and crept slowly towards the edge of the wall. They had reached the centre of the ancient maze, and the grand prize was a pair of helpless victims with nowhere left to run.

The two farmhands gave one last chortle of excitement before leaping around the corner. Fugris' large jaw dropped open to reveal a line of rotten teeth. Their handfuls of rocks stumbled to the ground.

A deserted wall stood before them — a completely empty space — where two small children had seemingly vanished without a trace. What would once have been the private quarters of a wealthy ruler was now a roofless square lined with rubble. A flock of crows cackled in the opening up above, mocking them, with their sharp, smirking beaks.

The confused brothers searched around in disbelief.

Could they really have disappeared? Had they just evaporated into thin air?

These were just some of the questions grazing the shallow surfaces of their simple minds. They were beginning to wonder whether the two children had ever existed at all.

It wasn't exactly unheard of for such an ancient structure to be haunted, especially one as ghostly as Lanbar. And there were few other explanations to come up with. As dim-witted as the two brothers were, even they knew that there was only one way out — and that was back the way they came.

As always, there were a lot of things that these two farm hands didn't know. Down in the ground below their feet, two tiny figures were making their way through a winding underground tunnel. Aran had discovered this secret passage quite some time ago. He suspected it had once served as an important escape route, a last resort that had been used to good effect during an infamous siege. Hundreds of years later, it had saved the day, once again, by outwitting two of the most clumsy and incompetent invaders to have ever graced Lanbar Castle.

The tunnels curled beneath the ground like a colony of earthworms. They chomped through the soil, twisting and turning, their insides dripping from the surrounding dampness.

Aran took great comfort from the fact that one of these earthy intestines would lead them all the way back out towards the other side of the hill (which is how he had discovered the secret passageways in the first place).

Sarwen stepped carefully over the small puddles beneath her feet. The traumatic experience on the ground above had made her unusually quiet (something that came as a soothing relief to her ever-suffering guide). All she cared about now was remaining out of harm's way.

Whilst she was more focused on the dryness of her toes, Aran was busy rubbing his hands across the dribbling walls on either side of them. He hoped that, somehow, they would eventually lead them in the right direction.

"My brother would have killed them both," muttered Sarwen.

Aran stiffened. He knew the silence had been too good to be true. They continued down another series of passageways until they were met with an unexpected fork in the path.

"It's this way," said Aran, who immediately turned right. Sarwen froze into place and folded up her arms.

"How do you know?" she asked.

Aran turned around. "Because that's the way out. I've done it before."

"But we'll just be heading back to where we came from." She pointed to the lefthand path. "Your way is heading west; we want to go east."

Aran was quickly losing his patience.

"How on earth can you tell which way is west or east?" he snapped. "You can't even see the sun from down here!"

Sarwen was taken aback. This was the first time her gentle companion had ever attempted to raise his voice at her. Not even those tormenting farm hands would have brought this side out of him — but *she* had.

Aran let out a deep sigh and turned to walk away.

"Fine," he said, "Go your own way. See if I care."

Sarwen didn't know whether to feel upset or angry. Her usual reaction would have been to bite the head off of anyone who even dared to speak to her the way Aran had just done. Even her overbearing father had always made sure to tread carefully whenever she was in a bad mood.

At this point, she was both very hungry and very tired. But she refused to let the growing urge to break down and sob get the better of her. She would show that good-for-nothing *horse boy*.

"Fine!" she called out.

Her determined frown melted away, as she watched him disappear into the darkness. Sarwen took a long, deep breath and turned around to follow her preferred route.

The tunnel up ahead was much darker than the previous one. Sarwen followed her palm against the rough stone, her small feet tiptoeing through the soggy mud. Drops of falling water echoed from either side, and the hollow silence sent a chill down the entire base of her quivering neck. Her eyes had barely adjusted to the lack of light, and the cold had now become unbearable. She tried hard to ignore the fact that she was now aimlessly wandering around the hidden bowels of an old, deserted castle (and a castle she hadn't much cared for in the first place).

It wasn't long, however, before her sinking heart had reignited into a dancing frenzy. Up ahead was a piercing stream of daylight — a ray of glimmering hope — creeping in through a small, rusted grate in the ceiling above.

She began to hurry, desperate for a closer look. With any luck, there might have been a chance to escape this forsaken prison after all.

She hopped and skipped across a series of tiny puddles, until something hard and solid caused her to freeze into place. Overcome by a surge of terror, she forced herself to look down.

Her mouth went dry. She realised now that the peculiar object brushing up against the ankle of her right foot was not actually a rock; it was a large, human hand.

3

THE SECRET OF LANBAR

S arwen screamed.

Her foot had gone sliding forwards through the mud, causing the rest of her body to fly backwards. Confused and disorientated, the small girl opened her eyes to find that she was now lying flat on her back in the wet dirt.

The sight of a pale face looking back at her prompted a second shriek.

"Sarwen!" cried the gentle voice. "It's *me...*"

Sarwen squinted through her blurred vision to find a concerned Aran crouched over her.

"Aran?" she said. "What are you doing here?"

"What do you think?" he replied, whilst pulling her up from the mud. "I thought you were in trouble."

After a short pause to recover from the shock, her eyes widened. She cried out and shoved him away.

"It's still there! That *thing* is still there!"

She pointed towards the large hand. It clawed its way up from the ground and reached out towards them. Sarwen squeezed her eyelids shut — she couldn't bear to look.

"It's a body — a horrible, dead body!"

Aran stared down at the hand. He had never seen a dead body before, and he was fairly certain Sarwen hadn't either. But he *had* seen a dead crow, and the smell of that had been bad enough. Still, it was not an odour that seemed to be present in *this* tunnel.

He was certain that his companion was very much mistaken (not that he'd ever tell her that).

"What are you doing?!" she cried.

She watched as Aran placed his hand on the body's forearm and wiped away the mud. Whatever it was, it had been buried there for quite some time.

Aran worked his way along the arm, digging at the dirt, until his fingers rested against a solid breastplate. This was no dead corpse.

"I can't believe you're actually touching it," said Sarwen. She covered up her mouth in an attempt not to gag. "You farm people are disgusting."

Aran looked back at her and smiled. His eyes twinkled in the spears of light coming down through the grate, as he gave the forearm a sudden tug.

Sarwen let out a revolted groan.

"You filthy monster!" she shrieked, "You pulled its arm off!"

Aran lifted up the separated hand that was now dangling from his own.

"It's a gauntlet," he said. "An empty one." His face had lit up so much that it could have quite easily illuminated the entire tunnel.

This was the first gauntlet he had ever come across. He had spent many hours over the years trying to make his own, of course, but his uncle wasn't best pleased at having his favourite pair of work gloves ruined.

Aran pulled away the rest of the so-called "corpse" so that it bathed in a pool of light. His throat drained away the last ounce of moisture it had left.

Lying there in the tunnel was a full suit of body armour, all with its various pieces still intact.

"Who on earth put that there?" asked Sarwen. "I could have broken my neck."

Her fear of this motionless body had at last been melted away by the revealing sunlight.

"Whoever it was," said Aran. "They're not from Galamere."

He admired the impressive craftsmanship before wiping his hand across the breastplate. The lumps of dirt fell away to reveal a bright, green-coloured metal.

"I've never seen armour like that before," said Sarwen.

Sarwen watched his fingertips caressing the smooth exterior, as if it were the scalp of a baby's head. It felt neither cold, nor warm. Sat in the middle of the breastplate was an insignia unlike anything he had ever come across.

His hands trembling, he tore out a single page from his tiny scrapbook and placed it directly across the middle of the plate. Then, he began frantically scrubbing a layer of thick dirt accross the thin paper, his muddy fingers tracing carefully along the well-defined edges of the deep grooves.

Sarwen watched with great fascination, as he held up the finished drawing against the nearby grate. Backlit by the glowing daylight, an elegant pattern was suddenly revealed. Aran grinned.

"Do you think it's from another kingdom?" he asked.

Sarwen shook her head and looked back at the armour.

"That rusty old thing?" said Sarwen kicking her foot against the hollow shell. She yelped out, having painfully underestimated its solid exterior.

"Someone must have hidden it here on purpose," said Aran. "Like buried treasure..."

He lifted up the gauntlet.

"Don't be so stupid," Sarwen snapped. "What would a little farm boy like you know about treasure?"

"I know what steel and iron looks like. This is definitely not any of those."

"If it's so valuable then why would someone just leave it here?" she asked.

"Maybe they're coming back."

Aran drew a short of breath. A surge of fear passed through his body.

What if the owner of this hidden treasure was still alive? What if they were... a cold-blooded murderer?

"We should probably get moving," he said.

"Well I hadn't exactly planned on staying in this wretched hole overnight," said Sarwen, who was still picking mud out from her hair.

She watched Aran scramble across the armour as he searched for the other arm. The various pieces were carefully sculpted to cover every ligament of the human body. They were also as light as a feather, a surprising weight considering that most armour was designed to withstand the fiercest blows from the sharpest of swords.

There was no doubt in Aran's mind that whatever this suit was made of, it had not been forged in the North Island of Morwallia — *that* was for certain. He felt a strange tingling sensation against his raw skin, as he searched each piece with the tips of his frozen fingers.

With a gentle click, he unhinged the second gauntlet and held up both pieces.

"I can't believe we found these by accident," he said.

"You mean I found them!" said Sarwen.

"Only because you were going the wrong way."

She couldn't deny that one; it was quite clear that they had reached a dead end.

Sarwen gazed at the two gauntlets, her eyes hypnotised by their dazzling colour. Their emerald surfaces were lit up by the beams of light creeping through behind her, and both artefacts were now reflecting in the centre of her enlarged pupils.

"I'll keep this one, and you can have the other," said Aran.

An intrigued smile crept across Sarwen's face, as he handed her a gauntlet. She clutched it tightly, its mysterious energy creeping over her for the very first time.

"We must never tell a living sole," Aran warned. "I'm sure there are people out there who would love to get their hands on one of these."

She saw the seriousness in his face.

"Well they won't," Sarwen replied. She held her new possession tight against her chest. "Because they belong to us now."

They both smiled.

Sarwen looked back at him with a newfound interest. She had greatly underestimated this peculiar stableboy from the edge of nowhere. There was a thirst for adventure inside of him that had somehow eluded her. She could see the excitement burning inside of him, longing to escape. This trip might well have proven worthwhile after all.

"I can keep a secret better than you can, *horse boy*."

Aran rolled his eyes. They both began digging up the earth below them until it covered up the remaining armour.

Sarwen didn't utter a single word on their entire journey back through the underground tunnels. This time, they took Aran's route with no protests or any disagreements. They headed all the way back to the other side of the ruins, until they were eventually greeted with the comforting glow of an evening sun across their grubby faces.

Those treasured new possessions, nestled deep at the

bottom of their trusty satchels, were so light, it was as if they were barely carrying anything at all.

From the moment they had left Lanbar's underground labyrinth, these two unlikely companions felt like the richest people in the entire kingdom. They both shared a secret that nobody else would ever know.

When they finally approached the front gates of Penarth Farm, Lord Falworth was stood in the middle of the yard. It was clear he had been waiting there for quite some time. His servant had already prepared the carriage for an imminent departure, and his expression was very different from the one he had presented earlier. He began pacing back and forth, his demeanour irritable and impatient.

Falworth watched his daughter making her way back into the yard. It wasn't long before her high spirits were dashed by her father's scornful frown.

"Where on earth have you two been?" asked Falworth. He had no interest in a reply. "We should have left this cursed place many hours ago."

Aran watched Sarwen being herded inside the carriage like a lost sheep. Something had severely ruffled this man's feathers whilst they had been away — so much so, that he was now grunting as he walked. He had barely acknowledged Aran's presence at all.

Before the stableboy knew it, the carriage was hurling away through the main gate. Sarwen peered out through the small window as it rode past him, her gaze honed in on Aran's. They exchanged an understanding nod.

It soon became apparent that Gwail was nowhere to be seen. Aran headed straight to the most likely place a person could find his uncle, which was surrounded by his beloved horses. Gwail had always preferred the company of these elegant animals (for they were far more reliable than any human being).

The art of conversation had never been the man's strongest attribute, and he found most discussions to be either dull, trivial, or a complete a waste of time. It was something Aran had grown perfectly used to. He would often spend most of his working days in the midst of a cold silence, and the only morsel of human speech he ever heard then was when he'd done something wrong. Indeed, Gwail was a man of few words — and harsh ones at that.

The two occupants of Penarth Farm shared very little in common, including their blood. According to Gwail, Aran had been dumped on him in an act of "pure cruelty". It was during the tail end of a harsh winter that the curious infant had landed on the farmer's doorstep. Gwail had already struggled to feed himself during that difficult season — let alone his animals — but someone had decided that the newborn was somehow better off with him than his own parents.

Gwail had always lived alone, and it was no secret amongst the locals of Galamere that he preferred to keep it that way. Although he knew nothing about raising a child, there had been countless thoroughbreds he had nurtured well into adulthood. As far as he saw it, horses required far more care and attention than any human being would ever need. If he was capable of raising the perfect stallion, then surely a newborn child would be no trouble at all.

As the years passed by, it soon became clear that this unique logic was also a very flawed one. Aran was not the perfect child, by any means. Gwail expected him to be the strongest, fastest and most skilled specimen that ever lived. Any failure of Aran's would also be his own. After a decade of ongoing frustration, and bitter disappointment, Gwail had come to a single, definitive conclusion: young foals, and small boys, were a very different breed.

Shortly after Lord Falworth's abrupt departure, Aran found

his uncle stomping around the stables with a furious expression on his face. He bashed his equipment and flung his tools through the air — actions that were normally a bad indication of an impending outburst. Aran knew better than to disturb him when his mood was this unstable, but something told him that there was more to this behaviour than a routine sulk.

"How dare that pathetic excuse for a man come into *my* home and insult me in such away," growled his uncle.

Aran was struggling to find the courage to speak. Instead, he merely stood back and watched, as the older man hobbled towards his favourite horse and patted him on the nose.

"Over my dead body will he ever get his dirty hands on you, boy."

Gwail brushed his rough fingers against Meaden's perfectly shaped snout. A great sadness washed over him. Even underneath all that overgrown hair, his eyes projected a look of growing sorrow. If Aran could have ever possessed the ability to read a person's mind, he would have done so right then.

The following day, life on the farm continued on as normal. Gwail was back to his muted, old self and the events of the previous day were never mentioned, nor spoken of, again.

Aran, on the other hand, had returned to his chores with a much reinvigorated enthusiasm. Even his uncle had noticed the unusual skip in his step, especially the cheerful way in which he shovelled horse manure into a rickety old wheelbarrow. It was back to the grindstone for Aran, but this time something was different.

Tucked underneath Aran's bed was his new secret, an artefact that he considered to be of epic proportions. Even as he lied awake at night, Aran could still feel the gauntlet's mighty presence, burning away beneath his mattress, calling out for it to be worn. He thought about the remaining pieces, and how they were still sleeping in a bed of dirt. Heaven forbid that the likes of

Pedrog or Fugris were to ever get their hands on them. Two imbeciles with a fortified breastplate was a sure recipe for chaos. Something had to be done, and Aran had decided that the rest of the armour would be far safer in his own possession.

The whereabouts of the gauntlet's previous owner was also a growing concern. If this person were indeed a cold-blooded killer, it would mean nothing to slit the throat of a thieving stableboy.

He lit up the candle by his bedside. Its warm glow shone against the scrap of torn paper he had used in the tunnel. Those traces of dried-up mud were now forming a unique glimpse into another world.

He couldn't wait any longer; Aran reached down and lifted up the gauntlet from underneath his bed, before he was once again mesmerised by its gentle beauty. His tiny arm had a long way to go before it would ever fit such a giant glove.

There were no scratches, no marks, and not a hint of any damage. It certainly did not feel like the kind of object that had been buried on a cold mountaintop for years on end. For all Aran knew, its furious owner was now scouring the nearby fields in search of the guilty thief. Aran tried his best not to give this idea too much thought, especially if he was going to try and get some sleep that night. With that in mind, he carefully placed the gauntlet back underneath the bed and blew out the candle.

4

THE GAUNTLET

Two days after his unpleasant altercation with Lord Falworth, Gwail had decided to take Meaden out for one of his regular excursions to the small town of Baladene. This journey to the next valley provided a straight enough ride that they could gallop most of the way. Horses hated being in one place for too long, as did Gwail. The farmer had never been quite the same since the Lord's visit, and a short ride across the vast plains to Baladene would do both himself and the horse the world of good.

Gwail set off long before dawn. His painful leg was now a distant memory, as he soared through the valley at great speed, his ragged hair blowing freely in the wind. Now he had four legs instead of two, and they were all far stronger than his own would ever be.

Aran watched his uncle go riding off into the distance. That long list of menial tasks he had been left with could now wait until the afternoon.

He stood outside the woodshed and held the gauntlet up towards the sun; it looked even more stunning in bright daylight. Along its edges were faint lines of silver patterns, like stars across an emerald sky. If the Gods themselves had been involved in the armour's creation, he would not have been surprised. It was hard to believe that something so sleek and beautiful had been designed to withstand such violence — not that it would need to any longer, Aran had assured himself.

He placed the gauntlet down against a wooden chopping block. Lifting up his uncle's favourite axe, he braced himself by clenching up his scrawny arms; he had to know for certain whether these nagging suspicions were true.

After a long, deep breath, he swung the blade high into the air. A deafening SMACK soon followed, which rattled his tiny eardrums. The backend of the heavy tool came bouncing back like a rubber mallet, and bashed its cowering user straight in the middle of the forehead.

Aran went flying backwards onto the floor. For a brief moment, he could have sworn he had been knocked out cold. Instead, he had nothing but a bulging red mark to show for it. After a moment of swirling stars, he climbed to his feet and clutched his sore head.

The gauntlet hadn't moved an inch. There it was, still lying there on the chopping block, without a scratch or dent in sight.

Aran was more than happy with the result to refrain from trying again. A single blow to the head would be enough for one morning. This painful experiment was all he had needed; that shining object in his hand was no ordinary piece of iron or steel. If the story of his favourite book was indeed true, no tool on the entire farm could ever hope to penetrate it.

A Rider can only be destroyed from within. The words from his favourite book whispered inside his mind.

Aran slid the gauntlet across his boney hand. He clenched his fist and waved it around as if it were no longer his own. It was now a force to be reckoned with, and he could swipe away any imaginary foe that dared to cross his path. He punched and chopped, hurling his body around the yard, until an accidental step sent him colliding into something hard, and solid.

Aran looked on in horror as his right fist went crashing through the middle of the woodshed door. He took one step back and admired the deep hole. His reinforced hand felt perfectly secure.

In a burst of increased confidence, Aran placed a wooden log down against the chopping block. He normally hated chopping wood (not that he ever hit his target), but now he had backup. He straightened his covered hand and sliced it downwards. With one foul swipe, the block of wood split straight into two pieces, like a freshly cut pork chop against the knife of a skilled butcher. Aran looked down at the gauntlet; he had felt nothing. An immense feeling of power washed over him.

After an afternoon of further experimentation, and far more wood chopping than he had ever done before, the sun had already began to dip down behind the surrounding hills.

"What the devil have you done to my woodshed?" growled his furious uncle upon his return.

"I was just... chopping some wood," replied a guilty looking Aran. "I suppose I missed."

They both stared at the gaping hole in the middle of the woodshed door. Gwail looked down at the small chopping block.

"You can say that again," he said. "Remind me never to let you handle that axe again, boy. Or you'll kill us all!"

Aran spent the rest of the night contemplating his great find. That mysterious shell had truly become one with his own body. He also began thinking about the remaining pieces that were still buried underneath the ruins, wasted, in piles of wet mud.

The thought of Sarwen also entered his mind. Did she also have an idea of what had gone home with her? Somehow these gauntlets gave them both a strange sense of connection. He could almost feel Sarwen clutching her own. Someday these two pieces would once again be reunited, and that gave him a strange sense of comfort.

Aran was certain that nobody else, at least from his own kingdom, had experienced anything quite like the power he had come across that afternoon. The way that warm substance had clung to the pores of his bare skin, pulsating, as if it were alive, almost breathing. It was a feeling no book, or poem, could ever hope to describe.

The following day, Aran made the steep excursion back towards Lanbar Castle. A large sack hung from his shoulders as he wove through the oaks of Skelbrei Forest. His body was camouflaged by a thick, green cloak. By passing through unde-tected, no ruin-dwelling predators would have any hope of tormenting him this time around.

It was an unusually clear morning up on the hillside. The ruins were far more visible than they had been on his last visit, and despite the peace and quiet, Aran had somehow found himself missing the continuous chatter of his former companion.

He had grown quite fond of Sarwen by the end of their eventful trip, and he had hoped that, somehow, the feeling might have been mutual. In many ways she had given him a courage he never knew he had. Being around Sarwen had made him feel safe (not that he would ever let *her* know this).

The orange sun was glaring against the edges of the crum-bling walls. What was normally an intimidating structure had now been stripped of its murky shadows and joyless colour.

Aran made his way through the labyrinth of underground tunnels, until he reached that all too familiar looking passage-way. The dead-end that Sarwen had previously discovered was as cold and dingy as they had left it. He dropped to his knees and began digging away at the layers of dirt. A nervous tingle caused him to pause.

What if it had gone? What if the owner had indeed returned, and was now lurking in the darkness behind him?

Soon enough he was hit with a wave of relief, as something hard and solid grazed the edge of his hand. It felt like the surface of a masked helmet.

Aran pulled up the first of many pieces, one for each body part. They were all as light as a feather, which meant carrying them back would be no problem at all. Had he been much larger in size, he could have quite easily have worn the entire suit without feeling a thing.

Not only was the armour strong, but it allowed for its small owner to be as loose or mobile as he or she wished (which could not be said for most other suits of armour). After collecting up the last piece, Aran hauled the entire bundle across his small back. With hardly any noticeable difference in weight, he felt stronger than a young horse (a rare feeling indeed).

He could hear clunking and rattling for the entire duration of his journey back down the hill. The pieces shook against his spine like a sack of iron kettles. The added noise was hardly a concern, for the boy was so light on his feet that he could quite easily have ran the remaining miles. He was so elated by his new discovery that even Meaden would have struggled to catch him.

By the time Aran had reached the last few fields, he had already come up with a suitable hiding place. He needed somewhere his uncle would never think to venture — somewhere secluded and hidden — where he knew the armour would be safe. Now that these instruments of warfare were at last in his possession, a creeping sense of responsibility had begun to take over. In the wrong hands, this clunking sack of metal could cause a lot of trouble indeed. It was far better off with him than to have been left around for some bandit to stumble on.

When he reached the farm gate, Gwail was nowhere to be seen. Aran made his way straight towards the back entrance of the house.

"Aran!"

The roar of his uncle's voice almost caused him to drop the entire sack.

"Aran!" called the voice again. "Don't play games with me, boy... I know it's you out there!"

Aran hauled up his sack and went rushing in the opposite direction. He darted across the yard, his back rattling away, until he passed the first corner.

The back door flew open. A series of pounding thuds became louder with each second.

In a burst of desperation, Aran continued around the house until he reached the front door. The sound of Gwail's boot followed after him. Soon there was nowhere left to hide, and he could feel the contents of his bag quivering as much as he was.

Aran looked up; the window above his head was wide open. With a last slither of hope, and one almighty heave, he lifted up the enormous sack and stuffed it straight through the small opening.

"Are you deaf, boy?"

Aran turned around to see his uncle standing there, only a few feet away. His piercing eyes sliced through him.

"Sorry, Uncle," he replied, trying to hide away his relief. "I thought you were in the stables."

The bushy eyebrow above Gwail's right eye curled up with suspicion.

"Well, we don't have time for any of your *thinking*," he said. "We need to be leaving."

Aran watched as he pushed past him with his crooked walking stick.

Moments later, they were scrambling around the kitchen,

gathering up any last useful objects they could find whilst stuffing them into old bags.

"But where are we going?" asked Aran.

Gwail bashed through the various cupboards above his head and began throwing a selection of cooking utensils into a pile.

"As far away from this cursed place as we can possibly get."

5

THE OUTLAW

"I should never have trusted that wretched snake in the first place."

Aran assumed that his uncle had been referring to Lord Falworth. He had experienced many of Gwail's tantrums over the years, but none had compared to the enormous outburst he had thrown that afternoon. The boy could sense that somewhere, deep down, beneath that raging anger was a sense of dread — or even fear. It was as if, somehow, he *knew* that something truly terrible was about to happen.

The farm had taken many years of hard labour to reach the standard it was in now. For his uncle to just dismiss the place so easily was a ruthless decision, even for him.

"We will leave at sunrise," said Gwail. "Anything that's not packed up will be left behind — no exceptions."

His last statement had come with very little objection. There were few possessions for Aran to even miss, and what he did own was of little value to anybody else.

That rather small book collection had provided many hours of escapism during those long winter evenings, but something told him that he wouldn't need escapism for very much longer. Those countless nights spent dreaming of other worlds was soon to be a distant memory. It was clear that Gwail had no intention of settling back down again any time soon.

"If we reach Tylbrek within the next three weeks, we can catch the first vessel we find to Kolwith," Gwail announced, before storming off into the next room.

Aran had heard a couple of references to Kolwith before, but none of them had been positive. It certainly didn't sound like a place that people ventured to in a hurry.

Located at the top end of the South Island, Kolwith Bay had long become a refuge for convicts, criminals and anyone with a past they would rather forget. For others, it was merely a stop-off point, a place to pass through, if no other route was available. It was not a destination that Aran had envisioned moving to at such short notice.

Distracted by his uncle's urgent need to abandon everything he had ever worked for, Aran had almost forgotten about the priceless bundle of armour that was still lying in the next room. Within the next few minutes, he had already thrown the entire load over his shoulder and was now hauling it up the stairs.

His bedroom was cramped enough as it was. Scattered across every corner was an assortment of odd trinkets and random artefacts. His bed had become a floating vessel in a swamp of collected items. It was quite surprising what a person could find whilst scavenging around the hills of Galamere. But nothing had even come close to his latest sack of treasure.

Behind the meagre bookshelf was a small opening. This squared hole, which had started life as a small fireplace, had provided the perfect hiding spot. After a short grunt, and a heavy clank, the entire sack of armour had soon found its new resting place.

Aran sat himself down on the bed. The news of his imminent departure had yet to fully sink in. It had come as quite a
shock for the boy who had barely left the surrounding valley, let
alone the North Island.

He turned to the book on his bedside table. Normally this
bundle of text had served as a direct portal into a world of
fantasy and legend. Now it was nothing more than a pile of
crumpled up pages. For tomorrow he would be embarking on
his own adventure. Rather than feel excited, he was instead
plagued by a series of endless questions.

*What had his uncle found out that day? Were they now in
danger? What on earth would make Gwail want to abandon their
home without a moment's hesitation?*

Gwail enjoyed nothing more than sitting in front of a roaring
fire with a hearty meal. He was a man of simple pleasures. Not
one who ran off into the night like some escaped convict. As far
as Aran was aware, the honest farmer had never hurt a sole in
his life (except maybe a few trespassing foxes).

Surely Gwail had nothing to worry about. And yet *something*
had clearly rattled the man. Whatever it was, Aran could sense
that he was very close to finding out.

THE NEXT TIME Aran opened his eyes, he was met with the fierce
expression of his uncle's face staring back at him.

"Aran! I won't tell you again — get up!"

Gwail jerked him back and forth, until his vision became
blurred.

"What time is it?" asked Aran, shaking off the grogginess.

"It's time to go," said Gwail.

A glowing lamp was hanging from the farmer's large hand.
He lowered it for a moment, before pushing his nephew back
from the window.

"Get down!" he snapped. The man peered over the stone windowsill with a pair of wide, bloodshot eyes.

Just as he was beginning to suspect that his uncle had finally lost his marbles, a series of metallic flashes caught the boy's attention.

"Damn it!" said Gwail. "They're already here!"

He blew out the light, grabbed his nephew by the arm and dragged him towards the doorway.

"Wait, I need to grab my bag!" Aran cried.

Gwail released his tight grip and let the boy go hurling towards the corner of the room.

Lines of armed men were gathered in the yard outside, their torches of fire lighting up the ground beneath their feet.

Aran pulled out a small satchel from underneath the bed and swung it over his shoulder.

"Gwail Saddler!" cried a voice from outside. "We know you are in there!"

Aran took a quick glance through the small window. What he hadn't expected to see was a face he recognised.

Standing with a group of soldiers on either side of him was a mounted knight in red-plated armour and heavy chain mail. His steely gaze caught the boy's eye for just a moment, as it had done once before. There was no denying that this was the very same Brenin he had come across in the forest.

"Come along, Aran!" growled his uncle, his crooked stick waving at him through the air.

Gwail led the way down a narrow staircase and stormed through into the kitchen. He swung his bad leg as quickly as it would allow, until they reached the back door of the house.

Aran followed closely behind, watching in horror as his uncle slipped a sharp chopping knife underneath his coat.

They both jumped at the sound of a loud thumping noise on the other side of the house. Gwail held Aran close whilst signalling for him to remain quiet. He swung the back door open, only for his face to drop at the sight of two soldiers blocking their doorway. One of them looked cautious, and the other clenched his sword with a firm, and ready, grip. The second shook his head; there would be no escape.

These two unlikely prisoners were soon marched outside towards the front of the house. The Brenin knight was still towering on the back of his great horse in the middle of the yard. His men were poised and awaited their orders. His chiselled face lit up at the sight of a reluctant Gwail limping his way towards him. A half-smile crept across his square jaw.

Aran glanced at the line of soldiers with their serious expressions and heavy looking armour. Surely there was no need for this many men, he thought. An old farmer and a small boy were hardly a threat, and it wasn't as if either of them could put up much of a fight.

The large emblem on the knight's chest glimmered in the moonlight — a mark of the Queen's finest. Gwail refused to look his nephew in the eye. Whatever trouble they both were in, it was very serious.

"Gwail of Galamere," said the Brenin. "I'm arresting you in the name of Her Majesty the Queen."

Gwail scoffed. He was in no mood to cooperate.

The knight's focus remained unbroken. Even under the distressing circumstances, Aran couldn't help but feel slightly disappointed; it was becoming clear that the Brenin had not yet recognised him.

"You are a criminal and a traitor," continued the knight.

Gwail looked up at him and smirked.

"With what proof?" he asked. "I am nothing but an honest farmer trying to make a living."

The Brenin said nothing for a moment. Aran admired his uncle's calmness. At that moment in time, nothing would have pleased the boy more than to return to the warmth of his bed. Instead, he found himself shivering in front of what appeared to be a small army.

The knight glided off his great horse with the elegance of a trained dancer. He marched forward with careful steps, until his cold breath clouded the air in front of Gwail's face.

"Search the house," he ordered.

Without a moment's hesitation, the men behind him broke away from their perfect line and went barging through the front door.

Aran and Gwail stood in the yard for what felt like an eternity. The knight remained frozen in his tall stance, and seemed quite happy to wait in silence until his soldiers returned. His fierce stare remained locked on Gwail's calm face.

The uncomfortable moment was soon interrupted by the appearance of a large sack being dragged outside through the broken doorframe. Aran's stomach went tight, as the bag was emptied out across the dirt in front of them.

The Brenin smiled. "Nothing but an honest farmer, you say?"

Gwail had no response. He had expected them to return empty handed, and, instead, they had presented him with a pile of armour even *he* was surprised to see. The Brenin and his team of disciplined soldiers stared in wonder at the various pieces, with their emerald surfaces and engraved patterns.

"There aren't many farmers I know who would have something like this in their possession," said the knight.

Aran could feel his uncle's horrified stare from the corner of his eye. Gwail stared at the armour as if it were the ashes of a deceased memory, and now it had come back to haunt him.

Had the boy known what was about to happen next, he would have left that bundle of hollow limbs buried where he had found them.

An air of caution spread out across the yard. Soldiers

clenched their sword handles, whilst the knight took a step backwards. Gwail remained still.

The Brenin turned back to his second in command.

"Nobody must know what was seen here tonight," he told him.

Aran's stomach tightened, once again, and he watched as the knight gathered up the remaining pieces of armour before launching back up on his horse. Those chilling words were still circulating around the boy's mind.

The commanding officer pulled out his sword and held it up towards Gwail's face. The man didn't even flinch.

"Whatever happens, you stay behind me," Gwail whispered to his nephew.

Aran looked up at him. He had a very bad feeling about what was to come.

It was quite clear by the hostile atmosphere that these men had no intention of keeping them alive. His uncle's calming words would never be enough to guarantee their safety (no matter what he secretly had planned).

The knight turned back to his lead soldier.

"Do not underestimate him, Delius," he said. "You are far too close for my liking."

The soldier nodded. He now had his blade held inches away from Gwail's bearded neck.

"Fear not, Sir," said the swordsman. "We can handle it from here."

The knight returned his nod. A fraction of a second later, Delius' weapon was thrusted away with the swiftness of an experienced pickpocketer. Aran looked down to see that his uncle's crooked stick was now lying in the dirt.

"I said get behind me, boy," Gwail growled.

Aran ran towards him without the slightest hesitation. His

uncle was clutching the sword like he'd held one every day of his life.

Two other men came charging towards them, only to be dismantled by a series of perfectly timed blows. The bashing of swords sent tremors through every bone in Aran's body. The idea that a person could be capable of such ruthless destruction would have seemed otherworldly only moments before. But if there *was* to be someone who possessed such a power, he was glad for it to be the very same man protecting him.

Gwail's hips fired back and forth like heavy pistons, jolting in time with every sharp deflection of his busy sword. Several clashes of steel later, a dozen more soldiers were on their backs, most of them dazed and confused at what had just happened.

The knight waited patiently on the back of his horse, admiring the skill of this older man, with his graceful strokes and elegant body movements. He was watching a warrior well past his prime, and yet one who could still hold his own against a wave of multiple attackers.

As efficient as Gwail had been at taking down half a squadron of trained soldiers, he knew that it would only be a matter of time before fatigue would get the better of him. Life on the farm had made him careless, and even sloppy.

His attention was soon distracted by a bright, green light in the centre of the yard. The pieces of glowing armour illuminated his entire face as he manoeuvred towards them. They had now become so bright that even the soldiers were struggling to resist their hypnotic glare. It was as if these old relics had awoken from a deep sleep, ready for the arrival of their new master.

The knight's face filled with dread.

"Don't let him touch it!" he cried out.

With only a small amount of adrenaline left in his body,

Gwail flung himself down towards the green glow, causing an enormous surge of energy that rippled out across the yard. This wave of immense power toppled over anyone within a dozen feet, leaving a confused Aran shaking against his uncle's back.

The yard fell silent.

6

THE MESSENGER

The only sound in the entire yard was the steady grunting of an exhausted Gwail. To the boy's surprise, the tired man was already clawing to his feet. Aran gazed around at the unconscious men, all scattered around him like toy soldiers. Even the Brenin knight had tumbled to the floor, and was now lying in the dirt beside his sedated horse.

He slid himself underneath his uncle's arm in an attempt to lift him up.

"What just happened?" he asked.

The impact of the giant flash had robbed any last remaining stores of energy that they had left.

"Why am I so tired?" Aran asked.

Gwail's weakened body did nothing to dampen his temper. "Come along, Aran," he said. "Enough wasting time. You have a long journey ahead of you."

Aran listened in disbelief. The man could barely push out his words. How his uncle could still be so focused on their journey south, after everything that he had just endured, was beyond the stableboy's understanding.

"Shouldn't you rest a little, Uncle?" asked Aran. "Just for a moment?"

"Don't talk daft, boy. Your carelessness has already caused enough trouble for one night. There's no time for resting."

Aran presumed that he was referring to the suit of armour. The man did have a point; had the boy known his little secret was going to cause an entire army to drop to its knees, outside his very own house, he might have thought twice.

"Hurry up and grab that bag," snapped the croaking voice.

Gwail pointed to the empty sack that was still lying in the mud. Aran scurried over to fetch it, before approaching the pile of armour with a newfound sense of caution. The thought of another explosion was too terrifying to imagine. They packed up the various pieces, each of them still warm with their waning glow.

"We need to move quickly," said Gwail. "They won't be down for much longer."

Aran looked around at the carnage this frail man had caused. Armoured soldiers were scattered around the yard, each one of them frozen in the night-time air. Whatever sorcery his uncle had performed, he knew that the armour would have played a large part.

"What did you do to them?" he dared to ask.

"I did what was necessary. This armour was built as a means of protection." He placed the final piece into the bag and looked around. "It has truly served its purpose here tonight. Come — we must move."

The warmth of the stables swept across Aran like a blanket of comfort. Normally the smell of rotting hay reminded him of hard labour and long winter nights. Now it was the smell of refuge, a safe haven from the horrors of the yard.

Gwail led the way inside, pulling his nephew along as the latter tried to prevent him from falling over. The sack of armour hung from his shoulder like a hunted animal. They hobbled their way to the final stall; it was the stall that Aran had dreaded the most.

Standing there, in his narrow home, was an eager looking Meaden.

"Up you get, boy," said Gwail as he reached for the saddle. Fortunately, the horse had already been prepared for the journey ahead. His master's well-organised nature had paid off once again that evening.

Aran looked up at the gigantic animal with a rush of panic. The last time he had climbed on the back of a horse, he had been thrown straight back off again. Ever since that dreadful day, he had sworn to never ride again. It was something Gwail himself had approved of at the time: "I'd much rather you stay on the same level as these horses anyway," his uncle had told him. "If you can't ride them properly, then you shouldn't be riding at all."

Aran had been quite adamant that the horse was mostly to blame, even when that horse had been the great and magnificent Meaden. The thought of climbing back aboard that death trap had made him quite sick to the stomach. As fortune would have it, he didn't have to contemplate this thought for very long. Gwail grabbed his nephew by the legs and flung him straight over the horse's back. The animal stirred, and was calmed only by the man's gentle voice.

"Whoa, boy," he whispered.

Once Aran had finally managed to swing the correct leg over, his uncle shook him by the trouser leg.

"Forget your dithering and listen to me, boy," he said.

The boy steadied himself by grabbing an entire handful of silver hair. The horse did not take kindly to this decision and jolted back his head as a stern warning.

"As soon as you've gone, those men out there will arrest me," his uncle continued.

The words struck Aran as quite odd. He could have sworn the man was implying that only one of them was leaving.

A quite serious face looked up at him. He couldn't even remember the last time his uncle had properly locked eyes on him. Now he could hardly look away. There was a sense of warmth and affection that he had never seen in him before.

Gwail whispered under his short breaths: "Aran..." His thick beard scratched against the boy's quivering cheek as he held him tight. "You must head straight to the South Island, to the port of Kolwith Bay. There you will find my brother — a man named Wyn Drathion. In my bag is a letter in a sealed envelope. *Drathion* — remember that name, Aran. You must tell him what happened here tonight. Tell him everything."

Aran gave him a reluctant nod.

"But *how* will I find him?" he asked.

"You must find a way." Gwail let out a chesty cough. "Promise me one thing — when you head past Lake Carreg — promise me that you will throw that cursed armour into the very bottom of those waters. Only bad things will ever come of it. You must promise me, Aran."

"I promise," said Aran. The words did not come easily for the boy who was still reeling in shock at his worsening situation.

"Find Drathion," Gwail whispered. "He is the only person I can still trust. You can trust him too."

The words made Aran very uncomfortable, even more than the rock-hard saddle bobbing around underneath him. He couldn't tell if his sniffling nose was the result of the freezing weather conditions or an urge to break down in tears.

Gwail's tight grip began to loosen. He untied the strap around Meaden's neck and gave him one last stroke on the nose. With a firm slap on the horse's backside, Aran was launched from the stables in an explosion of galloping hooves. The small rider clung for dear life as he passed a group of groggy looking soldiers.

By the time the Brenin knight had regained consciousness, Aran had vanished into the night without a trace. He turned to see a calm figure making his way back into the yard. Gwail showed no sign of resistance this time around, as he knelt himself down and waited to be handcuffed. The confused soldiers were more than happy to oblige. The Brenin, however, seemed more preoccupied with the empty yard.

"Where did it go?!" he cried.

The only response from Gwail was an amused smile.

The Brenin looked around again, before the answer slowly dawned on him. "The boy..." In a burst of panic, he signalled to his men: "Search the area! Bring me back that armour!"

Meanwhile, the stableboy and his horse were long gone. They rode through the cold air to the sound of thumping hoofs, and at a speed few human beings could ever hope to achieve. Aran clung to his new guardian for dear life, as the pounding movements sent a surge of nausea with every jump. He looked back towards the farm; it grew smaller with every passing second, and an unexpected sadness washed over him. It had only just occurred to the boy that he was unlikely to see the place ever again.

Meaden maintained his pace for several miles, which was helped mostly by the fact that Aran had yet to figure out quite how he was going to stop. He'd already tried slowing the horse down a number of times, and his gentle tugs had achieved very little; it appeared Meaden was very much in charge.

A glimmer of moonlight flickered in the far distance. This vast stretch of blue ripples meant that they were already approaching the shores of Lake Carreg. The town of Gala was only a few miles ahead, and Aran could hardly believe the distance they had already covered. What would normally have taken a whole afternoon had felt like no time at all. He knew that horses could run fast, but the most he had ever achieved in the past was a short trot.

He looked over across the great lake as their pace began to slow. A thin row of orange lights flickered on the other side. These faint beacons were the spires of Gala's town centre. Aran knew that somewhere amongst that strip of lighting was a sleeping Sarwen. He had heard no end of lengthy descriptions about the wonders of her hometown (or how much better the place was to his own home).

The horse slowly made his way to the edge of the lake. Aran could hear the splashing of his front hoofs as they touched the water. Meaden lowered his long head and took a drink. All that could be heard now was the sound of a large tongue splashing and slurping.

Aran shuddered. In that moment, his future had never felt so uncertain. Although he had always dreamed of the opportunity to leave the eternal boredom of Penarth Farm, he had also come to accept that his *real* destiny lied in shovelling horse manure for the rest of his life. Now everything was different. He barely knew where he'd be the very next day.

Meaden had offered little solace, and spent the next hour lying down in the comfort of the grass. Aran took the opportunity to release the bag of armour that was still tied against the saddle. He made his way to the edge of the lake and emptied the entire contents all over the wet gravel. The pieces seemed pale, and gloomy. Their green glow had all but dimmed, as they hibernated amongst the shadows. One by one, he threw the pieces as far as he could into the icy water, like pebbles that would never be seen again. Had it not been for these mysterious green plates, he might well have been tucked up in bed. So far, they had been nothing but a curse.

Fortunately for Aran, they were as light as a feather. It wasn't long before he had rid himself of the last piece — or *had* he?

Aran lifted up his satchel and pulled out the gauntlet. It clung to his hand like a limb that refused to leave him. He knew that the second gauntlet was but a short boat ride away. Somewhere, on the other side of that very lake, its owner was sleeping soundly.

He looked at the gauntlet again. To part ways with such a personal item would have felt like a betrayal. Aran opened up his satchel and slipped the gauntlet back inside; there was no harm in hanging on to it a little while longer.

The time had come to make a move. Meaden had quenched his thirst for long enough, and he had now grown restless. The night was cold, even for him, and the time for resting had now past.

Aran took a deep breath and grabbed hold of the reigns. He slotted his first foot through the stirrups and prayed for mercy. With a giant swing of his other leg, he pulled himself upwards with every ounce of strength he had left.

The horse soon began throwing his weight around, kicking and shaking in every direction. Aran clung on for dear life, swaying from side to side, to keep his balance. But it was no use: Meaden had already descended into a fit of uncontrollable panic, and this in turn had panicked his rider even more.

"Woah, boy!" he cried, trying desperately to imitate his uncle's calming voice.

The horse responded with a nervous trot — then a gallop — until eventually, Aran was barely touching the saddle at all. His sore backside bounced up and down, whilst a burst of wind slapped him in the face.

Just as he had managed to gain a small amount of control, Meaden kicked out his back legs and sent his wailing master flying upwards into the air. Aran landed with a heavy thud. The grass may have been damp, but it had struck his body like a bed of rocks.

With a disgruntled nicker and a chatter of teeth, the horse steadied himself before casually wandering over as if nothing had ever happened. His wet snout dangled across Aran's face and concluded his little tantrum with a proud snort.

Before long, Aran was walking along a winding, rocky path, away from the lights of Galamere, and down into the next valley. He knew that his best option was to head south. Fortunately, that sky of stars was the same exact one he had studied back on the farm. It had now become the last view that he still recognised, and his last hope of not getting lost. The only other familiar sight was Meaden's dribbling mouth, which was now bobbing away beside his cheek.

The boy had decided that there would be little chance of him climbing that great beast again. His initial concern had been correct — the horse was far more trouble than he was worth. There were many ways a life could be shortened, but he wasn't about to spend his last few moments flying across an animal's rear end. He would rather attempt the entire journey on foot. Once again, Meaden had won the day. Aran was back to his former role: the ever-abiding horse servant. Some things would never change.

Having found their common ground, literally, there were now far more pressing matters to be worried about. For on that very same night, a man had been arrested. His guilty accomplice was now making his way across a wilting countryside — a wanted fugitive –and an escaped outlaw. This same outlaw also happened to be embarking on the biggest journey of his entire life. Making it to Kolwith Bay would require far more than a pair of feet and four hoofs.

The Kingdom of Morwallia was broken in half by a great channel. To venture across these treacherous waters without a map, or guide, was an ambitious task, even for the most seasoned of travellers. Unfortunately, Aran was well aware that he had very little choice in the matter. All he had left was a promise — to find this *Wyn Draithon* and deliver his uncle's message. If there was to be a hefty price on his head from now on, he would need all the allies he could get.

In a single night, he had gone from stableboy to criminal. Now he was a postman. To be a glorified carrier pigeon was not quite the position he had always dreamt of, but after the night he had just had, the title of carrier pigeon would do just fine.

7

THE ORCHARD

I t had been almost two days since Aran had first started his journey south. The sun had already risen for the second time when he began to feel a series of stabbing pains along the pit of his stomach. The hunger that had plagued him since the night before had now become unbearable. His last proper meal had been one of Gwail's special stews — and that had barely stayed down in the first place.

Up ahead through the clearing were the early signs of a small town. The sight of thatched roofs and a smoking chimney brought a feeling of warmth and comfort, if only for a brief moment.

As reliable as the guiding stars had been, Aran had no idea where he was, and there was no guarantee he would ever reach the coast. He'd never even *seen* the sea, let alone sailed across one. His only point of reference had been the empty spaces of an old map that had been discarded in the back of a drawer on Penarth Farm. He had often studied it over the years, exploring its crumpled lines with the ease of an index finger: those mountainous regions of the North Island, and the expansive cities of the south. He had never dreamt in a million years that such knowledge would ever have become useful. That basic grasp of Morwallian geography was all he had left to go on.

The town of Aber's End had *not* been on Aran's map. And from what Aran had seen so far, it was unlikely to feature on *any* map at all. What had once been a prosperous mining community, had since deteriorated into a lifeless ghost town.

Having once boasted a wide range of rare minerals and precious metals, the surrounding hills had long been sapped dry of all their resources. All that remained now was the town's last few groups of lonely inhabitants, many of whom were still holding out hope of a quick fortune. The rest were aimless nomads, who could have cared less about the outcome of their shrivelling destinies, and were now more than happy to share in the misery of others. Aber's End was never one to pass judgement. Instead, it was willing to provide the perfect location for two of its two main activities: mining, and drinking (although, these days, the latter had proven far more popular).

Business at the only tavern in town was very much thriving. Any concerns, or worries, about the days ahead could instantly be washed away by a tall glass of local cider. Those thick stein handles would fill many an empty hand after the long, hard days toiling in the hills.

By the time Aran had reached the town square, a lonely church bell was chiming away the remains of an eerie silence. In the centre of the square was a stone monument. Four streets veered off from each corner, each one as empty as the other. Even with no sole in sight, Aran knew he was not alone. He could feel those curious eyes as they peered out from the darkened windows.

The sooner he could move on, the better. He felt lonelier there than he had done the night before. It was a far cry from the bustling streets of Gala, and he prayed that the frosty reception of Aber's End was not a sign of things to come.

"Where did you find him?" asked a voice.

Aran turned around. Sat on a rotting bench at the edge of the square was an old woman. She puffed away on her smoking pipe, whilst gazing up towards Meaden's towering head.

Aran was surprised he hadn't noticed her sooner. The woman was deathly still, more so than the stone monument beside them.

"I didn't find him!" snapped Aran. "He belongs to me."

His tone had become defensive, and even irritable. The hunger was still raging inside of him. He was in no mood for games, let alone some polite conversation.

The woman let out a croaky chuckle.

"I used to have a horse," she said. "Not a horse like yours, mind. But he was still a horse. He was *my* horse."

She took another breath of smoke and let it slowly drift out into the cold air.

Aran took a closer look at her, that hard face, and those drooping eyes. There was a trace of kindness he had not expected. He already felt bad for snapping.

They sat in silence for a while, the church bell still a faint echo after its last chime. He was surprised the church had even bothered. It wasn't like anyone in this town ever left the house.

Aran looked up at the monument. With no distinct shape or form, it was unlike any other statue he had seen before. He crouched down beside this giant lump of stone and clenched his stomach in pain.

The old woman's distant gaze had not changed, and yet she could feel his discomfort.

"You sound hungry," she said.

Aran looked up, surprised she had even noticed.

"I haven't eaten in a very long time," he said. "I tried eating grass for a while, like my horse. But it made me sick."

He squirmed and held his lower abdomen. The woman nodded.

"This fine specimen deserves better than *grass*," she said, pointing towards an absent-minded Meaden. "And perhaps you do, too."

She let out an amused laugh, followed by a series of chesty coughs. Aran, however, was not amused.

The woman grabbed her short walking stick and hauled herself up.

"Come along then," she said, her frail hand caressing the nearby wall for guidance.

It was soon brought to the boy's attention that the old woman was using the stone structure as a substitute for one of her five senses. She appeared to lack something he had always very much taken for granted

"Oh, you're... you're... blind," muttered Aran, slightly taken back.

His attention had now turned to her waving stick, clanking its way across the ground beneath her feet. Despite this woman's obvious limitations, her determined strides and confident spirit reminded him somewhat of his uncle.

"But, how — how did you know about my horse?" asked Aran.

He reflected back upon their brief conversation. By the time he'd finished pondering, the old woman had already reached a narrow side street. She paused without turning around.

"Are you two coming?" she asked. "Or are you planning on eating *that* great thing instead?"

Aran looked up towards the stone monument that he presumed she was referring to. With nothing left to lose, he rose to his feet and grabbed the drooping strap beneath his horse's chin. Tired and weary, he pulled him in the direction of the old woman.

Aran followed his new guide through a series of crooked passageways; the blind leading the blind, Aran thought. The woman's grey hair was as poorly maintained as the surrounding buildings. She continued her way around the dingy backstreets of this quiet town.

By this point, Aran was quite happy to let someone else to take the lead for a while (even if they were a little strange). The starvation had long diminished any last sense of pride or motivation that he might once have had.

He gazed at the endless stream of closed doors that passed them by. Each house had very little to differentiate it from the next. It seemed that variety was not something people craved in Aber's End.

Local residents popped out their heads to observe this curious, and unexpected, looking group. The trio ignored their suspicious glances and marched straight by them in single file, curling around each corner like a regiment of unlikely misfits: the boy, his horse, and a blind old woman.

The final stop was a walled courtyard with a single, dried-up well. Hollow windows overlooked them from high up above, and Aran could once again feel the gnawing presence of watchful eyes. An overgrowth of wild plants had completely taken over this long-forgotten corner of town, giving the crumbling stone its own layer of thick, prickly skin. Any hint of sunlight was completely blocked out by an enormous ten-foot wall, which dwarfed its new visitors like a towering ogre.

The old woman stopped. She lifted up her stick and prodded it against the imposing obstacle.

"What you seek," she said. "Is beyond that wall."

A confused Aran looked up at the giant structure. There was no chance in a million years, he thought. Scaling a wall that size would require a strong catapult and a pair of wings, both of which he did not have.

"Then what are we doing on *this* side of it?" he asked.

His patience had worn thin. At this point, he could have devoured an entire horse — including the one standing there beside him.

The woman coughed out a laugh and began sucking on her trusty pipe. Her amusement only aggravated her new companion even more.

"How are we supposed to get over a thing like that?" he asked again.

"*We*?" she asked back. "I never said we were *all* going."

"My horse has a better chance of getting over that thing than I have," said the boy.

He waited for her to finish another long gulp of smoke. She was in no hurry to answer.

"You know what your problem is, boy?" she eventually asked. "You use your eyes too much."

The woman let out a stream of cloudy breath and put away her pipe.

Aran watched as she strolled over to the wall, prodding away, until her stick reached a hedge. She bashed away at the layer of thorns until the stone behind it was finally exposed.

Was she raving mad? This was certainly one conclusion that Aran was leaning towards. Not only had he been led on a wild goose chase, but the person he was now stuck with had appeared to have lost her marbles (which, in a town like Aber's End, could happen to anyone).

"Are you going to just stand there?" the woman asked.

She was now pointing her stick towards the open hedge. Aran sighed. He dragged himself nearer in an effort to humour her.

And then, to his great surprise, he suddenly caught the glimpse of a narrow crack. Nestled behind the beaten down hedge was a small opening at the bottom of the wall, a slender hole, where the stone had crumbled away. Although it was narrow, surely it would be wide enough for a weedy boy like him to slip through.

"Off you go then," said the woman.

"But how..."

Aran didn't bother. In fact, he no longer cared. Nothing this old woman did, or said, had made any sense to him so far, anyway. And it seemed unlikely to change.

"Like I said," she added. "You only see what's in front of you."

She tapped the end of her stick against the wall as if it were a wand that could teleport him straight through.

"Aren't you coming?" asked Aran, apprehensive about what he might find on the other side.

The woman shook her head, her wild hair as overgrown as the hedge in front of them.

"There's nothing for me through there," she said. "I'm far too old to be crawling around in the dirt. I should be riding high, like this fellow here."

She lifted up her hand to Meaden's snout and stroked it.

"And what about him?" he asked, sticking out his finger towards the great horse, forgetting that the woman couldn't see him. But still, she knew.

"I'll look after your friend," said the woman, patting Meaden against the side of his muscular neck.

Aran had stalled for long enough, and he was hit by yet another unbearable stomach clench. At that moment, he would have been quite happy to leap off the nearest cliff had there been a chance of food at the bottom.

He held his breath as if he were plunging into a pool of murky water. Brambles scraped the surface of his fragile skin. An awkward limbo soon followed, as he lunged his tiny body underneath an even tinier crack. A web of thorns clawed at his small satchel. After a series of tugs and shakes, the bag came hurling towards him, bringing along with it a cloud of dirt and needles. His eyes stung from the impact. He hoped that this had all been worth it.

He emerged on the other side like a cat from a flooded river. Branches and weeds still clung to his sore body. Aran wiped his eyes and dusted himself off.

What appeared in front of him was a sight far more magnificent than he could have ever imagined: lined in a series of horizontal rows were dozens upon dozens of carefully grown trees — and not just *any* old trees. These spirals of winding branches were covered in an infinite selection of the most juicy, and succulent, apples that Aran had ever laid eyes upon. His heart was beating with an uncontrollable excitement, and his mouth watered like an open tap.

What the boy had stumbled on was a great orchard, and inside of it were the finest apples a person could hope for. Fruit had been a rare luxury back on Penarth Farm. Gwail had always been more of a meat-and-potatoes man, and preferred to wash down his meals with an enormous mug of mead, as opposed to a cold pint of cider.

Aran was now faced with more apples than he could have ever hope to eat, and the way his stomach was feeling at that exact moment, the timing could not have been better. After a morning spent roaming the saturated streets of Aber's End, the bombardment of bright colours was too much to handle.

Before his eyes could even begin to adjust, he was already charging towards those luscious trees, with their reds, pinks and greens. He braced himself for what would soon become a long-awaited feeding frenzy. Moisture from the damp air soaked up against his quivering cheeks, as he ran through the long grass.

Before he knew it, his mouth was erupting with the sweet and sour flavours of cool, watery pulp, as it dribbled down his cheeks whilst he chomped into the first of a dozen apples.

Aran collapsed to the ground in a euphoric daze. It seemed that fruit tasted a lot better when you were on the brink of starvation. He rolled around, bathing in the fallen apples, like a pig in mud, laughing away at his incredible stroke of good fortune.

He thought about how much he had doubted the old woman and her bizarre ways, and how she had still been willing to throw him a lifeline, despite his moaning. It would be a favour he would never to forget.

After a rejuvenating feast, he began stuffing his satchel with as many apples has he could possibly fit. Within minutes, he had six down his trousers, four up his sleeves and at least a dozen along the inside of his clothes. This may have seemed excessive, but the boy knew that if he were ever going to make it to the coast, he would need every last morsel of food he could lay his hands on. Such a journey could take months, or even longer without the help of a strong horse. Meaden may have slowed him down so far, but he could never abandon the only friend he had left (even if those feelings weren't necessarily reciprocated). Hopefully they would someday find a home that Meaden deserved. Until then, they would continue on together.

Lying with his back against the fallen apples, he looked up at the overcast sky. The branches from the surrounding trees formed a perfect frame around the gathering dark clouds, like veins closing in on him.

At that very moment he could have quite easily been lying in the rich earth of Skelbrei Forest, enjoying a free afternoon's rest from his long list of chores. Now there were no chores whatsoever, and he was free to do exactly as he pleased. Unfortunately, this new revelation brought him very little comfort, and his eyes squinted as a heavy raindrop splashed the tip of his cold nose; the heavens were about to open. He should have known that such a blissful moment could only last so long. Good things would be a rare pleasure from now on.

These negative feelings were strengthened by a loud cry from the other side of the orchard. Aran leapt to his feet. Robbed from his nostalgic dream, the shouting gradually became louder with every turn of his head. All he could see now were the lines upon lines of apple trees. The place had morphed into a house of mirrors, an infinite maze that he could no longer navigate. Any sense of direction had completely evaporated.

"Where's the hole?" he asked himself.

His precious feeding ground had now become a prison. Something told him that the owner of these fruitful trees was anything but generous, and the furious calls were soon accompanied by two more angry voices.

8

THE GUIDE

Aran went charging through the trees, ducking and weaving, the branches scraping through his hair like a wall of sharp combs. Apples bobbed against the top of his head until he was drenched in their juicy moisture. The hostile cries echoed around the orchard, making it impossible to plan his next move.

"I know you're in here!" cried the voice. "Nobody trespasses on my soil without paying for it, you thieving little rat!"

Aran rested his back against one of the more bloated tree trunks. He could hear the rustling of leaves as the man edged closer with every step. With no sign of a way out, he remained still for as long as his nerves would allow. There must have been close to a hundred trees in this walled garden, and it would take forever to search them all.

His heart jumped at the sight of a snaking trail of stolen apples now following him across the grass. Not only had he consumed the forbidden fruit, but he had also provided a long line of evidence. He looked up at a snarling face staring back at him from behind the opposing tree.

"Gotcha, you filthy vermin!" growled the face, before lifting up a rusty chopping knife.

Aran made a frantic dash towards the nearest wall. Two other men appeared from either side of him, almost simultaneously. The shortest of the two assailants struggled to catch up, his bulging waistline bouncing as he ran. The other man was hot on Aran's heels, laughing under his deep, heavy breaths. His target was heading straight for the ten-foot obstacle up ahead, and he called out in a burst of excitement.

"There's nowhere left to run, little man!"

But Aran kept running. Apples poured down from his flapping trouser legs as he searched, desperately, for the small hole. With not a single opening in sight, he made a valiant leap towards the layer of overgrown vines that covered the nearby wall. He crawled up the creeping plants with more energy and determination than he had ever mustered in his entire life. The initial hesitation he experienced earlier had completely vanished, and it was amazing how much confidence a climber could have when his life depended on it. He pulled and clawed like a lost squirrel, scaling the first half with surprising ease, whilst he kept his sights firmly locked in on the goal above.

Just as he was about to make progress, he felt a sudden jolt in one of his legs. Grasped around his left ankle was a grubby hand that appeared to have spent most of its days covered in soil.

"Come here, you little thief!" cried the voice below.

Aran looked down to see the fuming orchard worker yanking at his ankle with an evil grin. Although he had made it further up the wall than he had ever first expected, there was little time to celebrate. The man below had secured himself a firm grip and was unlikely to release it without a fight.

Aran looked down at his dangling satchel. He lifted up the bag and began throwing its entire contents towards the solid forehead beneath his feet. The man grunted in disapproval, as apples bombarded him in the face with a rapid-fire burst.

With every last ounce of hope draining out from his tired body, Aran peered inside the satchel to see the glistening shine of the green gauntlet.

One foul swoop of his arm was followed by a loud CRACK. The man below went tumbling backwards and landed with a heavy thud against the wet grass. His obese colleague let out a sympathetic gasp at the sight of his forehead, which was now so swollen and purple that it stuck out further than his large nose.

Aran plummeted down into the nearby weeds, the gauntlet still fastened around his right hand. He slipped it into his satchel and sat up in a confused daze. Through the distant rumbles of his muffled hearing, he could begin to make out the angry wails of a furious orchard keeper. The man came running towards him, his rusty chopping knife shaking through the air.

With his mind spinning and his heart thumping, Aran turned his focus to the eastern wall. Peeping at him from beneath the neglected brickwork was the gaping hole he had first entered. After one last look at the hysterical figure coming his way, he hauled himself up for a desperate sprint.

The overweight worker wiped off a layer of sweat from his shining brow, before charging over to intercept. Aran swung his own shaking legs, backwards and forwards, with everything they had left. He could hear the pounding of heavy work boots, their thick heels only meters away from his own tiny shoes.

The moisture in the air burned through his lungs, whilst the terror of what was behind him consumed his every move. The hole had become smaller with every stride. As his muscles went numb with unbearable fatigue, he committed his entire body to a horizontal dive. The downward leap sent him sliding through the narrow gap just in the nick of time.

"Get back here!" cried the furious voice.

Aran sat up in disbelief. He could hear the clawing of large hands against the wall behind him. Somehow, he had made it to the other side. The orchard keeper was still fumbling around on his hands and knees, only inches away from his very own. A handful of chubby fingers poked out through the tiny gap.

Aran looked back up at the great wall. What had previously caused him so much grief had now become his saviour. Before he had time to comprehend his lucky escape, he was soon struck by a terrible realisation: the courtyard before him was completely empty. There was no old woman, and no Meaden. His stomach clenched.

He had been tricked, he thought. *Tricked by an old blind woman!*

He knew there had been something about her from the moment they first spoke. His belly was full, but it had come with a hefty price.

Had she been plotting to steal Meaden from the very beginning? Was she really even blind?

These were just some of the questions he had little time to answer. The boy looked up to see a familiar figure stumbling into the main courtyard. The furious orchard keeper had been let loose from his walled cage, and he was now more than ready to secure his revenge.

"Stop him!" he cried. "Thief! Thief!!"

Residents popped out their heads from the windows above. They glared down with frowns of passing judgement, pointing their fingers in great disapproval at this guilty looking child.

Aran ran for the nearest side street, his small feet clattering away along the cobbled path. He turned at each passing alleyway — left, then right — then left again. He weaved through this great urban labyrinth, desperate to outwit his fuming assailant once and for all.

The words "Stop!" and "Thief!" followed him the entire way. No matter how far he ran, the echoes still chased him.

Pointed fingers continued to expose his location, like curling, fleshy sign posts leading the way. As usual, the boy had no idea where he was heading. Either side of him were lines of endless windows, all of them darkened by rickety shutters and closed curtains. The locals of Aber's End offered very little sympathy to helpless children. In this town, he was well and truly alone.

Aran eventually found himself running towards an old, neglected church. It was hidden away, as if not to be disturbed. Its empty courtyard was similar to the one he had just escaped from. He threw himself against the panes of solid oak, and slammed away at the thick, circular door handles. The doors were locked tight. This had soon become a dead-end in more ways than one.

Aran leaned himself back against the church door. He had very little knowledge of religion, but at that very moment he prayed harder than any priest or churchgoer had ever done. What awaited him in that narrow passageway was the angriest, most vengeful, man he had ever encountered. The orchard keeper's scaly, yellow teeth grinned in the reflection of his blade, as he emerged from the shadows in the company of his portly assistant. The last route to freedom had well and truly been blocked off.

"Caught like the thieving little rat that you are!" growled the keeper.

He savoured the moment and flicked the edge of his knife against his long, dirty finger nails.

"I wasn't stealing!" Aran cried. "I was starving hungry!"

The man turned to his colleague and scoffed.

"Did you hear that Bolden?" he said. "The boy was hungry!"

"So am I," said Bolden, who was struggling to hide his

exhaustion from the brief foot chase. He clutched his rounded belly and let out a hearty chuckle.

"You hear that, boy?" said the orchard keeper. "Bolden, over here, is *always* hungry. But if Bolden were to eat every time he was hungry — I wouldn't have anything left." The two men moved closer. "And if I didn't eradicate every last pest that made it through my walls, that little orchard would be nothing but a field of empty branches."

The man was close enough now that his hot breath was emanating across Aran's face. It reeked of stale cider and burnt gravy. The sight of his knife created a thick lump in the back of the boy's throat. Aran did his best to swallow.

"And that's exactly what you are, boy," the man continued. "Nothing but a *pest*. And pests need to be exterminated..."

Aran closed his eyes and prepared for the worst. He felt the rusty knife go upwards towards his throat, his sweat dripping down across the blade. What followed next was the sound of a galloping horse. He would recognise those thumping hoofs anywhere. The echoes of bashed cobbles were soon drowned out by the wails of a startled Bolden.

Aran opened his eyes to see Meaden's valiant head, charging towards them at breakneck speed. The widest of the two men was trampled down as if he were a bale of stuffed hay, as the horse leapt into the courtyard with the majestic flair that only he could ever possess. It was the kind of display that would have once filled the stableboy with a feeling of sheer terror — now it came as a welcome sight.

Sat upon this heroic beast was the old woman, who appeared to be controlling her horse with remarkable ease. It was a gift that Aran could only admire with great envy.

As for the orchard keeper, he had barely moved. The surprise appearance had frozen him to the ground like a helpless fly.

"Close your eyes, boy!" cried the woman.

The strange command had only confused Aran's captor even more.

"Mind your own business!" he growled at her. "You *old hag*! I'll turn that animal of yours into horse meat!"

Aran was more than happy to keep his eyes well and truly shut, although he had little faith that it would do him much good. Through the tiny cracks of his loosened eyelids, he could see the old woman reaching into her pocket. She pulled out an entire fistful of mysterious granules, before throwing out her palm to release a pale cloud across the man's grizzly face.

Aran had never heard a grown adult cry before. But the high-pitched squeals coming from the man standing there in the middle of the courtyard could have quite easily rivalled those of a screaming newborn.

The boy opened up his eyes to see his former tormentor now clasping his face with both hands, wailing at the top of his lungs for the agony to stop. What had initially felt like a spray of dry sand was now burning through his flesh like a hot rash. The orchard keeper dropped to his knees as the tears streamed out through his bony fingers.

"Climb aboard, lad!" cried the old woman, who was now steering her horse back towards the entrance.

Aran took a running jump towards the horse's back, severely misjudging the enormity of its large rear-end. He clung on for dear life, as Meaden darted forward towards the street ahead. They flew through the long passageway in a matter of seconds. Although he was far from being comfortable, Aran had somehow managed to secure himself a seat.

"Arch your back," said the old woman.

She could feel him shuffling behind her the whole way back to the town centre. Passers-by turned their heads in admiration at this powerful animal, hurling its way across the stone cobbles at a dramatic pace. Aran could feel the horse's beating heart, as it vibrated beneath him at regular intervals. The back and forth action of Meaden's pumping torso gave him a jolt of nausea with every movement, and it wasn't long before they were galloping out into the surrounding wilderness.

Aran looked back at the shrinking rooftops. There were only a couple of towns he had visited over the course of his sheltered childhood, but he had never been so glad to see the back of a place as he had Aber's End. He could safely say that he had no intention of a second visit, and he was quite certain that Aber's End would have little objection.

The sun had already begun to set by the time they had reached the nearest clearing. Beyond the bare trees of the surrounding woodland was a vast stretch of land that appeared to go on for miles. Either side of them were a variety of looming rock formations, blending seamlessly into the barren landscape. With no vegetation, and few signs of life, it was not an environment that Aran was used to. He felt an eerie shudder running down the back of his spine. Having grown up around the mountains of Lanbar, the boy had never known such flatness. The only noticeable feature of this infinite brown valley was a narrow river; it ran straight through its centre like an everlasting ribbon. The skies above had grown harsh and raw, and their blood-red colour unsettled the young traveller.

"Where are we?" he asked.

The old woman had been facing away from him the entire journey.

"By this point, I would say we're heading deep into the Ailman Valley," she said. "Better known as *The Devil's Basin*."

Aran pondered her answer for a moment.

"How can you be so sure?" he asked, knowing full well that it was a pointless question.

"I know the North Island better than you know yourself, boy.

I've been travelling through these lands since before you were born."

She pulled on the reigns and slowed them down to a grinding halt.

"I'd say this is a good spot, wouldn't you?" she said.

Aran took one look around the bleak surroundings and almost slipped out a laugh. There was nothing but wide-open space for miles in every direction. He assumed she must have been joking.

"A good spot for what?" asked Aran. "Starving to death?"

The long day full of trauma and stress had taken its toll. He had little patience left, and was beyond irritable. Meaden walked over to the shallow riverbank and dipped his head down for a well-earned drink.

The old woman laughed.

"No, my dear boy!" she said. "I have no intention of dying. Not out here, at least. There'll be plenty of time for that later."

Aran watched, as she slipped down from her saddle like a heavy sack of vegetables.

"Now, we sleep. It's been a very long day indeed."

Aran couldn't agree more. It *had* been a long day.

"But we can't stop here!" he protested. "I don't even know where *here* is!"

"What does it matter *where* we are? We are right *here*!" She raised her hands to the sky and inhaled the fresh air. "Have you anywhere else you need to be?"

"Actually, I do," said Aran, and folded up his arms. "I'm heading to the South Island."

"The South Island?" asked the woman. "Then what the devil were you doing in *Aber's End*?"

Aran went silent for a moment. The tone in her voice indicated that she indeed knew far more about the geography of Morwallia than he did.

"Because I was on my way to Tylbrek," he snapped.

The old woman laughed.

"Tylbrek! Oh my dear, dear boy..."

She shook her head and began pulling out various sticks and branches from her tattered bag. Aran had wondered why she had been collecting them on their way through the woodlands.

"Only a lost person would call Aber's End *on the way* to anywhere," she continued. "If I were you, I would get yourself a new map!"

She unleashed an enormous cackle. Aran hated being made fun of. At that exact moment, he felt like a complete fool The worst part of all was that the woman was right; he *didn't* have a clue where he was going. He had been walking along blindly, as blind as she was. The only thing that had kept him going so far was the faint hope that he might one day reach the south coast. Now he had received confirmation that his greatest fear had come true: he was well and truly lost. It didn't help that the same person who had delivered this depressing news was also the one laughing in his face.

Aran threw her a miserable glance. Somehow, even with her lack of sight, the woman could still feel the boy's frustration.

"Now come down here, you silly boy," she said, with a dismissive wave. "It's time to prepare some supper."

Aran looked at her in disbelief; first at the deluded idea of supper, and then at the daunting reminder of how high up he was. He had as much fear of getting down from a horse as he did climbing up one. He scrambled to his stomach like a beached amphibian, wiggling and squirming, until he came tumbling down in the most awkward position imaginable.

The old woman cringed at the sound of crunching knees as he hit the ground.

"You move with the grace of an old hag," she said, with a shake of her head. "And I should know!"

Aran dusted off his legs, and watched her gather the wood into a small pile. She continued to chuckle whilst drowning out the awkward silence with a range of disturbing noises. Her large posterior swung itself towards his face as she bent over. The woman had more in common with Meaden than she did himself.

"Tell me, boy," she said. "What do you call yourself?"

"I call myself, Aran," he replied, still sulking. "Because that's my name."

"Aran!" said the woman, "I prefer — *boy*."

She knelt down by the shore of the murky river and clasped her head in a peculiar position. "I knew a king called Aran. A strange king! You are not a king. You are a boy. A peculiar boy!"

Aran was struggling to contain his bad mood.

"I was named after the *River Aran*," he said with pride. "They say it breathes life into the people of Calon."

"Quite right!" she said, and placed her hand into the flowing water. "Rivers are a marvellous thing."

Her comment took Aran by surprise. It was the first time they had both been in agreement on something.

"Rivers are like horses," she added. Aran sighed. They were back to disagreeing. "A river is like a vein of blood. And blood gives us life."

Aran watched her reflection in the rippling water, her eyes motionless in the dark surface. She moved her hands in a delicate and hypnotic manner, before lowering them deeper into the harsh current.

"And just like blood... It can also drain life away." She let out a smile.

Aran dropped his jaw, as she gently lifted up a slender looking creature, with brown scales that glistened in the fading light. Its gills opened and closed, whilst it wriggled against the surface of her wrinkled fingers.

"But how — " Aran cut himself off. His hunger far outweighed his disbelief. He didn't care whether it was a miracle or a cheap trick. They now had a source of food, and his next meal was squirming away in the old woman's hands. His stomach could not have been more grateful.

By the time the skies had turned black, the two companions had already settled themselves underneath a large, woollen blanket. Their backs rested against Meaden's sleeping body. Even Aran could agree that the horse was a generous source of heat in this cold and unforgiving valley. He could feel every breath of Meaden's inflating stomach, as he tucked into his juicy fish in front of a glowing fire. How the old woman had even managed to *start* a fire was beyond him. But whilst chewing on his first piece of meat in many days, the boy had never felt happier.

"Aran..." muttered the old woman. She mulled over the name again, whilst the oils from her meal dripped down across her slimy chin. "Aran, of the River Aran! Ha-ha!"

Pieces of meat sprayed out whilst she chuckled.

Aran did his best to ignore the loud chomping noises and incoherent songs, which seemed to come along at any given moment. He had never met a more irritating person in all his life (and he had met more than his fair share).

"Aran!" she cried again, this time at the top of her lungs. Aran jumped with fright, the spontaneous cry nearly costing him most of his dinner. "Aran — the greatest river of them all. How I miss it."

Her startled companion wiped the spit from his face.

"You've seen — I mean — you've actually *been* to the River Aran?" he asked.

"Been to it?" she said. "I've swam in its clear, blue waters, at the height of summer."

The word summer filled them both with a tingling nostalgia.

They sat in silence for a moment, shivering underneath their rough blanket.

Aran stared into the burning firewood. He didn't know whether to believe the woman's tales or not — for she had many of them to tell. For the time being, at least, these incoherent stories were the only comfort he had left. Despite her constant rambling, and unpleasant noises, she had yet to let him down. She had twice promised him food, and both times she had delivered. However annoying her behaviour was, he knew she wasn't to be underestimated. After hours spent listening to her long stories, it soon became clear that she had visited far more of this vast kingdom than he ever had. Her relentless optimism offered him a feeling of hope during these troubled times (not that he would ever admit it).

After all, Aran had become the accomplice of a wanted outlaw. And that, in turn, made *him* an outlaw. He was now lost on an aimless mission, all so he could honour the promise of a man he no longer felt he even knew. The Gwail *he* had known was a grumpy old farmer — not a trained killer — a killer who could take on an entire army at short notice.

The old woman, on the other hand, didn't really seem to have a care or worry in the world.

"How are you there, King Aran?" she said with a laugh. "All hail, King Aran!" She touched his quivering shoulder and grunted. "Ah... My dear King Aran looks cold."

Aran shuddered in agreement, as she centred her body.

"Come, breathe with me." The woman began puffing out her chest and let out a series of deep breaths. They both inhaled the cold air together, in and out, in and out, until they found the perfect rhythm. This continued for a few minutes.

Aran's mind lit up from the burst of extra oxygen, and his muscles went numb with a strange euphoria. He had never felt such a sensation. Breathing had always come very naturally to him in the past — in fact, he practiced it all day long. But this was something very different. His heart rate began to slow, and his thoughts had completely mellowed. The fire in front of them danced around in a blur of vibrant colours, streaming and swaying like his confused body.

"I once knew a king," said the old woman. Her face gazed up towards a cluster of stars. "He was a proper king of course. Not like you, King Aran."

Such a comment would normally have irritated the boy. But tonight, he was willing to humour this persistent storyteller.

"Where did he live?" he asked.

His speech was stilted, and his lips had turned blue.

"He lived where all the other great kings have lived," replied the woman. "In the towers of Calon Castle."

Aran tried to focus his senses for a moment.

"You've been to Calon?" he asked.

"I had the most important role in the entire kingdom," she said. "I was a royal midwife. I brought into this world some of the finest people to have ever walked those white stones. For I never saw stones as white as those of Calon."

Aran listened with both wonder and disbelief. Something told him, by the look of sadness in her face, that she may well have been telling the truth. If this story was indeed true, it had been quite the revelation.

"I brought in my fair share of trouble too, of course," she continued. Her jolly tone had quickly descended into a cold seriousness. "There was one infant in particular that still troubles me to this very day. If evil could ever be born human, then that child's mother could have spawned the devil himself — and she might well have done. I could feel his black heart from the moment I first held him. I will never forget it." She fell silent for a while.

"What was the baby's name?" asked Aran.

"They named him, Morgelyn. A foul name that suited him well."

Aran went cold. The name she had just mentioned was a name he had heard many times before. For Morgelyn was the name of a prince. His mother was the queen of Morwallia, and her father, King Rowe, had sat on the throne for most of his life.

To hear such treacherous words against an heir to the most powerful position in the entire kingdom made him uneasy. This was a dynasty he had spent his entire childhood dreaming of a chance to serve. The young prince had seemed as pure as any of the royal family members. *Surely this bar me old woman was mistaken?*

"What is *your* name?" Aran asked.

The woman remained still. He couldn't believe he had spent this much time in the woman's company and not even thought to ask her name. To be fair, she had hardly used his own name very much either. *King Aran* may have been a strange nickname, but it was far better than *Boy*.

"I have been called many names in my time," said the woman, who had returned to her more jovial mood. "Some of which are far too rude to repeat here!"

She startled her companion with another laugh.

"But you may call me, Corwel. For that is the name given to me by my mother. The name I give only to my friends."

Aran turned to look at her. This stranger had done nothing but help him, and all he had ever done in return was dismiss her as a mad old woman.

"Then I will call you, Corwel," he said.

The old woman smiled.

"I haven't been called that in many years," she said. "It's good to hear it once again."

They both said nothing for a while. The crackles of the burning firewood filled their comfortable silence.

"I must confess..." Aran said eventually. "There was a moment where I thought you had stolen from me."

"Why, that was because I *had* stolen from you!"

Aran frowned at the unexpected response. Corwel laughed and gave him a playful shove.

"A magnificent beast like him should be ridden like a phoenix — not walked like a dog." She patted Meaden's stomach. "I was doing the poor sole a favour."

"So why the change of heart?" asked Aran.

"Bah! It was too easy," she replied. "It would have been like stealing a large block of cheese from a tiny field mouse. You should never steal from those who are helpless. Especially lost little boys."

Aran felt a surge of anger light up inside of him. His pride had taken a blow, and he struggled to hide it.

"I'm not as helpless as you might think," he said.

"Noooooo?" asked Corwel in a high-pitched voice.

"No," said Aran. He rested the satchel underneath his left hand. The thought of its contents brought him more warmth than a fire ever could. "I have seen crimes you wouldn't believe."

"Is that so?"

She decided to humour him. He had acquired her full attention. Whether she actually believed him or not was another matter.

"And what crimes has the brave, King Aran, committed that are so terrible?" she asked. "Don't tell me that this great horse is in fact *stolen*. It's cruel enough that you make him walk for miles on end, like some wandering old fool." Despite the cold breeze, she took out her pipe and lit it with great ease. "If you're not careful, you'll end up like me! An aimless old bat with no purpose but to torment others for her own amusement. People like you, King Aran! You are by far the most entertaining king I have ever met."

She slapped her palm against the boy's puny shoulder. Aran tried to maintain his dignity by pretending he had not felt anything.

"I do have a purpose," he said, his gaze still transfixed by the dancing flames.

"Well, good for you," said Cornel.

"I must continue my journey towards the town of Kolwith Bay."

Corwel went silent for a moment. She felt the seriousness in his voice and decided to spare him more ridicule.

"Kolwith Bay..." The old woman nodded. "There aren't many who would tread that way without a purpose. Only lost souls with nowhere better to be."

Aran reached into his purse and pulled out his uncle's envelope. Gwail's blood-red seal had miraculously remained unbroken.

"I have a promise to keep," Aran said. He slid his fingertips along its crumpled edges. "Tomorrow, I will continue south towards the coast."

Corwel shook her head in dismay.

"You think you can make it to the coast? On *those* two feet?" She pointed towards his worn-out shoes. The soles were already beginning to fall apart at the edges, whilst a great hole in the front corner exposed his white toe.

"I have covered a great distance already," Aran said. He looked up at the clear sky and located his trusty southern star. "If I keep going, I should make it in a few days."

He pointed south. In the distance was the open valley of the *Devil's Basin*, stretching out into the great unknown.

"Do you know what awaits you at the other end of this valley, boy?" Corwel asked.

She already knew the answer herself; Aran fell silent, for he did not.

"They don't call this part of the kingdom the *Northern Peaks* for nothing. Unless you know a better route, there will be many mountains to climb before you reach the coast. And what do you intend to do afterwards? Swim across to Kolwith? To the *South Island*? With your great, big friend over here?" She patted Meaden's thick fur. "Turn back, King Aran. Go back to your castle. Back to the place you once called home."

"It's too late," said Aran. "I can no longer go back, even if I wanted to."

The saddest part was that he knew everything the woman had just told him was true; he could never make it over the mountains on foot, and certainly not on his own. He would likely perish before he even reached the first summit.

The boy turned to face the old woman who was now stroking Meaden's dusty mane. She felt his pain. For she, too, had once called a place home.

"I can see he is very fond of you," said Aran.

Meaden's head was curled around her waist as he slept.

"The feeling is mutual," she said. "I have often felt closer with these creatures than I have with people."

Aran took one last look at the letter before slipping it back into his satchel.

"Tomorrow I will continue south," he said. "If Meaden means that much to you, then you are welcome keep him."

Corwel's mouth opened wide. A serious expression washed over her entire face, as her body went still.

"You would let me keep him?" she asked, in disbelief.

"It's the least I can do," said Aran. He turned back to look at the enormous animal behind him; that strong body, with those powerful back legs, stretching out into the dirt like mechanical pistons waiting to fire up again. "You are a better master than I could ever hope to become."

"Horses don't need masters," said Corwel, with a grin. "They need looking after."

"Which is exactly why Meaden is better off with you," replied Aran. "Take him as a gift. You have done more for us than I could ever hope to repay."

Corwel shook her head.

"My dear boy," she said, with a tap of his shoulder. "You have a kind heart. And that means you have a great deal to learn. For a kind heart is a rare thing in this world. No living sole has ever given me such a magnificent gift." She stopped to think. "Or *any* gift, for that matter. If it is south you must head, then it is south you must go. And I shall be the person to show you the way."

Aran turned his head to face her. It was an offer he hadn't expected. He was also surprised that she was insisting, and not asking.

"You can help me get to Tylbrek?" he asked.

"*Tylbrek*?" asked Corwel in return. "My dear Aran, I can get you all the way to the South Island! All that way across that treacherous sea they call Balog!" She leapt to her feet and saluted the air with a burst of excitement. "We have no need for the flimsy ferries of Tylbrek!"

She performed an enthusiastic dance in front of her confused observer. Aran didn't know whether to be pleased or terrified. But he *was* certain of one thing: he stood a better chance of survival with the help of this mad old woman than he ever did on his own. Not that it filled him with *that* much more confidence.

"I will provide you with the finest vessel this side of Morwallia!" the woman cried. "And the finest seaman to go along with it!" She began swirling her imaginary ship through its imaginary storm. "Commander Simlee — the most decorated sailor this side of the southern coast. Or at least, he was before he became fat and lazy!"

Aran watched her steer the invisible ship around the roaring fire.

"But why would he want to help *me*?" asked Aran.

"Because that old pirate owes me a favour," replied Corwel. "And a good pirate never likes to owe *anyone*."

She let out an uncontrollable laugh. Her light-hearted tone worried the boy even more. But if what she said was true, it was more of a plan than *he* had ever come up with. He hadn't a single piece of coin to offer anyone, and so, an old pirate's favour would be good enough for him (not that the word *pirate* was particularly reassuring).

It wasn't long before the two companions were fast asleep in a cosy heap, bundled together, beneath an impressive spread of watchful stars.

9

THE BRONCAT

Aran woke up to find a slither of orange sunlight creeping up over the horizon's edge. The gentle sound of running water was drowned out by Corwel's heavy snores. He took a moment to splash his face in the shallow river, hoping it would cure his tiredness after a disrupted night's sleep. The icy sensation also helped to wash away the growing feeling of dread. He hoped that the weeks ahead would be far less eventful than they had been the day before, but knew it was unlikely.

They set off at a steady pace. The Devil's Basin was as flat and dreary as it had been the day before. Meaden stormed over its rocky surface as if he'd been let loose for the first time in weeks. His thumping hoofs churned away at the dry gravel, causing it to rise up into clouds of thick dust.

Aran clung to his saddle for dear life. The landscape either side of him passed by in a giant blur, causing his newly discovered travel sickness to worsen with every gallop. He tried his best to look up over Corwel's bouncing shoulder, not that there was very much to see.

Over in the far distance was a line of colourless peaks. What

Aran had initially assumed were rocks, were actually the great mountains he had been warned about the night before. The Northern Heights, as they were so aptly named, curved around like a magnificent wall, an imposing fortress for anyone brave enough to approach them. Their intimidating presence had no effect on Corwel, who had been singing away for the entire duration of their ride.

"Fear not, King Aran!" she cried, raising her voice to compete with the beating rumbles of Meaden's hoofs. "I would know these mountains blindfolded!"

Aran felt her entire body shake from the explosive laughter. For someone who was supposed to be blind, her eyesight was proving to be far more reliable than his own. Still, he had long abandoned the will to question her. Whatever senses she *did* possess were far superior than all five of his own, and they were much more reliable than the old map at Penarth Farm had turned out to be. It amazed the boy how something so flat on a piece of paper was, in reality, a hundred square miles of vertigo-inducing elevation.

The dark horizon thickened with every passing hour. Heavy clouds hung low above the line of varied peaks and dominated what was once a clear sky. The temperature dropped into a bitter chill, as they made their way closer to the first of many mountain tops.

So far, Meaden had maintained a fairly steady pace. The Devil's Basin was already a distant memory. After a terrible night's sleep on its unforgiving surface, it was a memory that Aran preferred to leave far behind. The gravel beneath their feet soon morphed into luscious, green grass. The air was damp, which came as a welcome relief after breathing in clouds of dust for miles on end.

Aran looked over at the first great peak coming towards them. The towering mound reached high into the murky heavens, its sharp edge piercing through them like a mighty dagger.

Swirls of mist unleashed a shower of heavy rain across the three unfortunate soles who happened to be passing through their shadows. Aran attempted to shield himself from the sudden burst of falling raindrops. They fell heavy, and they hit hard. He scrunched up his face, as they tore through his hair and grazed the surface of his raw skin. Resistance was useless, and the drenching only got worse the deeper they entered the mountains.

Corwel, on the other hand, was in her element. She tilted back her head and embraced the rush of heavy rainfall, letting it wash over her wrinkled features like a cascading waterfall.

"Can you feel that, Aran?" she cried. "We are being baptised into The Northern Heights!" She celebrated with a high-pitched howl. "There's no feeling like it!"

Aran agreed; there *was* no feeling like it. He just wished it had been a feeling he enjoyed. He drooped down into his seat, like a soaked kitten, and continued to observe the hysterical performance of the woman in front with a miserable expression. Corwel swung out her arms like a mad sorcerer, as if summoning the bad weather with her waving stick.

Meaden's steady canter decreased into a gentle trot. The grassland beneath his feet steepened into an everlasting slope towards the dark skies. He soldiered on across the increasingly muddy terrain, and fought back against a series of gale-force winds. The impact of the storm was so powerful that it had lifted him off the ground on numerous occasions.

"Corwel!" Aran called, at the top of his empty lungs. But his cries were no match for the howls of the increasing winds. "Corwel!" he shouted again. "I see a cave!"

Corwel was hugged tight against her horse's neck, egging

him forward with every step. She would not be defeated by a spot of rain and wind.

"Now is not the time for sightseeing, King Aran!" she called back.

The invisible force of nature nearly threw the boy clean off his saddle, yet again. Aran held his driver tight and leaned forward to call in her ear.

"We need to find shelter, Corwel! Or we'll never make it!"

After a stubborn grunt, and a reluctant shrug, Corwel yanked hard on the slippery reigns. She sent them hurling back down towards the bottom of a steep cliff. The enormous rock-face stuck out like a drooping gravestone. Underneath its rigid surface was the gaping entrance to a dark cavern. Despite its eerie blackness, the hope of shelter filled Aran with a long-overdue feeling of joy.

"Keep going!" he cried. "We're almost there!"

Meaden hobbled his way into the cave, relieved to have found some refuge from the hellish conditions. Now that the three travellers were finally safe and dry, the storm outside appeared worse than ever. A transparent curtain of heavy rainwater flowed down across the entire entrance. This circular window to the outside world provided a tranquil water feature that lasted for many hours. The soggy cave dwellers sat in silence for the rest of the afternoon, and listened to the regular intervals of loud thunder as it echoed like music throughout the cavern walls.

In some ways, Aran found the whole experience quite peaceful; in other ways, he felt trapped. *How long would the storm last? Days? Weeks?*

Behind him was complete darkness. Every so often, he turned around to peer into the deep unknown. He couldn't help but wonder how far the cave would go.

"We shouldn't stay still for too long," said Corwel. The

exhaustion had made her unusually quiet. She pulled out her pipe and began puffing away. The fact that she could still manage to ignite her precious pipe during a terrible thunderstorm fascinated the boy.

"These mountains are crawling with broncats," she continued. "This is *their* territory, after all. We'll be sitting ducks in here."

At that precise moment, Aran longed for a far more comforting conversation. He had never seen a wild broncat before, and he was in no rush to meet one.

"Well... if we're going to be sitting ducks..." Aran muttered, with a gulp. "At least it's the perfect weather for it!"

Corwel tilted her head and lifted up those grey, bushy eyebrows.

"So!" she said. "Our King Aran *does* possess a sense of humour, after all!" She filled the cave with a cackle of laughter. "Who would have thought it?"

Aran struggled to keep a straight face. He couldn't tell if he was genuinely amused, or just delirious from the prospect of being eaten alive. By this point he had started to doubt his own sanity. Was he becoming as mad as the old woman? Either way, he didn't really care. He knew the isolation was going to get the better of him in the end.

Corwel continued to roll around in the dirt, her uncontrollable laughter causing a shortness of breath that broke out into fits of coughing. This only tickled Aran even more, and before long, his own back was also twisting against the floor.

The rain continued to pour well into the evening. Aran closed his eyes and listened to its hypnotic rhythm. Drips and drops began to sound louder with each passing minute, whilst their steady beats maintained perfect timing with his own heart.

The smoke from Corwel's pipe drifted around him with a misty haze. Aran was quite certain that this potent smoke was probably not doing his heightened senses any good, but it was useless asking her to stop. The smoking also provided a brief interval to her disjointed rambling. From time to time, her sporadic noises would alternate between serious conversation and meaningless chatter. It was as if she had a switch inside of her that flipped back and forth, turning her from a mad old woman to her wiser, more serious self. There were clearly two sides to this woman, and Aran was never quite sure which one he would be talking to next.

"So what does the great King Aran seek when he reaches the shores of Kolwith Bay?" Corwel asked.

Aran was taken by surprise. The question had just broken an entire hour of blissful silence.

"I hope to find a man named Wyn Drathion," replied Aran.

Corwel pondered for a moment. She had heard that name before.

"*Drathion*, you say?"

Aran sat up and turned to face her.

"You know that name?" he asked.

"I hear many names over the course of my travels. Some I forget, some I remember."

"And what about *that* name?"

Corwel took her time with the reply.

"From what I hear, this Wyn Drathion is not a man someone would wish to cross paths with. In this kingdom, a person is either a friend or an enemy. Unless of course... you have yet to cross paths." She gave him a pat on the shoulder. "If I were you, I would stick with the latter on this one."

Aran frowned. Once again she was testing his patience.

"Well, I don't have a choice," he said. " One way or another, I have to find this man. I must do it for my uncle."

"Is that so?" she asked. "So this uncle of yours knows him, does he? Well in that case he must have chosen the *friend* option.

Tell me, where is your uncle now?"

"He's... he was arrested."

Being forced to utter those words made Aran furious. It was as if she had known the answer already. For all he knew, Corwel had never even *heard* of the name Drathion. He had become tired of her cryptic tales and boastful manner.

Corwel may have been a more seasoned traveller than he was, but Aran was still convinced that she didn't know everything. For instance, she had no idea about the hidden wonders of his treasured satchel; the secret letter; the otherworldly gauntlet with its unique abilities. These two items he would keep to himself.

Although he had come to trust Corwel with his life at this point, there was still so much about this mysterious woman he had yet to discover. Her motives (if she even had any) remained vague, and each time Aran was a step closer to understanding her complex behaviour, she would somehow manage to knock him back a dozen steps more. The hard truth was that he would never get the chance to really know Corwel at all. And for the time being, he preferred to keep it that way.

The storm continued well into the night. The heavy thunder rumbled throughout the cave, its damp ceiling trickling in all directions, like melting stone. Aran lay awake and listened to the raindrops. They fell at regular intervals, like a ticking clock, or grains of sand inside a hollow egg timer.

His eyes soon fell heavy, and it wasn't long before he was snoring as loud as his companion. The humid conditions allowed for a deep sleep that lasted until the early hours of the morning.

Aran woke up to a deathly silence. Corwel and Meaden were nowhere to be found. The rainfall outside had also vanished, having been replaced by a warm sunrise. Birdsong filled the cave, and rays of comforting daylight spilled out across Aran's weary face. It was a miracle, he thought. He felt as if he had just survived a catastrophic shipwreck and was now resting on the gentle shores of a tranquil beach.

The boy sat up to find a pair of narrow, yellow eyes staring back at him. He let out a short gasp. Lurking in the darkness was a creature that turned the insides of his stomach into a pit of watery jelly. Even in the pitch-blackness he could still catch sight of those white fangs snarling back at him underneath a pair of quivering, pink lips. Whatever the animal's intention was, it did not appear friendly.

Aran threw himself backwards, cornering himself further into the cave. The beast stepped out from the shadows, its beefy paws scratching at the ground with razor-sharp claws. The creature forced its cowering prey back against the opposing wall, and let out a high-pitched growl that sent a chill down the boy's neck. Aran looked on in horror as its dark fur spiked up into a coat of sharp needles. He required no further warning; he slipped his trembling hand straight into the bottom of the satchel, and deep inside the gauntlet. With his forearm secure, he began swiping away as hard as he could.

Feline screams echoed around the cave. The boy's desperate strikes were no match for the sharp reflexes of this agile beast. Those pointed ears twitched and jolted from side to side, as the large target bobbed and weaved with effortless movement.

It was no use; Aran was now but a helpless mouse, and the giant cat had long grown tired of playing with its food. The hungry beast was a wild broncat, and wild broncats did not take too kindly to being provoked. Crouched on its front claws, with its tail raised high in the air, the furious animal braced itself for an almighty pounce.

Stood behind him, in the brightness of the cave's mouth, was the black silhouette of an old woman. Streams of daylight lit up her waving silver hair, as she raised her hand up with a slow and precise movement.

The broncat backed away without a moment's hesitation, much to the surprise of its former prey. This fierce aggressor had now been reduced to a whimpering kitten. The sight of Corwel's motionless expression haunted the boy. Her white, hollow eyes scared him as much as it had the animal.

Corwel circled the cave and herded the confused broncat back towards the opening. She reached out towards her helpless puppet, her steady hands in complete control over their invisible strings. The enormous tail went limp. Like a wounded animal, the broncat went scurrying out of the cave and back into the safety of the outside world.

Aran turned to the woman next to him as if she had morphed into a complete stranger. Corwel remained fixed in her unusual stance, her body frozen into place like a lifeless statue. Eventually, she lowered her arms and relaxed her muscles.

They stood in silence for a while, until eventually the woman spoke: "It's time we got moving now."

10

THE NORTHERN HEIGHTS

Corwel had broken through her strange trance with a deep and commanding voice. Aran said nothing in return. After what he had just witnessed, he was more than happy to oblige; it was time to move on.

Outside the cave, Meaden was busy munching on wet grass whilst enjoying the morning sun. The warm light glistened against his bright coat, as his two passengers climbed up onto the arch of his back. Corwel clipped the side of her heels, and before the boy knew it, they were galloping through the dwarfing shadows of the Northern Heights. Those great summits became pointed beacons, marking the way through the blinding sunlight, as it pierced down against the overlooking crests. Aran spent most of his journey gazing upwards; the skies above had cleared into an everlasting sea of tranquil blue.

After miles of steady riding, Corwel had returned to her usual, noisier, self. She laughed and sang, as though the events of that same morning had never happened.

Aran, however, remained quiet. It had been difficult enough to forget the traumatic experience of the hungry broncat, let alone the memory of what had saved him. All he could picture now was the image of Corwel in her hypnotic trance, her white pupils glowing in the darkness of the cave. She had connected with that animal in a way he could never understand. It had felt otherworldly, or even magical. If there was ever a moment to believe in the supernatural, it was during the midst of that ghostly performance in the cave. The event had left a scar in the depths of his sole, and he would never quite look at the eccentric old woman in the same way again.

"Cheer up, King Aran!" Corwel cried, leaping in her saddle and swinging on the reigns. "We will be dining by the sea in no time!"

Although the sound of crashing waves seemed like a long way off from the nauseating altitude of the Northern Heights, it was hard not to appreciate the vast distance they had already covered. By the time they had stopped again for another night's rest, the dream of salty air and wailing seagulls were starting to feel like a possible reality.

That evening, they sat upon the edge of an enormous ridge, one that overlooked an entire mountain range. The view had a long history of embedding itself permanently into the memory of anyone fortunate enough to witness it. Despite having his bony legs hovering over a deadly drop, Aran was, for the first time in his life, completely without fear. If he could look into the eyes of a wild broncat and still live to tell the tale, then surely he had little to worry about. Even Meaden was starting to grow on him by this stage. Bobbing around on a shaky saddle had become a very natural part of Aran's day. He sometimes wondered whether his newfound confidence was actually the result of a mysterious spell, and with Corwel around, one could never be too sure.

Aran tucked into his small supper beside the flames of a roaring fire. Corwel's effortless fire making skills were still a mystery. For now, he was more interested in the crispy meat of his succulent poultry, which only a few hours before had been scurrying along the same clifftop they were sat on. He looked up at the scorching sunset and smiled. It was certainly a moment to remember.

The steady progress continued for many days. Their success had been the result of two key factors: a brief patch of merciful weather and Corwel's incredible sense of direction. The woman's navigation skills had so far been impeccable. They weaved around the Northern Heights as if they were a field of small mole hills.

"You know the best way to conquer these mountains, Aran?" asked Corwel, as they descended a sharp ridge. "You avoid them altogether!" This was followed by an amused laugh. "They will eat you alive if you're not careful! There's only one way over these great monsters and that is to go *around* them."

Aran had no objection. He was no mountaineer, but her theory had worked well for them so far. They had spent entire days circling some very wide bases, but had also managed to avoid a series of treacherous rocks and disappearing paths. Aran would much rather be crossing the wide rivers of the valleys below than attempt the everlasting trails of the summits above.

The weeks dragged by with every passing mountain. Every other day, a brand new peak reared its ugly head. The higher they climbed, the deeper Aran's heart sank. The thought of being trapped in an eternal loop of passing mountains had become a newfound fear of his. Despite their great beauty and impressive views, Aran was growing sick of them.

Corwel, on the other hand, was as excitable as she had been on the very first day. The high altitude and fresh smell of evergreen pines made her giddier than her favourite pipe. Given the choice, she would have been perfectly happy circling these mountains for all eternity. Aran prayed that this would not end up being the case.

Although his lower half had become slightly more accustomed to the unbearable saddle soreness, his upper body was a different matter. The winding trails had given him a motion sickness that never seemed to go away. His diet, which consisted of any shrub, weed or fungus that Corwel could lay her hands on, was also not helping. He knew that beggars could not be choosers, but if he never had to eat a barbecued toad again he would have been quite happy.

Aran spent all of his days longing for the peace and tranquillity of the long nights. Lying awake, under a starry sky, he could still feel the heavy pounding of Meaden's footsteps, as if his body hadn't yet grasped the fact that they were no longer moving. He hoped that this would only turn out to be a temporary issue.

Each steady climb was inevitably interrupted by an abrupt descent; going up would always mean coming back down again, a hard fact of nature that did very little for the boy's moral. The mountain of Lanbar, the first mountain Aran had ever conquered, was a mere foothill compared to the daily grind of the Northern Heights.

By the time they had scaled one of the final stretches of near-vertical rock, Aran had begun to lose all sense of time and place. After a month-long marathon of physical torture, the Northern Heights had become a true test of both body and mind.

"Not long now!" Corwel cried. She hauled her horse up the steepest track they had come across so far. It was so steep that they eventually had to resort to the use of their own human legs. Meaden, who welcomed the rare break, was quite content to stroll alongside them.

Corwel continued with her usual selection of personal

ballads — those same repetitive melodies — which somehow managed to get stuck on an endless loop. Aran was in a particularly bad frame of mind that day, and the bombardment of high-pitched vocals was severely testing his patience. He had started to wonder whether the blind old woman had also acquired a hearing problem, not that he dared to mention it. His sore toes slipped and scraped against the harsh gravel, forcing him to stumble around on his raw hands for support.

"Come along, King Aran!" she said. "A young lad like you should fly over this mound with no trouble. There's no time for dawdling."

Aran looked at her with a harsh scowl. The misery he felt was only exasperated further by the freezing cold wind blowing in the direction of his face. For an elderly woman, with short legs and hunched-up shoulders, Corwel appeared to have the balance and grace of a young bird. Aran often imagined her sprouting a pair of wings and taking off into the air, never to be seen again. The exhaustion had hit an all-time record, and he was reaching such a delirious state of fatigue that he very nearly stumbled off a nearby ledge.

"Corwel!" Aran called. "I can't walk any further."

He dropped to his knees and began gasping for air. His head felt light, his body heavier than an iron skeleton.

Corwel had already reached the top, and was shaking her head in bitter disappointment.

"I thought you were made of tougher stuff than this, King Aran!" she cried back, before turning around to admire the view.

"We've been travelling for weeks!" Aran said. "I can barely stand! I have nothing left!"

Corwel tutted. "Nearly there. Not much further."

"You said that at the last mountain — *and* the mountain before that. I can't take any more mountains, Corwel. They're killing me!"

Corwel's gave him a grave look and shook her head.

"If these mountains wanted to kill you, they would," she said. "They have beaten entire armies!" The great clusters of rising earth stood tall behind her. She took a step back and raised up her arms in victory. "And yet here we both stand!" Aran looked up at her. He was not as convinced. She scurried down the path and reached out her hand. "Now the least you can do is come up here and admire their magnificent beauty."

Aran unleashed a long, exhausted sigh and let her drag him by the arm. He hauled his weary body over the last remaining steps, which felt to him like an entire lifetime. As he reached the end of their vertical climb, Aran dropped to his knees, gasping for oxygen, like he had just escaped from an underwater tank.

Corwel tapped her hand against his scrawny shoulder. "You see," she said. "There is always more fight left in you, lad. We are capable of so much more than we will ever know."

Aran raised his heavy head and came to notice something quite unexpected. Over on the southern horizon was a streak of dark blue, a blue much darker in shade than the blue of the sky above. The tall peaks parted ways to create a large opening. He was witnessing a sheer miracle; the Northern Heights had listened to his cries of mercy, and were melting away into a distant shoreline.

"It's... it's the sea..." Aran said, his mouth dangling in complete shock. He couldn't believe it. "We made it... We've made it to the southern coast!"

"Your eyes are far more reliable than mine," said Corwel, with a laugh. "I doubt they deceive you at this point."

Aran had never seen the sea before. And yet, he still knew, with all of his heart, that what awaited him beyond the next mountain were the vast salt waters he had always read about. Those stories he had studied in such great detail back on the farm, those famous pirates and brave explorers — they had all depicted an infinite world that dwarfed their own.

Corwel inhaled a nose full of salty air and smiled.

"I never get tired of that smell," she said. "Come on, lad. We are off to meet a drunken old pirate who still owes me a favour."

11

THE PIRATE HUNTER

Corwel threw herself up into the saddle. For a short and corpulent old woman, she could certainly move quickly when she needed to. Aran soon joined her by flinging his delicate body across a solid back of white hair.

The ground began to descend quickly, as they set off down a steep hill. Aran had no interest in bidding the Northern Heights a final farewell and chose to keep his full attention on the road below. He had seen more than enough mountains for one lifetime, and would much rather take his chances on the mysterious high seas than attempt another climb.

Before long, the salty air was filling his lungs and soothing his tired soul, an entirely new sensation that the boy could get quite used to. That horizontal, blue line had grown thicker with every mile. Clusters of tiny, triangular shapes morphed into focus, a sight that later turned out to be a fleet of fishing boats gathered around a small harbour.

"Did you say your friend was a pirate?" asked Aran.

"He describes himself as more of a pirate *hunter*, actually," Corwel replied. "Or at least... he was in his youth — a damn good one too — a member of the *Royal Sharkskins*, a crew of elite sailors, who brought in some of the most feared outlaws the sea has ever seen. Had they been fishermen, they would have come back with a great whale. Although, I hear my friend is a little more partial to shrimp these days!"

Aran was filled with an all too familiar feeling of dread. Corwel had managed to get him out of some fairly sticky situations so far in their journey, but she had also got him *into* many of those situations in the first place. Life with this woman had certainly not been dull.

"I don't think I've ever met a *pirate hunter* before," said Aran. He thought about it further.

"And neither would you want to," said Corwel. "The only time you come across a pirate hunter is when you're on his list."

"Then how did *you* meet him?" asked Aran.

"Ah, well." Corwel laughed. "For a while there, I think I was actually on his list." The news was hardly reassuring, and Aran had a horrible feeling that she wasn't joking this time.

Port Linion was situated in between two cliffs that curved outwards on either side. They rose up from the crashing waters, their white surfaces glaring from the sunshine. It was the same raw material that formed the coastal town's pale buildings. The wild calls of circling seagulls were a far cry from the serenity of the mountains.

They rode through the middle of the bustling harbour, with its idle vessels and crowded pier. Although it was far enough away from the manic atmosphere of Tylbrek's busy docks, it was the largest taste of civilisation that Aran had encountered in a very long time. On the shores of Port Linion, goods were being unloaded and deals were being struck; nobody had any idea of the epic journey these two travellers had just made, and nobody would ever care. It was an anonymity that Aran had become very grateful for. Despite all the frantic groups of busy seamen and impatient merchants, not one of them had even batted an eyelid at the passing strangers and their trusty steed. Life in Port Linion would continue as it always had.

Once they had made it past the lively seafront, and through the series of dusty streets, they headed upwards, towards the small hills overlooking the town. Meaden stomped his hoofs towards a stretch of sweeping sand dunes.

"How do you know he'll be home?" asked Aran, as they weaved around the prickly overgrowth. It was a very alien sight to a boy from Galamere.

"Because he has nowhere better to be!" replied Corwel. "The only friends he ever had were his old crew. I can't imagine any of *them* are still around. That man will die a sad and lonely death. If he is not dead already, of course!"

"But what about you?" asked Aran. "You said *you* were his friend."

Corwel frowned and turned her head around. "Is that what I said?" Aran nodded. "Well..." she mumbled. "Perhaps *friend* was the wrong word."

A sudden sadness washed over her.

"I thought he owed you a favour?"

"That he does," she said. "Friendships can melt away, but a favour lasts forever. They are like pieces of granite underneath a blanket of snow. You'll be wise to remember that, Aran."

Aran was relieved. For a moment he had thought the journey to see this mysterious sailor had been wasted. Only time would tell.

"Well, I owe you more favours than I dare count," he said. "If a favour lasts forever, then I'll be indebted to you for the rest of my life."

"I wouldn't worry too much. I'd say your life expectancy on this earth is pretty short if you hope to find your Drathion man."

Aran swallowed an enormous gulp. The sound of Corwel's cruel laughter rang loudly through his ears.

After a few more miles, a small cottage appeared across the dunes. What would once have been a quaint, little home by the seaside was now a dilapidated old shack. Outside the neglected house was an enormous scrapyard; it boasted an assortment of battered old boats, rusted naval equipment and piles of mysterious junk. Aran had never come across a shipwreck before, but if the worst wreckage in the entire world had been gathered up and placed in one, giant heap outside some unfortunate person's house, he imagined it would probably look something like this.

Meaden pulled up outside the front door. The property was as isolated as Penarth Farm. There was nothing around but rising mounds of sand and hovering seagulls.

"So this must be the place," said Aran, squinting at the arrival of a giant dust cloud.

Corwel dropped down from the tired horse and began waving her short stick towards the house. After a few loud knocks against the peeling door panels, they waited for a response. Minutes past, and after several more attempts, she stepped forward and placed her mouth against the rotting wood.

"Simlee!" she called out. "I know you're in there!"

Aran looked up at the dark windows and caught a glimmer of something sharp and pointy. He went flying from the back of his horse, as a large arrow went darting past his scalp. It passed so close to him that he had felt it blowing against the side of his hair. After a heavy fall, he looked up to see a bearded face looking down at them from the bedroom window.

"That was a warning shot!" cried the man. "If you don't leave now, the next one will be lodged right in the middle of your forehead"

Aran crawled through Meaden's long legs and took cover underneath his giant stomach. He felt bad sacrificing his own horse, but he knew the animal had a better chance of surviving another arrow than he did. The man in the window was holding up an old bow in his hand and had already begun to reload. A leather eye patch covered half of his face, and on his bald head was a crooked sailing hat.

"Simlee, you old fool!" cried Corwel. "It's *me*!"

"I know it's *you*!" replied Simlee. "And had it been *you* in my range I'd have gone straight for the heart!"

Aran cowered underneath the horse. He was beginning to doubt this so called 'friendship' he had been told about. Corwel's face had turned a shade of red.

"Now you listen here!" she called back. "Don't forget what happened the last time you made me angry!"

Simlee's face puffed up as if it were about to burst.

"Spare me your threats, you old witch!" he said. "Or I'll shoot that horse in its big, ugly face!"

He lifted up a blue bottle full of liquid and took a large swig. His speech was slurred and his eyes were almost glowing in a shade of purple. The potent substance that occupied his half-empty bottle had far more bite than a glass of drinking water. The dishevelled man climbed up to the edge of the windowsill and took aim.

"I'm warning you, Simlee!" called Corwel. "If anybody deserves an arrow in the head — it's you!"

Simlee took no notice. He lifted up the bow and pulled back on the tight drawstring. The tension from his long weapon caused him to sway from side to side, whilst his large, hairy feet barely kept themselves on the ledge. As he took his shot, Corwel turned her face to the nearby horse and closed her eyes.

Meaden exploded onto his hind legs and lifted his enormous body high into the air. Aran was now fully exposed as the horse's piercing cry caused Simlee to completely lose his balance. Startled by the sudden screech, he went flying off the windowsill before landing in a trough of murky water.

12

THE CROSSING

S imlee opened his eyes to find himself tangled in a web of thick ropes. His arms and legs were both tied with an excessive amount of strange knots, and his bald head was now fully exposed with the absence of the old hat. He looked up to see a stern face looming up above him.

"Wake up, you old crook," Corwel said. She prodded his sore legs with the end of her stick. The man's confused expression quickly turned to anger.

"I told you never to call me that," he snapped, whilst trying to shake away the drowsiness. "I've captured some of the most feared outlaws who ever lived. I deserve a lot more than *crook*."

"You're a drunken old pirate!"

"What would you know about pirates?"

"I know that it *takes* a pirate to find a pirate. And you have found many! How sad to see you are now living like a poor scavenger."

Simlee unleashed a wicked smile, and revealed a mouth full of gold teeth.

"I clearly must be dangerous enough for you to restrain me," he said.

Corwel prodded him in the cheek with her stick.

"The reason you're all tied up is to stop you from hurting *yourself*. You're lucky to be alive after that fall."

"I've survived greater falls than that windowsill." He looked up to see Aran inspecting the long bow, the same one he had been so keen to shoot him with earlier on. "You know who that bow belonged to, boy?"

"Whoever it was, I doubt they remember you," Corwel interjected.

"It belonged to Elgar-the-Quickshot!" cried Simlee, spitting as he spoke. "The most notorious assassin in all of Morwallia. And he's far too busy rotting in the king's dungeons to remember anything! All thanks to yours truly!"

Aran looked down at the bow and inspected the indecipherable carvings along its slender back. He had heard the stories. Could it really have belonged to Elgar Quickshot? The notorious assassin had been the stuff of legend, an infamous name that had inspired many a budding archer. Could this rambling old sailor really have turned in one of the most iconic outlaws in the last hundred years? In some ways, the boy wanted to believe it. In many other ways, he did not.

"And what have you got to show for it all now?" asked Corwel. "You've wasted away every fortune you ever made."

"You think I lived that life for fame and fortune?" asked the sailor, who was still wriggling around on the floor. "I hunted those outlaws — not for the wealth or reward — but because it made me feel *alive*. It gave me a purpose — *that* was my reward."

Corwel fell silent for a moment. It was clear that this volatile man had brought out a different side in her.

"The great Captain Simlee!" she declared. "Cooped up like an old hen. It's a sorry sight to see."

Simlee rested his head against the floor and gave the expression of a wounded animal. "I've tried hard to lead a normal life.

It's taking its toll on me, I'll admit. I had a better chance of survival when chasing down villains." He unleashed a delirious laugh.

Corwel peered at him through the smoke of her pipe. "If you think rotting away in here is a normal existence, then perhaps you really have lost your mind."

The living room around her was cramped and dingy, with barely any room to move. Pieces of old junk and clutter were piled high in every corner. Corwel picked up an old, wooden baton from a nearby stack of forgotten artefacts and began studying the craftmanship.

"Still holding on to the ghosts of the past, I see," she continued. "I know the feeling well."

"Either tell me what you've come here for, or leave me in peace," growled Simlee.

Corwel took her time with the response. She was rather enjoying the discomfort of her bitter, old friend. Simlee watched her eyelids gradually close.

"Don't you even think about getting inside my head," he warned, bashing the back of his skull against the hard floor. "You've done enough damage in there already. I know your tricks all too well."

Corwel slowly opened her eyes and spoke in a cold tone: "I need you to take this boy to Kolwith Bay."

Simlee burst into laughter. "Kolwith Bay? *Him?*" He looked the boy up and down. "He'd get eaten alive. That place is more like an open prison these days — a refuge for the wicked! He wouldn't last a day."

Aran felt his knees go weak. He was yet to hear a promising opinion of Kolwith Bay, and this may have been the most brutal one yet.

"Besides," Simlee continued. "I'm a retired naval officer, not a ferry captain. I have no desire to go anywhere. Why should I?"

"Because you owe me a favour," said Corwel.

Simlee shook his head. "I don't owe a penny to anyone."

"You owe me your life," she said in a raised voice.

"That was a very long time ago." The old sailor went quiet for a moment. "That was back when I had a life worth living. Now your favour is worthless."

Corwel puffed on her pipe and tried to contain herself. Simlee really was a mere shadow of his former self. She had underestimated the damage a life in the Sharkskins had taken on him.

Aran's heart sank. The one thread of hope he had clung on to over the last few weeks had been this so-called *favour* Corwel had spoken of. Now, it had turned out to be worthless. He had made it to the southern coast but with no way of crossing.

"What if this boy has something he can offer in return?" Corwel asked.

Simlee scoffed at the mere notion of it.

"What could such a puny thing like him ever have to offer someone like me?" he asked. "I own treasures from the far corners of distant lands — and beyond! No amount of gold in the world would cause me to set sail again. If I wanted to travel across to the bays of the Southern Island, I would have done it."

Aran grew nervous. *Did Corwel know about the gauntlet?* He hadn't let the satchel out of his sight the entire journey, but she always seemed to know everything. There was nothing else he could think of that would be of any interest to someone. He would do almost anything in the world to complete his mission for Gwail, but giving up the piece of armour might have been a stretch too far.

"Aran has an acquaintance that might interest you," said Corwel.

"I very much doubt that," muttered Simlee, before shooting out an enormous wad of spit to the other side of the room.

"Does the name, Wyn Drathion, mean anything to you?" she asked.

The room fell silent for a moment. Simlee took a moment to digest the name. He lied there in a bundle of ropes and began vibrating with heavy chuckles.

"*Wyn Drathion*? Are you telling me that this shrimp of a boy associates himself with the likes of *Wyn Drathion*?" He looked over towards Aran and choked out another one of his chesty laughs. "That man is currently the most wanted outlaw in the entire kingdom. The Queen herself has requested his capture, *personally*. The latest reward is obscene. You say that this mallard of a boy knows where to find him? He can barely pull the drawstring on that bow!"

Aran looked down at the firm spine of the infamous weapon in his hand. He had forgotten he was even still holding it. He placed the longbow down and tried to hide his frustration from the cackling observer. It had become apparent, once again, that Corwel knew more than she had let on.

It had also occurred to Aran that the only purpose he had left since leaving Penarth had been to find a man he knew very little about. The fact that Wyn Drathion's bounty had been common knowledge (or at least, it had been to a washed-up navy officer and a blind old woman) made him even angrier.

"Not only does this boy search for Wyn Drathion, but he knows his exact whereabouts," said Corwel.

Aran watched her spin out a web of lies like a cunning spider.

"You said you wouldn't tell him!" Aran called out, in his best attempt at an outraged reaction. He could see what Corwel was doing, but if they were to ever convince his last hope of getting to Kolwith Bay, he would have to play along.

Corwel smiled.

"And what makes this boy so different to everyone else trying to find Drathion?" barked Simlee.

"He has a letter," replied Corwel. She turned to Aran before uttering a few words that he never thought he would hear her say: "It's written by Drathion's most trusted ally, a farmer, going by the name *Gwail of Galamere.*"

Aran looked back at her in genuine shock; they were no longer playing along. He had never once mentioned his uncle's name to her — let alone the letter.

"But how... How do you know that name?" Aran asked her, in a state of disbelief.

Simlee let out a hurl of wicked laughter.

"Corwel — you old blood hound!" he cried, before rolling onto his large stomach. "I knew that gift of yours would pay off one of these days. If what you say is true, then you've really outdone yourself this time."

Corwel blew out a puff of smoke into the air.

"It's all true," she said. "A subconscious thought tells no lies. Shortly before his arrest, this Gwail fellow instructed the boy to deliver his letter — at all costs."

"Then we'd better make sure he does," said Simlee, with a sinister smile on his face.

Aran turned to look at Corwel. He felt a rush of betrayal rise up from the pit of his stomach as she untied her excited friend.

He charged towards the front door. After slamming himself against the solid wooden panels, it became clear that his only exit was bolted shut. He turned around to see a sharp arrow being pointed towards his heart.

"Spare your energy, boy," said Simlee, his bowstring yanked tight against his wide frame. Covering his arms and feet were a variety of faded tattoos. These vague patterns clung to his scarred flesh like overgrown ivy, and continued across the rest of his body. "We have a long journey ahead of us."

Aran stared into Corwel's lifeless face. She tied his hands together as if he were a piece of captured livestock.

"I think you'll find I've practically handed Drathion to you on a plate," she said. "Another worthy name for your precious list of conquests. Now it's time I received my own fee. You know what I've come here for."

Simlee gave her a knowing frown.

"First, I need to see the letter!" he cried. "I've fallen foul of your tricks before, old woman. I need to know for certain."

Simlee pulled away Aran's satchel. The boy cried out in protest as his uncle's envelope was swiftly torn open. Simlee lowered his bow and unfolded the page inside. His sharp pupils squinted towards the mysterious writing.

"I can't understand a word of it," he said.

"I'm sure you'll find someone on the South Island who can translate," said Corwel.

Simlee reached the bottom of the page to find a large signature. "The letter is signed *Kelion Drathion*."

The room went quiet.

"I told you he was a close ally," said Corwel. "The man is Wyn Drathion's brother — the second most wanted man in Morwallia."

Simlee struggled to contain his excitement. "You're telling me this was written by *him*? Drathion's *brother*?"

"So it would seem," replied Corwel. "It doesn't surprise me that he changed his identity. Drathion is not a name you would want to keep with a brother like his." The sailor noticed the surprise in Aran's face. The boy was left speechless, once again. "As you can now see, the letter is completely genuine. There is no greater proof you could have."

"Perhaps," Simlee replied. "But you've provided me with little more than the seeds of a new bounty. It's a good start, I'll grant you that. But it's hardly a fair trade for what you seek."

Corwel began shaking from the anger bubbling up inside of her.

"Simlee, you ungrateful swine!" she screamed, much to the sailor's surprise. "So be it!" She opened up Aran's bag and lifted out the emerald gauntlet. The boy's heart sank. "I shall throw in a piece of Drathion himself."

Simlee's eyes burst open as she handed him an unusual piece of body armour. His stained fingertips inspected its smooth exterior.

"This belongs to the outlaw, you say?" he asked with a grunt. "Looks like a piece of old junk to me."

"What I have given you is the opportunity of a lifetime," Corwel insisted. "I have provided a key for what will inevitably become the highlight of your pathetic excuse for a life."

The sailor went quiet, whilst he took another close examination of the letter's mysterious scribblings. He had spent his entire life chasing after famous outlaws and had come close to apprehending them all. But there was one famous individual he had yet to encounter.

Simlee's expression went from excitement to uncontrollable euphoria. The other two watched, as his beady gaze gradually made its way down the paper. Aran jumped with fright as the man let out a deafening howl.

"Who would have believed it? The call of adventure is summoning me, once again!"

What followed was a style of naval dance that only a former seaman could ever truly express. Simlee circled the room in a burst of boundless energy.

"Cheer up, boy!" he told Aran, who was looking more miserable than he had done through the entire journey over the Northern Heights. "I'm taking us to the South Island! You're going to help me make history!"

He dangled the piece of stained paper above Aran's lowered head before quickly swiping it back again.

"Enough!" growled Corwel.

Her giddy associate composed himself for a moment before taking a deep breath.

"Very well," he said to her. "You shall have your reward."

"You will give me what's rightfully mine in the first place, you mean," said Corwel. Her patience had worn thinner than Simlee's hair.

The strong winds outside the cottage had caused a mild sandstorm. Aran was soon making his way down a steep foot-path, one that snaked its way all the way down towards the shore. His wrists were now sore from the old rope rubbing against his skin. Granules of harsh sand scratched at his face as he reluctantly followed his cheerful captor. Simlee whistled a merry tune as he walked, and the gauntlet was now covering the tattoos on his bulging forearm.

A small cove with a pebbled beach had dug itself deep into the side of the eroded cliff. The rising tide continued to push further in with every wave. About a mile out to sea were the masts of a sunken ship. The shell of this great vessel rose up from the water like an enormous carcass of rotting wood. Its sails were long gone, but the skeleton of this mighty vessel stood strong for all to see. Its curved stern pointed up towards the grey skies, still holding out a faint hope that one day it would set sail once again.

Aran looked over towards Corwel. She had not said a word since they left the cottage, and the boy could hardly recognise her as she made her way down the cliff beside him. Even after all the countless weeks they had spent scaling the Northern Heights, he knew less about her now than he did back then.

"Are you really even blind?" he asked her, deciding to settle the nagging suspicion once and for all. She released a deep sigh.

"You mean, are my eyes incapable of seeing all the wondrous shapes and colours, as most people do?" she asked back. "Then the answer is yes."

Aran shook his head, still not knowing what quite to believe.

"I can promise you one thing," she continued, "My eyes may not see the light, but I can see far more than most people."

"Is that how you knew about my uncle?" he asked. "About Gwail?"

"The people where I come from have learnt to harness many of our senses. Morwallian people have barely scratched the surface of what is really possible. It has always been such a primitive culture."

Aran tugged at the rope behind his back and gave her a disgusted scowl.

"Why are you doing this, Corwel?" he asked. "*Why?* After everything we've been through. You promised me you'd help me find Wyn Drathion."

"And I have kept that promise," she replied. "I have given you one of the most skilled head-hunters I have ever known. If anyone can find your Wyn Drathion, it's him."

"I'd rather do it on my own," snapped Aran. "I am not some goat you can use to barter with."

"One day you'll understand. This is your best chance at reaching the South Island."

"You told him I know where to find Drathion. All I have to go on is the name of a town I've never even *been* to!"

"I would avoid mentioning that part if I were you. The more he thinks you know about Drathion, the better. Otherwise he might as well throw you overboard."

Aran shook his head. He could see that there had been more to her motives all along. Whatever it was that she was willing to trade him for, it was clearly far more important than his own well-being. In that moment, he knew he would be resenting the woman for as long as he lived.

When they finally reached the stone-covered shores, Simlee was already knee-high in seawater. The large sack of belongings that had been hanging from his shoulder was now thrown to one side. He removed his grubby shirt to reveal a heavily painted torso; the same tattoos that covered his thick forearms were now stretching well over his bulging potbelly. He took one last look through a long viewfinder before diving, head first, through the incoming waves.

For a man who had let his health suffer in recent years, Simlee could crawl through the sea quicker than the fittest of swimmers. Aran watched him glide away towards the shipwreck, kicking and splashing, like a frantic rescue dog.

"Is that the ship we're supposed to be taking?" Aran asked, in his most sarcastic of tones. Corwel said nothing.

When Simlee finally reached the gaping hull of this formidable ship, he flung his toes high into the air before diving down towards the murky seabed.

The determined seaman had been gone for quite some time. Aran started to wonder whether he would ever see the man again (a thought that gave him a glint of hope). After what had felt like several minutes, a record for any diver, the boy could just about make out a cluster of tiny bubbles. They continued to rise up above the top deck, until Simlee's gasping face came shooting out from the water for a breath of air. After a surge of oxygen through his tired lungs, he lifted up a tiny metal chest that was attached to a loose chain. With one final inhalation, he threw out his heavy arms and splashed them against the powerful current. Soon he was making steady progress back towards the shore, his most prized possession in toe.

Corwel eagerly awaited his return, and was pleased to hear the crashing of wet pebbles against a wall of loose flesh. Simlee had come ashore face-first, and was now panting on the ground like a beached whale.

Aran could barely take his eyes off the glimmering gauntlet still fastened around the man's arm. The boy looked on with a nagging sense of curiosity. Simlee rummaged through his old sack, only to pull out a tiny set of keys. It was clear that the small chest had been sat at the bottom of the shipwreck for quite some time. Pieces of wet seaweed poured off the lid as it was gradually forced open with the help of a successful key. Inside was a peculiar locket with a carved symbol on the front. Simlee lifted it up towards the sunlight and grinned.

"More blood has been spilled over this one item than any of my other possessions combined," he said. "For years I have never understood its value." He took one last look at its brass exterior before handing it over. "Some call it the *widow's compass*. There's only one thing I know for certain, though — it's the worst rotten compass *I've* ever used! Lousy piece of junk."

Corwel took the treasured artefact into her wrinkled hands and rubbed against its soft casing. She flipped open the lid to reveal half of a white sphere that rose up like a hollow eye staring up at the sun.

"It's called an Olyiason," said Corwel with a frown. "It's only useless to those who are too ignorant to use it."

Simlee scoffed.

"Well, I hope you get more use out of it than I have," he said. "If it gets you lost then it's no fault of mine." He lifted up his arm to admire the gauntlet. "You've given away something far greater if you ask me. That boy is about to lead me to the greatest prize of them all." Aran stared back at him with a complete void of emotion. "I shall forever be known as — Captain Simlee — the man who caught Wyn Drathion!"

13

THE BLUE DUCHESS

By the time he was floating in the middle of the Balog Sea, Aran had lost the will to speak. He had not uttered a single word since they had left the shore. The conversations on the beach had hit him like a punch to the stomach. He didn't know whether to feel surprised or foolish.

It had been quite clear on the night he had left Penarth Farm that Gwail was more than just a humble farmer. But never in a million years had he ever expected him to be the sibling of a famous outlaw — and a dangerous one at that. It still explained very little about the green armour, or why it had been buried within a short range of Gwail's doorstep. He suspected that many of his questions would be left unanswered.

"Cheer up, boy," said the man at the front of their tiny rowing boat. "You're part of *my* crew now. I need a first mate who doesn't look like he's going to throw himself overboard."

Simlee was rowing heavily against the rough tide. He pulled back and forth in a steady rhythm, his oars crashing down against the rising waves.

After another long pause, he dropped his giant levers and rested for a moment. Aran watched him pull out an enormous blade. The boy's throat went dry, as the knife glared in the harsh sunlight and came gliding towards him.

"Have it your way, then," said Simlee. "Turn around."

Aran did as he was told. He turned his back for what he presumed would be the last time. A second later, he felt a sharp yank against his bound wrists. Suddenly his hands were free.

"Call it an act of faith," said the sailor. "You and I are partners in crime now. If I'm going to hunt down the most dangerous man who ever lived, I might as well have a witness."

"I am not your partner," snapped Aran. The frustration of Corwel's betrayal had left the boy far too angry to be afraid. He had been abandoned once again, left to continue his travels with a man who could quite easily slit his throat at the drop of a hat. In a moment of sudden realisation, it dawned on the boy that he didn't need to worry at all. "Besides, you need my help a lot more than I need yours."

Simlee let out a voracious laugh and sat back down. "That's the spirit!" he cried. "Although, how you ever intended to cross these waters alone is beyond me!" He leant forward and lifted up his knife. "You see, boy, what I can offer you is protection. No harm will ever come of you with me by your side. Your death would not be in my best interest. There are plenty of cold-blooded criminals who would love the opportunity to come across a lonely little boy like you. Believe me, I've met most of them."

He flicked up the knife-edge in between his rotten teeth; a lethal toothpick, for a lethal hunter.

"I doubt we will ever make it to the South Island to find out," Aran said. "Crossing the sea of Balog in a rowing boat was not exactly what I had in mind. I thought you were supposed to be a captain? You don't even have a ship!"

"If you'd like to keep your tongue, I'd be careful on how you use it," Simlee growled. The disgruntled seaman lifted up his oars again and continued rowing. The thick veins across his bare arms popped out with every rotation. Beads of sweat flickered from his forehead with each new grinding pullback. Something had clearly touched a nerve. "And I'll have you know I *do* have a ship."

"The same ship I saw buried under water?"

"She's called *The Wild Rose!*" Simlee snapped. He took a pause and tried to compose himself. "And as for her crew, well..." He looked up at the surrounding water. There was nothing to be seen for miles in every direction. "They chose their own fates the minute they decided to betray their own captain."

Aran sensed a darkness in his eyes that he hadn't yet come across. What he had previously dismissed as a drunken, old fool was now baring the scars of a lifetime of horrors.

"Let this be lesson to you, Aran," the man continued. "Those who decide to cross me will never last long. They always pay the price in the end. You're either with me, or against me." Any hint of courage that Aran had so far developed was suddenly decimated by the threatening stare coming from the other end of the boat. With just one look at the vibrant gauntlet on his right arm, Simlee had flipped back to his previous jolly mood. "But now is not the time to dwell on such unpleasantness." He reached for the blue bottle beside his leg. "Now is a time for celebration." He took one large swig before handing it to Aran. "Come! Have a drink with me, boy. This is the finest lewpetal juice you will ever come across."

Aran took hold of the bottle's thick neck and took a whiff. He had never drunk lewpetal juice before, and even the potent fragrance brought tears to his eyes. He suspected that the sailor had drunk more than his fair share over the years, which would explain the disturbing wildness in the man's eyes. With one foul lift of the bottle, Aran swallowed an entire mouthful. The burning liquid ate at the back of his throat like a blaze of fire. Simlee burst into a fit of laughter.

"That's it, boy! We'll make a proper seaman out of you yet."

He couldn't help but admire the boy's defiance. The loneliness and isolation of his cottage had been difficult for the man who had once boasted a loyal crew of able seamen. In Aran he saw the early makings of a new shipmate, or even an apprentice. Sitting before him was a piece of raw clay still pliable enough to mould, but cheap enough to cast away. It was early days, of course, but Simlee knew that catching a fish as slippery as Drathion would require more than just a single pair of hands (even if the other hands in question were small and weak). This was his opportunity to gain trust, something Wyn Drathion had yet to earn. With enough time and patience, Aran's loyalty would ultimately lie with him.

"Do you know the difference between an outlaw and a sailor?" Simlee asked, after yet another gulp of lewpetal juice. "An outlaw can live forever. They become a figment of the public's imagination. They are no longer flesh and blood." He wiped away the excess dribble from his chin and leant forward. "But I have witnessed, first-hand, that an outlaw does in fact bleed, just like the rest of us. Some of them are little more than petty thieves with a catchy title. Everyone knows the name *Snake-Skinned Sam*, but do they ever talk about the man who brought him to justice? Captain Simlee, and his crew of fearless seamen? Never!"

The drunken rower began to slur and sway, even more than he had done already. The potent drink was coursing through his whole body now, his eyes wide with a strange, fluorescent colour.

"But I'll tell you one thing," continued Simlee. "They will all remember the man who caught Wyn Drathion. They will sing songs and write poems. I will become known as a slayer of dragons. For every legend needs a good ending."

Aran listened to the man's incoherent rambling until the sea grew dark and the air grew cold. Blackness had finally descended upon them, almost without warning.

After a short doze in the back of his new floating home, Aran woke up to the sound of heavy snoring. Lying flat on his back against the wooden floor was Simlee's and his oversized stomach, which fluctuated up and down like a struggling bagpipe. How easy it would be, Aran thought, for him to reach across and grab the giant fishing knife. How easy it would be to put an end to his new predicament, right there and then. He imagined the piercing sound of that enormous belly and almost vomited from the horrible reality.

He shuffled closer towards the sleeping captain, whilst keeping every movement of his body as silent as possible. Apart from his creaking footsteps, the only other noticeable sounds were the irregular splashes against the side of the boat. The steady crawl felt like an entire lifetime. When he finally reached a pair of large, hairy feet, those dirty soles only inches away from his own face, he lifted up his quivering hand and reached for the knife. With the blade held high, he looked down at his snoring kidnapper and clenched the handle.

A surge of hesitation filled his tightening body. *What would he do afterwards? What would become of him then?* He had no plan, whatsoever. A simple farm boy with such limited knowledge of the sea would surely perish. Simlee had been right; Aran *did* need this cold-blooded madman far more than he needed him. To continue on alone would surely be suicide. Then there was the small matter of slaying a man in his sleep, something he had never pictured himself ever contemplating in a million years.

As the boy lowered his weapon and released a slow, calming exhale, he caught sight of something that made him leap up with fright. Down below was a large eyeball. It was staring straight back at him, wide and open. Moonlight glistened against that long and toothy grin.

Aran struck his back against the side of the deck as an oversized body mounted him to the floor. Simlee's amused face was quickly brushed up against his own, his sour breath invading the corners of two reluctant nostrils.

"What's the matter?" Simlee asked. "Didn't you have the guts?" He dragged the back edge of his knife against the side of Aran's hair. "How about I spill yours all over this here boat? I've done much worse for far less. If you're going to slit a man's throat while he sleeps you'd better do it right."

"I wasn't..." Aran could barely spit out the words as a firm grip clenched his throat. "I couldn't do it!"

"No?" asked Simlee. "Then what *were* you going to do? Give me a clean shave?"

"I mean — I was, but... I changed my mind."

Aran was soon hoisted up by the scruff of his neck and thrown overboard into the cold sea. Before he could come to terms with what had just happened, the salty waters were already engulfing his small lungs.

"How do you prefer it out there?" Simlee called out. "Perhaps I have *also* changed my mind. Perhaps I don't need you, after all." He leant down against the side of the boat and peered down at his helpless companion. Aran splashed for dear life, his tiny arms proving little match for the strong current. Each time he inched a little closer to the underside of the hull, a large wave threw him straight back again.

Simlee let out a cruel laugh and began teasing him with a dangling rope.

"Help me, please!" cried Aran. "Let me back on board!"

After a number of false throws, Simlee lassoed the boy's neck and pulled him inwards. The long rope dragged Aran up from the water, like a noose that was slowly choking him to death, until he was back within the safe confinement of the rowing boat.

"Well this here is a pathetic catch if ever I saw one," said Simlee . Aran lied against his feet whilst throwing up seawater and pleading for air. "Perhaps I should throw this one back!"

"I didn't even do anything!" Aran cried, his chest on the verge of collapsing from the influx of water. "I wasn't trying to kill you."

Simlee sat himself back down and watched the boy suffer. "You didn't kill me, because you didn't have the guts," he said. "It's that same spineless attitude that nearly had you sleeping with the sharks tonight."

"If I wanted to kill you, then I would have done it," Aran spat out. He rested his freezing chest against the wooden floor. "I know more violence than you think — I've seen a whole army drop to its knees!"

For a moment he wished he hadn't said anything. Simlee stared at him for a while before letting out an amused grunt.

"Is that so?" he said. "An army of rabbits, perhaps?" He chuckled. "Bah! Knowing you, it was probably a horde of maggots!"

"They were led by a knight of the Brenin guard." Aran knew the old pirate hunter would never believe him. But it felt good to say it in front of a man who would probably be the death of him. He no longer had anything to lose, not even his treasured gauntlet. The act of sorcery he had witnessed on that dreaded night continued to plague him to this very day.

"A Brenin?" asked Simlee. "You're telling me that a worm like you has come face-to-face with a knight of Calon? I'll tell you one thing, boy — you're a damn good source of entertainment!"

Aran ignored his cries of laughter and sat back against the side of the boat. His attention was no longer on his tormentor, but on the vision that plagued his dreams.

"I saw my uncle defeat over a dozen armed men," Aran continued. "In a flash of light, they all fell down like toy soldiers. If my uncle were here now you would not be laughing."

Simlee listened intently. He slurped his drink before wiping off his wet chin. He sensed the boy's pain, like a shark smelling blood. Perhaps he had underestimated this child.

"You have the voice of a guilty man," he said, examining the boy's face. "I've seen that look many times before. They are the eyes of a criminal."

"I was given no choice," snapped Aran. "We had to escape."

"Oh, there's always a choice." Simlee had stumbled on a weakness, and he was determined to take advantage. The sailor put down his bottle and moved forwards. Aran looked up for a moment and caught his serious gaze. "You see, Aran, we're not so different, you and I."

"I am nothing like you."

Simlee rose to his feet in a burst of excitement.

"Oh, but you are!" cried the pirate hunter. "It's like looking in the mirror."

Drops of rain began falling from the black skies up above.

"We are not like regular people," he continued. "The laws of society only hold us back from reaching our true potential. They try to lock us away, like animals, and yet we are more free than they will ever be. You think Wyn Drathion answers to the Brenin? It's not in his nature. It's that same instinct that caused you to climb on top of me and reach for that knife. You were taking matters into your own hands."

"You're wrong." Aran was trying hard not to listen.

"Am I?" asked Simlee. "Your Gwail man is a killer, just like his brother. And he is a liar!"

"He is not!" Aran's words rang out over the rumbling thunder. The boat began to rock with the increasing waves.

"No?" Simlee reached into the inside of his trousers and

pulled out the rolled up envelope. "Then why did he not tell you who he really was?"

The boy went silent. Water streamed down from his wet hair. His vision started to blur.

"You know nothing about my uncle," he said eventually.

"I know enough." Simlee relished in the boy's frustration. "He has been lying from the beginning. The man wasn't even your uncle. He had you believe he was a farmer. He turned you into a cold-blooded outlaw — an enemy of the crown."

"Stop it!" Aran cried, holding back his tears.

"Why? I am the only person left you can trust, the only person who will ever tell you the truth. And I've saved the best secret until last." Simlee towered over him like a commanding god, the gathering thunderstorm framing his every movement. Water cascaded down his bare torso like a disturbing waterfall. "That mark on the back of your neck..."

Aran clutched the back of his long hair. "What mark?"

Simlee crouched down to the same level. He grabbed the side of the boy's head and lifted up the large fishing knife. Aran looked down at the sharp blade and began tugging with all his might.

"Trust me, boy," said Simlee in his most calming voice. "Or you'll never learn a thing."

He lifted up his brass periscope and held it behind the boy's neck. With the knife in one hand, and a polished brass surface in the other, he presented him with a narrow reflection. Aran gazed into the glimmering blade to see peculiar markings on the back of his own neck. With his hair raised up like an all-revealing curtain, he could make out a cluster of dark blotches. They swirled across the surface of his pale skin, as if an insect covered in black ink had been crawling its way around the back of his skull.

"I saw it when I pulled you out from the water," said Simlee.

Aran felt a tingle of goosebumps. He couldn't believe he had never seen these markings before. Penarth Farm had very few mirrors (they were a sign of vanity, according to Gwail) and it would have required at least two of them before he would have ever caught a glimpse — not to mention a good haircut. His uncle had certainly never pointed them out to him.

Simlee peered at the back of his neck with wide eyes. "Do you know what these markings mean, lad?" There was an excitement in his rough voice.

A spellbound Aran eagerly awaited the answer, as the boat shook them with a merciless force of nature. The two passengers went flying to their hands and knees, as the wooden floor beneath them began to elevate.

Aran looked up to see the largest wave he had ever seen. It curled towards them at an incredible speed. The giant mouth created a large opening in the water beneath, a drop so vast, it seemed to go on forever.

"Get down as low as you can!" cried Simlee, who grabbed his oars and began frantically steering the boat away. Aran took cover, bracing himself for the inevitable impact. With an explosive jolt, they went tumbling over to one side, rotating several times in mid-air.

Aran felt as though he had been swallowed whole, as the water, once again, began to fill his lungs and burn his eyes. The world around him had descended into an everlasting slow motion. He was flung around in a number of different directions, leaving it impossible to tell which way was up.

Just as he was destined to be trapped in this underwater void for all eternity — never to see the light of day again — he was struck by a flash of bright green. Before he even had time to make out the full shape, a giant, powerful hand grabbed him by the shoulder. In one smooth motion, Aran was lifted into the air and dumped onto the familiar safety of the rowing boat.

"I told you to stay low!" cried an amused Simlee, who was fighting off the incoming waves like a single soldier, fighting off an army. He pummelled his remaining oar from one side of the boat to the other, changing its direction with every new obstacle. "Ready for another ride?" His shaken crew member did not answer. As harsh as this terrible situation was, the old sailor appeared to be relishing every moment. The high likelihood of a slow and painful death made Simlee more alive than ever. To him, this bitter fight for survival was just another one of life's cruel games. For a brief moment, it was a game he also seemed to be winning. His sadistic howls echoed out over the deafening winds.

Aran held on for dear life, as Simlee began rowing towards the next wave like a madman with a death wish. The boat glided over its foaming head with an ease that only a skilled rower could ever hope to achieve.

Simlee cackled at another easy victory. But the premature celebration was soon to be interrupted by the appearance of yet another mountain of water. The rising wave curved towards them, drooling at the mouth, until it chomped away at the help- less boat.

This time, any hope of recovery was soon washed away, and the small wooden vessel was instantly devoured, sending both its passengers flying into the sea.

Aran swam with all his might to stay above water. Only a few yards away was a floating Simlee. Stranded and alone, with no sign of a boat, the bobbing seaman had clearly taken a large blow to the head. He was now at the mercy of Mother Nature.

The boy began frantically splashing his arms. The sea had become a heavy-breathing monster, rising and lowering with its unpredictable gasps. With a determination that he never knew he had, Aran fought against his exhausted body, which felt as if it had been cased with a layer of lead. With a final kick of his tired legs, he pushed forward and wrapped himself around Simlee's bulging limbs. After a drastic attempt at keeping them both from drowning, Aran was surprised to come across a pair of beady eyes glaring back at him.

"It would appear our fate has been sealed," said a mellow sounding Simlee. Barely held together, they both drifted in the middle of the ocean, like two pieces of forgotten debris. "This is where our journey ends. Don't fight it, Aran. There's no finer way to go out than at the hands of Glandra, goddess of the high seas! Embrace her glorious wrath!" He gave his companion a fatalistic smile before lying back to accept the final moments.

As the urge to keep on swimming slowly drained away, Aran looked up at the colossal black shadow coming towards them. Cruising through the heavy rain at an incredible speed, the imposing vessel grew larger in size with every passing second. With the narrow silhouette becoming more and more recognisable, Aran's waning heartbeat burst back into life with a miraculous second wind.

Ascending above him was the comforting sight of an enormous galleon. Its pointed masts were accompanied by a layer of beating sails, which shook in the ferocious winds with a mighty resistance. Leading the way was a long stern; it pierced through the fog, sharp and ready to cut through anything brave enough to obstruct its path.

Despite this small glimmer of hope, the desperate cries from Aran's strained mouth were muted by an invasion of seawater. With his throat full, and his muscles numb, he plummeted downwards until there was nothing but darkness. The crashes from the storm above were muffled into a gentle murmur, and his mind slowed into a calm and meditative state.

As the boy began to drift off into an everlasting slumber, his legs became caught in a layer of thick netting. The mysterious web wrapped itself around him, and, like a helpless fly, he was lifted upwards with great force. Within seconds, a disorientated Aran found himself rising above the sea as though he had been gifted with a pair of wings. Soaring through the air, it became apparent that he had been plucked from the sea by the largest fishing net he had ever seen. Before he knew it, Aran was dangling above the deck of a great sailing ship. Nestled beside him was a drowsy looking Simlee, who seemed oblivious of their narrow escape.

Below them was an entire crew of drenched seamen, who were looking up at their unusual catch with great interest. Standing in the middle of this hardened group was a tall captain in a pointed hat and a faded naval uniform. The dangling locks of hair on either side of his face quivered in the gale force winds. His wicked smile revealed a line of blackened teeth, and he seemed to be paying particular attention to the washed-up pirate hunter hanging above him.

"Looks like we've caught ourselves a deadman!" he called out, before turning to his second in command. "Cut them both down."

Without a moment's hesitation, the cold and miserable crew members lowered their fishing net and cut open the bottom. The two captives went crashing to the deck with a loud slap. The amused captain glared at Simlee as if he were a piece of treasure in a pile of fish.

"Well, if it isn't the great, Captain Simlee!" he said. "The pirate who became a pirate hunter."

Simlee nursed his sore backside after the heavy fall, and groaned at the familiar face that was smiling there before him. "Wettytoes..." he muttered, rolling his eyes at the stroke of bad fortune. The captain's confident demeanour became flattened by a sudden bout of insecurity. He widened his eyes in anger.

"It's Captain *Wettiman* to you, Simrat!" barked the captain, trying desperately to shake away some painful memories. "It's been many years since I've been addressed otherwise. Especially by that name..."

Simlee chuckled to himself, which only seemed to infuriate Wettman further. The captain turned around to address his crew. Many were quite confused by the obscure reference.

"This here," he continued. "This is the man that sold out his entire crew — all in exchange for a mere promotion!"

Aran turned to look at the man beside him, surprised by the new piece of information. To his great disappointment, Simlee denied nothing, and merely looked out towards the rumbling skies.

"That's right!" cried Wettman. "This pathetic excuse for a human being is also a coward and a traitor. I know this because I was there, the very same day he handed over his own former captain to the Royal Sharkskins."

He waited for a reaction and received nothing in return. Simlee remained calm and still, right before an amusing memory slipped into his mind. "Have you told them why we used to call you Wettytoes?" he asked the captain. Wettman gave him a threatening scowl. "We called him Wettytoes because, as a young lad, he used to scrub the entire deck of our ship in his bare feet. The boy would wet himself every single time." He let out a short snigger. "Do you not remember that, Wettytoes? It used to come pouring out the bottom of your trousers like snot from a toddler's nose. You were a spineless little toe rag who hated the water." Wettman pulled out his sword and planted it an inch away from Simlee's neck.

"Enough of your talking, Simrat!" he said. "No amount of your lying drivel will hide what you really are — a traitor!" Simlee smiled at him. His words had clearly struck a nerve with the old acquaintance. He had no more respect for the man now than he had for him all those years ago. Wettman decided to hide his embarrassment by turning everyone's attention to the boy. "And I see our water rat has scraped together an accomplice. You have been quite a fool to put your faith in this parasite, boy."

Aran could see that Simlee's capture had brought a lot of joy to the young captain. Whatever plans he had in mind for them, he suspected that they did not involve a warm bed and a hearty supper.

"He is no partner of mine," Aran declared. "I have been taken hostage."

Simlee turned to him like a rabid dog. He could quite easily have bitten into the boy's throat and never let him go. "Mind your tongue, boy," he growled. "I warned you never to cross me." His head cocked forward, as he was immediately struck on the back of the neck by a wooden bat. Stood behind him was one of the larger members of the crew, a man so muscular that he looked like he could carry the entire ship across his broad shoulders.

"Silence, Simrat!" cried Wettman. He threw the boy a wink. "So... the pirate hunter is preying on small children, now? That doesn't surprise me. Fear not, boy; you have nothing to worry about on this here ship. In fact, we are in need of a new deck hand. How are you at scrubbing floors?"

"Far better than you were, Wettytoes!" called Simlee, bracing himself, quite rightly, for yet another punishing blow. Aran cringed at the cracking sound of a wooden baton against a hard scalp. Despite the immediate punishment, the cheap heckle had exasperated Wettman's fragile temper.

"Take him away!" he cried, with a swoop of his sword.

Simlee's tired body was dragged across the wet floor and thrown through an open trapdoor. Wettman turned back to face Aran, who was still dripping from head to foot in seawater. The captain summoned a short man with a complexion as pale as the beating sails up above.

"This is Roaf," announced the captain. "He will be your new guardian. Everywhere he goes, you go."

Aran looked over at the excited deckhand, who glared at him like a new toy. The man used a stained sleeve to wipe against his running nose.

"Aye, captain... Hmmm... Aye..." said Roaf, grunting in between his words. The grunts were a strange mixture of sniggers and half-congested breaths.

"Roaf knows this ship better than anyone," added Wettman. "He'll show you where he sleeps. You'll need all the rest you can get."

The pirate looked up to see his men had already returned from the lower cabin. Clutched in one of their hands was the green gauntlet. "He had this on him, Captain," he said, handing it over to his superior. Wettman took hold of the piece of armour as if it were a glass ornament. His eyes glimmered at the shining surface. "We also found this, hidden on the inside."

Aran lit up at the sight of Gwail's crumpled old letter, which, due to its solid layer of protection, had miraculously survived the onslaught of the deep sea. The captain inspected its mysterious handwriting. His long, bony fingers and their assortment of stolen rings flickered their way across the paper with great intrigue. The small presence behind him eventually caused the captain to turn around, only to find Aran's mesmerised gaze.

"You know something about these, boy?" asked Wettman.

"I know nothing," Aran replied. It was a half-hearted response that did very little to convince the suspicious captain. Aran had always been a terrible liar, and his envious look towards the treasured gauntlet told Wettman everything he needed to know.

"We shall see." Wettman analysed every movement in the boy's face, like a jeweller with a precious stone. "Get yourself a good night's sleep, lad. You're going to need it."

14

THE DECKHAND

The Blue Duchess was layered with five main decks, each one stretching out across the entire length of its deep hull. It had become apparent that Aran was to spend his first night in one of the lower levels of the ship.

He followed his new shipmate with great reluctance. Roaf, it had turned out, said very little but the words "*Aye*" and "*Duchess*". These were often accompanied by a string of incoherent mumbles, or some short, stilted sentences. It had dawned on Aran that he had been placed with this particular crew member for a reason. He was like a loyal watchdog, determined to follow his master's orders — and at any cost.

Roaf was shorter than the average seaman, yet he was as strong as a bull when the situation called for it. He was a child in a grown man's body, a body that could lift whole anchors as though they were made of wood. The man was as loyal as they came, which, for a pirate, was a rare find indeed. Aran had also noticed that he seemed to have a rather unhealthy obsession with the contents of his floating home. Referring to the ship only ever as "Duchess", it was a manner of speaking that some would use when talking about their own mother.

"Duchess likes it clean!" he said, pointing to a misplaced bucket in one of the doorways. The journey towards the holding deck involved a steady descent through a myriad of cramped passageways. These narrow hallways crept along the side of the hull like tunnels through a gigantic ant's nest. It was a harsh reminder of each crew member's worth; the less important a person was, the deeper the climb. Unfortunately for Aran, Roaf's sleeping quarters were located on the lowest deck but one. These bottom decks were mainly reserved for worthless cargo and caged prisoners, one of whom Aran knew quite well.

He followed his muttering leader past an endless line of stacked-up barrels, the contents of which he presumed had not been sourced legally. The deck above contained rows of sleeping crew members, all dangling down from their grubby sheets. By the time they had finally reached Roaf's hammock, they were deeper than the outside water line and hidden away towards the stern side of the ship. The makeshift bed was tied between two wooden beams and surrounded by bags of worthless loot and strange trinkets. Just as Aran was about to take pity on the man's meagre sleeping quarters, the reveal of his own bed spared him the trouble.

"Sleep!" cried Roaf. He pointed his meaty finger towards the floor. "Sleep, like Duchess!"

Aran looked down to see nothing but a crusted, old rag. He assumed there would be no pillow.

His place on board the ship had officially been cemented and it was far below the lowest ranking member of the crew. Pirates were not known for keeping a strict and regimented system like they did in the navy. But there was always a pecking order, one that Aran had plummeted to the very bottom of on this occasion. Unlike Roaf, however, he had been greatly under-estimated. His plan of escape was already brewing in the subconscious of his mind and it wouldn't be long before he could put it into motion.

IF SOMEONE WERE try and find the worst location for the worst night's sleep, ever in existence, the Blue Duchess would have been a worthy choice. Aran clung to his midsection for hours on end, as his stomach churned in time with the frantic movements of the raging storm. If seasickness had been a disease, the boy was well and truly riddled with it.

Roaf, on the other hand, was sleeping soundly.

Aran tossed and turned, trying desperately not to vomit over his one-and-only blanket. The shadows from the surrounding cargo rocked and swayed with heightened movements.

With a jolt of his stomach muscles, the boy leapt for the wooden bucket that Roaf had stumbled on earlier. Fortunately, he had consumed very little food over the last few days and was grateful for the short evacuation.

Aran wiped his mouth and sat back against a hard crate. He was surprised to find that Roaf was still sound asleep in his dangling cocoon. A lifetime onboard an active sea vessel had enabled him to snooze through the nosiest of hurricanes. If anything, he was more likely to be disrupted by a moment of silence than he was by a bout of vomiting.

Aran climbed to his feet and gently crept away towards the other end of the deck. He placed his palms against the rough panelling to his left-hand side. It was hard to believe that on the other side of this great wall was a vast ocean, a sea of angry waves that were prepared to enact severe punishment on all the puny land-dwellers who dared to challenge their power. Despite the severe lack of light, Aran's eyesight had adjusted remarkably well. With the edges of his fingertips, he was able to navigate himself quite smoothly to the deck below.

If he had thought the previous deck was rather neglected, this lower level, a deck known simply as 'the hold', did not seem to contain any contents at all. The hold was normally an area that would be packed to the rafters with precious cargo, and after the recent disaster of a poor campaign, the pirates had nothing more to show than a few barrels full of lewpetal juice and some crates of old junk.

Apart from two sacks of grain (both of which had already fallen victim to the resident rats), the only object of note were two cages. Hidden away on the far end of the hold, these solid structures appeared empty and disused, their horizontal bars like blackened teeth, growling at him to keep away. Aran gradually made his way towards them, stumbling as he went on discarded containers and half-empty crates. Rats scurried past his feet at regular intervals, until his face was right up against the metal bars. After a short pause, he leapt back in fright, as a raging figure came charging out from the darkness.

"You double-crossing snake!" growled the prisoner, throwing himself against the bars and shaking them with all of his might. A startled Aran looked back at a furious Simlee, who more resembled a caged primate than he did a human being. "I warned you never to cross me, boy." The man leaned forward as if he were about to start chewing on the cold iron.

Aran shook away the initial surprise and reminded himself that he was perfectly safe. Simlee could throw as many tantrums as he liked, but there was no way he was escaping that cell.

"Thought you'd come down here to gloat, did you?" he asked. "Watch me suffer — like a filthy animal?!"

Aran took a step closer. "I came here to tell you how we're going to escape," he said, trying hard to conceal the enormous lump in his throat.

Simlee scoffed. "You told that idiot captain that I was your hostage."

"Which I was," said Aran, slowly regaining his confidence. "Now you can call us even."

The tables had truly turned; nobody was more surprised at the boy's change in behaviour than Aran himself.

"So you have come to watch me suffer?" asked Simlee.

"I've come to help you escape," said Aran.

Simlee peered into the boy's assured eyes with a careful squint. Years in the company of Morwallia's most unsavoury characters had enabled him to detect an outright lie when he heard one. "Help me escape, really? Now why would you want to do that..."

"Because I need to find Wyn Drathion." Aran leant forward and placed his hands against the bars. "You were right; the only way I will ever find this man is with your help. He's the only person who can tell me the truth; the truth about Gwail, the armour and... the truth about me."

An excited expression washed over Simlee's face. He had been right; the boy *had* needed him as much as he needed the boy. "You want to know more about you? Then let your Uncle Simlee tell you."

"How on earth would *you* know?" asked Aran.

"That mark on the back of your head...." Simlee grinned. Aran felt a chill that turned the surface of his skin into a rash of goosebumps. He placed his hand over the back of his neck. "That there is a birthmark. A famous birthmark! Your precious Gwail never told you, did he?" He relished in the boy's discomfort and frustration. "I'm not surprised. Of all the secrets those Drathions ever carried, you must have been the greatest one of all."

Aran was now pressed up against the bars, entranced by

every word that came out of the man's lips. "Tell me," he said. "Tell me what it means."

With only a row of steel bars now separating them, he could smell the stench of Simlee's rotten breath as it spewed out across his damp skin. He prepared himself for the worst, only to have his captivated gaze broken by a loud wailing noise.

Aran turned around to see a glowing lantern. Stood at the other end of the deck was a screeching Roaf.

"Bad!!" he cried. "Bad, bad, bad!!!"

Roaf made a dash backwards towards the open doorway, his light source rattling as he went. His movements were heavy-footed and clumsy, and the more he tried to hurry, the more unstable he became. Aran soon caught him up and grabbed the back of his loose shirt.

"Roaf, please!" he called. "Please — stop shouting!"

They stumbled their way up the crooked staircase with both making very little progress. For every grab of Roaf's clothing, the boy received a hard shove in return. The struggle continued for several more steps, until the furious deckhand exploded with an elbow to Aran's face. The mighty blow sent the boy tumbling back down the stairs with a landing that closely resembled a limp scarecrow who had tried to take flight. When he finally opened his eyes, the brief struggle had become a distant memory. All he could see now was a blurred face.

"Wake up, wake up!" cried Roaf's groaning voice. "Wake up, or Captain will be angry!"

With every shake of Aran's body, the frantic face gradually moved into focus. The throbbing lump at the back of the boy's head was a painful reminder of the fall he had just taken.

"Roaf, stop it!" Aran cried. "I'm awake! *I'm awake!*"

The forceful jerks from Roaf's powerful hands finally ceased. Roaf dropped to his knees and sobbed at the boy's feet like a traumatised child.

Aran took a moment to assess his surroundings. They were no longer on the stairs, and there appeared to be barrels in every direction. The barrels were a very good sign indeed, as they meant he was still in the hidden confines of the lower holding decks. Somehow, despite Roaf's high-pitched screams, no other members of the crew had been alerted to his visit with Simlee.

"Roaf, what's the matter?" he asked, crawling towards the large man who was now sobbing in the far corner.

Roaf looked up, his face surprised. He was reacting as though this was the first time someone had ever asked him a question.

"Captain..." he whimpered. "Captain said, if I break boy... he will hurt Roaf."

Aran watched him wipe away the tears with his grubby sleeve. This was the longest sentence he had ever heard the man string together.

"It's okay, Roaf," Aran said. "I'm not broken — look!" He jingled his limbs from side to side like a dancing puppet.

"No! *You* be broken!" Roaf pointed towards the back of his prisoner's head. Aran reached back and felt a huge bulge sticking out through his long hair. The bump was certainly painful, but he had experienced a lot worse.

"You mean — *this*?" He leant over to show him the bruise.

The sight of the great lump only worsened Roaf's fragile mood and caused him to break out into a terrified cry. "Boy be broken!" He dropped to his knees and covered his eyes; if at least *he* could not see the swollen mark, then surely it didn't exist.

Aran watched him curl up into a large ball. He had witnessed a hedgehog do this once before, only there was nothing cute about the sight of a man cowering in sheer terror. He observed him with a newfound feeling of sympathy, and even pity. But he also saw a glimmer of opportunity.

Roaf had spent his entire adult life being treated for what he ultimately was; a child in a grown man's body. This was also a child who had been severely mistreated — so much so that he was more terrified of being punished than he was of being judged. And, as the boy knew all too well, children should never be underestimated. Sometimes, all they ever needed was a little trust.

"Roaf, listen to me..." Aran whispered. He crawled towards him and placed a gentle hand on his quivering shoulder. "Captain doesn't need to know anything." Roaf glanced up in surprise. He stopped weeping for a moment and sniffed his dribbling nose. Aran glared back at him, his eyes focused and full of warmth. "It can be our little secret."

Roaf lit up, shaken by such an unfamiliar concept. "Secret?"

"*Our* secret. Roaf and Aran's secret." The boy gave him a reassuring wink.

A narrow smile worked its way across Roaf's drooping jaw. It cracked the edge of his cheeks like a sharp chisel on a bed of rock. "Secret..."

Roaf had never kept a secret before. He had barely been trusted with chopping vegetables, let alone withholding a piece of information. The sight of Aran kneeling down before him, crouched at the same level, was a completely new phenomenon. The other crew members had always spoken down to him as if he was nothing more than a rodent that lived aboard the ship. Roaf chuckled to himself and climbed to his feet. He was as giddy as a young puppy.

"Come!" he said, dragging the boy by his arm and leading him through the towers of wooden barrels. They wove their way around the enormous kegs of precious liquid. "It's time we be sleeping now."

As they approached Roaf's makeshift resting quarters, an unexpected crew member was already lying in his hammock.

"What's the matter?" said the stranger. "Jump in your grave, did I?"

The drunken looking pirate was none other than the captain's first mate, Leftenant Loxrin. He stared back at them and exposed his metallic teeth with a crooked smile. His uniform was a giant medley of different cloths and materials, a broad selection of clothes that had once belonged to a variety of deceased navy officers. He wore the outfit as a reminder of his past triumphs; a mark of his precious seniority onboard this corrupted watercraft of thieves and murderers. It had taken Loxrin many years to climb such an unstable ladder of criminal hierarchy, and he enjoyed nothing more than to flaunt his position with great pride, especially to the more unfortunate individuals of the lower ranks.

"You two look about as guilty as a pair of cats covered in feathers," said Loxrin. "Trying to escape this floating cesspit, are you, boy?" He rose to his feet and stretched out his tight neck.

Aran shook his head. "No," he replied. "I just got lost."

Loxrin let out a dismissive grunt and continued to crack away at the rest of his weary joints. "Lost, aboard a lost ship... How unfortunate."

The intoxicated pirate swayed towards one of the sealed barrels. Aran detected a certain tone in his voice that was different from the other seamen he had encountered. It was more refined, more articulate. He would not have been surprised if this meandering existence of plundering and pillaging was a more recent phase in his life.

"You wouldn't get very far even if you *were* trying to escape," Loxrin continued. "Why else do you think you've been given this idiot to watch over you." He pointed towards Roaf, who cowered at the very movement of his hand. "The only people who escape this ship are the ones thrown from it."

The slurring leftenant had now begun casually helping

himself to one of the giant kegs. He arched his head back and allowed the fluorescent liquid to flow across the entire bottom half of his face. Roaf gasped. Aran had seen this purple substance before; it was lewpetal juice.

"Arghhh!" came the disturbed noise from the deckhand's mouth. "Captain said..."

His superior gave a sharp turn of his head.

"Captain said... what?" asked Loxrin, who came stomping towards Roaf with a burst of uncontrollable rage. "You think I answer to *that* buffoon?" He pulled out his sword and aimed it at Roaf's neck. "Have you forgotten to whom you are speaking with? *I* am your superior, *deckhand*. And I order you to remain quiet."

Loxrin watched, as the terrified man quivered in a layer of sweat. He paused for a moment, for no other reason than the simple pleasure of watching him suffer just a little while longer. Eventually, he lifted up his solid boot and kicked him to the floor.

"If I wish to have a drink, I will have a drink!" declared Loxrin. "Because I can tell you now — I wouldn't be caught dead down here, otherwise. The people who tread these lower decks are worth less than the cargo."

He danced his way back to the open barrel and took another gulp. Aran stood in silence, disgusted by his behaviour. The drunken pirate came charging towards him with his sword raised. He swung the blade and stopped it, only inches away from the boy's nose.

Even though he was shaking on the inside, Aran was determined not to show any fear. Being openly scared of this man had not worked out very well for Roaf, and it was clear that this bitter leftenant thrived on weakness. Instead, he gazed back at him with the blankest expression he could muster.

Loxrin squinted in return with his thick, black eyebrows.

"Have you got something you want to say, boy?" he snarled. Aran shook his head. "Then you are a wiser man than him." Roaf was still lying on the floor, huddled up into a tiny ball. "Not that it takes much to be smarter than a sack of dung."

The leftenant lowered his sword, leaned back and spat an enormous wad of saliva towards the cowering deckhand. "If you ever question my actions again, maggot," he told him, "I will drain every last one of these precious barrels and declare *you* solely responsible." He wandered over to the wooden containers and stroked their smooth surface. "Or maybe I'll just let you drown in the stuff. A death far too good for the likes of you!"

He sniggered at the mere thought of it; the sheer irony of suffocating in such an expensive spirit, all whilst being surrounded by an entire ocean. Only Roaf would be stupid enough, he decided.

Aran watched, as he unbuttoned his filthy trousers and began relieving himself all over the floor of the deck.

"Now, this is the stuff you should be drowning in!" the man cried, nodding at the long, yellow stream. The stench was unbearable.

Aran still struggled to understand how a person could take such pleasure in the misery of others. The fact that a senior officer (a term used fairly loosely onboard a pirate ship) could be so amused by the suffering of an innocent deckhand made little sense to the boy. Aran had been a victim of such cruelty himself, and Loxrin's dramatic display had flared up a whole host of painful memories. This rash of old wounds had triggered an anger inside him that he never knew he possessed. If he had possessed the power to stop this Loxrin man, he would have done so in a heartbeat.

Roaf was busy listening to the dripping sound of the warm, stinking fluid, as it ruined his meticulously cleaned floor, causing him to shudder and snivel with every splash. Loxrin cackled in amusement, before yanking his trousers back up and storming off into the darkness. He left them with little more than an oozing, yellow puddle to remember him by. The faint murmurs of his slurring voice continued to echo long after he had left.

Aran turned to Roaf, who was still curled up in pain from his heavy beating. The boy reached for a wooden bucket underneath the hammock and headed over to the small puddle. He squeezed out an old rag and began dabbing up the recent spillage. He did his best to pretend it was something other than a trail of bodily waste, which had been quite hard considering it was still warm.

Roaf had gone very quiet. He sat up and watched with great fascination, as his tormentor's mess was carefully mopped up to the very last drop. Aran placed the soggy rag back inside the bucket and gave his observer a respectful nod.

"Duchess needs to stay clean," he said.

Roaf looked at him with an excited grin. For a brief moment, the pain from Loxrin's heavy boot had all but vanished amongst the distraction. His heart rate slowed to a steady rhythm, as he watched a small hand opening out in front of him. Confused at first, he lifted up his meaty fingers. The two hands embraced each other with a short squeeze, and the deckhand allowed himself to be hauled up from the floor. Roaf grunted in appreciation, and after an awkward nod, he collapsed into the safety of his hammock.

15

THE CAPTAIN

The next morning, Aran had found himself back on his hands and knees, only this time he was scrubbing his way across the boards of the main deck. Sprawled out, in a stream of soapy water, he scrubbed away at the rough surface, panting and sweating from the hours of hard labour.

"You're slowing down, boy!" cried the voice above him. "I want this entire deck sparkling by sundown."

Aran scoured harder with his foaming brush, its soft bristles worn down from the years of overuse and were currently in dire need of replacing. He dreaded to think how many other unfortunate souls over the years had also found themselves cursing at the same tool. Whoever these people were, they weren't scrubbing any longer.

The cool breeze was certainly a welcome change from the humidity of the lower decks. Last night's storm was already a distant memory, and the skies above were as clear as the calm surface of the deep, blue sea below. The horizon stretched out into a perfectly straight line and circled the great ship from every direction. It was a spectacular sight to behold, and had it not been for the abusive cursing every five minutes, Aran would have appreciated it even more.

Kneeling beside him was Roaf, who appeared to be perfectly at home in the situation. Scrubbing the miles of endless decking had become a daily routine for the seasoned deckhand, and by the time he had reached the end of one deck, it was time to start another. "*Keeping Duchess clean*" was one of the few small pleasures he had left. After all, a clean Duchess was a happy Duchess. And if Duchess was happy, then so was Roaf.

Aran, on the other hand, took no pleasure in his new activity, whatsoever. The repetitive and continuous movements had already burned two holes in the knees of his trousers, and his sore back was starting to resemble the shape of Corwel's crooked walking stick.

He looked up at the man barking orders. Of all the crew members on the entire ship, it *had* to have been the one he despised most.

"What are you looking at, boy?" asked Loxrin. The leftenant's bloodshot eyes were failing to hide his throbbing hangover. He had painfully misjudged his private binge the night before (counting servings was difficult when you were drinking from a barrel), and he knew it would not bode well for him if his sober crew were to find out. It wasn't easy sleeping above several gallons of lewpetal juice when you were gasping for a quick nightcap. A pirate's greatest enemy on these high seas had always been boredom, and it was for this very reason that any man caught dipping his beak inside the crew's hard-earned booty would suffer severe punishment.

Aran returned to his brush. He hadn't muttered a word, but he knew his hateful look would be enough to infuriate the leftenant. Roaf, on the other hand, knew better than to raise his eyes from the ground; a wise deckhand always kept his thoughts to himself.

The expression on Aran's face had said it all. Loxrin kicked over the boy's bucket and covered him in a wave of soapy water.

"Come on then, boy," he said. "Speak up, you coward!"

Aran took a deep breath and tried to calm his nerves. He shook off the layer of foam and turned to face him. "I didn't say anything," he replied, in a firm and determined voice. "You must still be drunk."

The veins across Loxrin's neck rose up until they were almost at the point of bursting. He felt the stares of his fellow crew members. Some of them were even in earshot and had grown rather curious from the lack of scrubbing.

"What did you just say?" asked Loxrin. No deckhand had ever dared answer him back before. The highly-ranked seaman had always relied on fear and weakness to get what he wanted, and the sudden absence of both factors had caught him off guard.

He pulled out his sword and swung it through the air. The long weapon was just about to slice through Aran's shoulder when it became narrowly deflected by a second blade. Loxrin looked up. His attack had been halted by a menacing figure with arms the size of two pillars. This brutish looking seaman, a man who went by the name of Dewin, was a bronzed sailor with heavy earrings and a tattooed face. He lifted up his unusually thick sword and flung the opposing blade back towards its owner.

"The captain has asked for the boy," Dewin announced. He had a deep voice and a piercing stare. "Preferably, all in one piece."

The two men locked eyes until Loxrin reluctantly took a step back. Dewin had never been fond of his superior, and it had given him great satisfaction to overrule him on this occasion.

"Why would he want to waste time on this puny, little runt?" asked Loxrin with a scoff.

"I could ask you the same question," Dewin muttered.

The leftenant shrugged, as if he couldn't care less about what the captain wanted.

Meanwhile, Aran was still flinching from the recent strike that had almost shredded him in half. He was pulled up by the scruff of the neck and marched straight across the main deck towards the great cabin. It was a place only a select few onboard the Blue Duchess would ever get to visit.

Captain Wettman was slumped behind his large desk. Maps were spread out across every inch of the table, and his workspace was littered with an assortment of brass measuring tools and smoked tobacco. Daylight burst through the windows behind him, creating a dark silhouette that shrouded his grave face. He had been awake the entire night, buried in stacks of papers that were still piled high wherever there was space.

When Aran finally entered the room, the captain remained still and composed. It became clear that he was clutching something very precious, and the man had become so lost in his own thoughts that the short cough from his large crew member did nothing to break his concentration.

Dewin began to lose his patience, and gave Aran a small nudge towards the middle of the room. He left the boy to suffer a long, uncomfortable silence.

Aran looked around at the walls on either side of him. Both were covered in a collage of documents and maps, each with their own unique set of notes and scribblings. Much of the writing appeared to be in a different language and one he had come across somewhere before. These familiar inscriptions jumped out at him like a swarm of insects. Each stroke of dark ink became a chain of humming sounds, like voices calling out to him from past memories.

Aran looked over at the captain. The man was still hunched

over in the darkness, the rings around his bony fingers clicking away against the old gauntlet.

"You ever seen that language before?" asked Wettman. He looked up towards the wall. The splashes of papers had become footprints of his unhealthy obsession. Aran took one more glance at the mysterious phrases and shook his head.

"You're lying to a pirate, boy," the captain reminded him. "And you're not very good at it." He got up from his chair and lifted up the gauntlet. "What about this?" The gleaming piece of armour caught Aran's gaze.

"It belongs to me." The words flung out of Aran's mouth quicker than he had expected. He had intended to deny all knowledge, but it was now too late. Something had risen up inside of him, a protective instinct for what was rightfully his.

"It belongs to you, does it?" asked Wettman. He walked towards him, until the treasured artefact was dangling above the tip of the boy's nose. "Well I knew it didn't belong to that old shiprat, down there in the hold."

He placed his hand against the wall in front of them and rubbed it with his fingertips.

"You know what all this is?" asked the captain. Aran followed his guiding hand across the endless amounts of notes and symbols, until eventually he pointed towards a familiar marking scratched out in black charcoal. "A lifetime of searching." Wettman turned over the gauntlet to reveal an identical looking emblem engraved into its green surface. Aran's eyes darted from side to side in an effort to compare the two symbols; there was not a trace of difference between them. A tornado of butterflies circled the inside of his stomach.

"I've sailed across vast waters to put this information together. Until now, it was all just a bunch of meaningless scratches in a pile of scrap paper. An endless puzzle I could never hope to solve." They walked along the wall of papers until it dissolved into a section of sketches. Each drawing formed the basis of a large map. In the centre were some shapes that Aran presumed were a cluster of small islands. "And then you come along..."

An excited smile slid across Wettman's tired face. He lifted up Gwail's letter. Aran jumped in fright as he slammed it against the wall.

"Years of searching and the answer comes washing up on my very own deck!" Wettman unleashed a hysterical laugh. "They told me it didn't exist, that it was nothing more than an old legend." He lifted up the gauntlet and waved it in Aran's face. "And thanks to you, I now have proof!" They listened to the clinking sound of fingernails against the solid metal. "This here, is just a tiny piece of it!"

"A piece of what?" Aran asked.

Wettman turned to him, niggled by what was surely just another calculated display of ignorance. He grabbed the boy's arms and flung him against the wall.

"Why, the Kingdom of Emlon, of course!" cried the captain. The sleep deprivation from his unhealthy obsession had got the better of him. His pupils were wide open, and the whiteness in his eyes had turned a shade of red; the wild stare of an unstable madman. "You know what I'm talking about, don't you? I can see it. You know it to be true."

Aran couldn't bring himself to reply. He knew that whatever he said next would have a serious impact on his fate aboard the Duchess. Instead, he said nothing. He turned his head and looked towards the map. Even in the company of this unstable pirate, he couldn't help but feel intrigued. Could it really be true? Ever since he had first stumbled on that buried suit in the ruins of Lanbar, he knew anything was possible.

Wettman released his grip and marched towards the

window. He leant his tired body against the narrow ledge and stared out. There was nothing to be seen but sky and water.

"My time as captain aboard this ship is coming to an end," Wettman eventually said.

Aran waited for him to elaborate but was met with another long silence. "Why is that?"

"There's a mutiny brewing. You can smell it in the air. It's been bubbling away for quite some time. That slithering snake, Loxrin, hasn't helped matters."

The mere mention of the leftenant's name caused Aran to feel queasy. He was relieved that someone else also shared his disdain.

"We've been looting for months," Wettman continued. "And all we have to show for it are some barrels of lewpetal juice. The men grow tired, and they long for shore. I promised them more fortune than they could ever dream of, and all I gave them in return was peanuts. Right now, we are heading to the nearest port: Kolwith Bay — a dead-end if ever there was one." Aran tried his best not to look surprised. It seemed that he was still on course, after all. The last thing he wanted was a change of plan, and he had a horrible feeling that a change of plan was exactly what the captain had in mind.

"There, my men will fight over pathetic scraps before wasting it all away on drink and gambling. All the while, Loxrin will be plotting and scheming to overthrow the very same man who helped acquire their reward in the first place. He's been planting his seeds for quite some time. But this ship deserves a better captain than him." He marched over towards the great map and pulled it down from the wall. "It deserves someone with ambition!" He pointed towards a black cross at the centre of a patch of ocean. "Someone who is willing to go further than any pirate from these waters has ever travelled before, to a place where few people even believe in!" Wettman lifted up the gauntlet. "There is far more where this came from; they say that the mountains of Emlon are filled with it."

"They also say it's heavily protected," said Aran.

Wettman paused for a moment. Aran's words had lit a spark of interest. "So you *do* know what I'm talking about?"

"I know the story," said Aran. "They say the men who wear this material are also sworn to protect it." He knew that engaging in an argument at this stage would be pointless; the captain had already made up his mind. But Aran was determined not to let his chances of reaching Kolwith Bay slip away on the dream of a delusional pirate. "I have read the story a hundred times, as have most people, I'm sure. Anyone who searches for the Kingdom of Emlon is doomed to fail. Nobody has ever come back."

Wettman listened to every word with keen interest. "So you do believe."

"I have believed in Emlon long before I needed any proof," said Aran. "But if there's one thing I've learnt from that piece of armour, it is that some things are best left alone."

The captain held him tight and pointed towards the main deck. "And *that* is the difference between us — and them!" he cried.

The man walked back to his cluttered desk and collapsed into the worn-out chair behind it. "I need people I can trust. The men are divided into those who are with me and those who listen to Loxrin. Which is why I'm putting together a new crew. It's time to flush out the rats — to weed out the rotten apples! You can either join me or be thrown out like the rest." He lifted up the gauntlet and twirled it around in the light. "First, you will tell me everything you know about this gauntlet — *where* you found it and *who* it belongs to."

"I've already told you," said Aran. He paused for a moment before considering his next words wisely: "I'm just a hostage."

"Do you know what an Emlon Rider's armour is capable of?"

The captain slipped the gauntlet across his own forearm for a moment. "They say it can lead a Rider home."

He pointed to an insignia in the middle of his paperwork. It was sketched out in great detail. Aran had seen this symbol before; it had featured in the middle of the emlon breastplate.

"They say it glows," the man continued. "The closer you get, the more it will glow — like a mighty compass! Can you imagine such a thing?"

Aran tried not to look him in the eye; he *could* imagine such a thing. When it came to that suit he could imagine *anything*. For the benefit of the pirate, he shook his head.

"This here gauntlet must have come with a breastplate," continued Wettman. "Have you seen it?"

Aran shook his head again. The captain studied his expression before letting out a disappointed sigh.

"You are a terrible liar, boy," he said, "which makes you a terrible pirate."

The two remained silent, until Whitman eventually climbed to his feet.

"Very well," he said. "Perhaps another night in the lower decks will help you think about it."

Aran walked out of the great cabin more confused than ever. By the time he had returned to his post, Roaf had already scrubbed half of the main deck. The boy did his best to ignore the cold stare of Leftenant Loxrin. His suspicious eyes had followed him from the moment he stepped foot outside. The pirate studied his every move; the way he picked up his brush, the tone of his expression.

The boy kept his focus firmly on the wet floorboards. His mind continued to race, as he spent the rest of the day scouring every inch of the upper deck.

16

THE ESCAPE

When it came time to rest his aching muscles, the sun had long descended into the sleeping waters. Aran's new bed, which consisted of a hard floor and a discarded old sack, had never felt so comfortable. He breathed out a sigh of relief, as the edges of his weary spine cracked out against the damp floorboards. The peacefulness of the night had come with a great sense of relief. It was a moment to become lost in his own thoughts, to contemplate the few options he had left in his unfortunate situation. The moment he closed his eyes was a moment he was no longer a prisoner; in the darkness he could escape to a much happier place.

His dreams that night consisted of a face he had not seen in quite some time. The sight of the emlon armour on the captain's desk had flared up a whole host of unanswered questions and painful memories. He wondered, as he often did, about the owner of that second gauntlet and whether she was also thinking of him at that moment. As he drifted off into a well-earned sleep, the image of Sarwen still fresh in his mind, he was soon disrupted by the sound of hollow footsteps rattling in his ears.

Aran opened his eyes. Standing above him was a face he had grown to detest; the face of a furious Leftenant Loxrin. He squirmed as a pair of grubby hands wrapped around his collar. In one foul swoop, he was lifted up and pinned against one of the surrounding barrels.

"Trouble sleeping?" asked Loxrin, his grip a tightening vice around the boy's throat. Aran could smell the stench of lewpetal juice fuming out from the pirate's rotting mouth.

"Let go of me!" Aran choked.

Loxrin sniggered at his defiant expression and swung him hard against a second barrel.

"What did the captain want with you?" he asked.

Roaf jumped up from his hammock, startled by the sudden commotion. He cowered at the sight of Loxrin and retreated to the safety of his bed.

Aran remained silent, which only seemed to exacerbate the leftenant even more.

"You see these?" asked Loxrin, who pulled out a set of gigantic keys. "I have the power to lock you away in one of those cages for the rest of your days. It will make scrubbing the deck seem like a holiday." Aran groaned as the largest of the iron keys was shoved up against his right nostril. "Now tell me everything that pathetic captain said to you."

Roaf whimpered at the boy's suffering. He hated violence, of any kind. To him, it was worse than the untidiness of a badly maintained ship. Violence was messy and unpredictable, whilst the deckhand lived only for order and routine.

Aran took a moment to answer, before he bit back at his interrogator with an angry shout. "Ask him yourself!"

Loxrin laughed. The boy had more spirit than he had expected.

"Very well," he said. "You want to be a man? Then we shall discuss this like men. Over a drink..."

Aran dug in his heels as he was dragged over to another barrel. The pirate pulled out his sword and wiped its smooth surface against his victim's delicate cheek. The razor-sharp edge was only a few millimetres away from slicing through the boy's pale skin. Aran squirmed at the sight of his own terrified eyeball reflecting back at him from the blade's gleaming reflection.

Loxrin lifted up the sword and used it to pierce through the barrel's wooden base. A spray of purple liquid came gushing out, like blood from an open wound. He cupped his hands together and took a drink.

"*Your* turn," he said, before shoving his victim's mouth across the small hole.

Aran coughed and spluttered; the pressure was too much. The liquid sprayed out from the side of his aching lips as he tried not to swallow.

Loxrin pulled his mouth away, letting him gasp for air before pushing it back down again. With his face held firmly against the barrel, Aran felt his mind begin to slow. His senses grew numb and the world around him began to blur and distort.

"Had enough yet?" asked the muffled voice.

Roaf groaned from the safety of his hammock. The excess liquid now spewing out across the entire floor had been too much for the deckhand to handle. He covered his eyes and did his best not to interfere.

Just as he was about to lose consciousness, Aran was flung to the ground and left to heave and cough. Loxrin crouched on top of him whilst shaking his head back and forth.

"Do you want to tell me *now* what you and the captain talked about?" he asked.

Aran looked back at the blurred face with delirious eyes.

"He told me you're nothing but a jealous traitor!" the boy cried. By this point he had lost all control. The overdose of lewpetal juice had eradicated any fears or hesitations he might once have had. "You're going to be thrown out like the rotten apple that you are! You have no power on board this ship — and you never will!"

The leftenant listened to every word in a furious rage. His hands began to quiver. "You want to see how much *power* I have?"

Loxrin slowly climbed to his feet. Aran watched, as he drew his sword and began slicing through every barrel that he could find. Streams of bright purple began shooting out in all directions.

"If I want to drink, I will drink!" The man danced around and let the sprays of lewpetal juice shower his whole body, like a carefree child in a public fountain. "If I want to do anything aboard this ship — I will do it!"

Roaf cried out in protest, his screeches becoming louder with each new penetrated barrel.

The pirate continued his great keg slaughter, stabbing away at the surrounding cargo and drenching himself in the process. Giddy and out of breath, he strolled over towards his confused observer.

"And if I want to kill... I will kill," he growled.

His jovial voice had turned cold. Aran leant back against the barrel behind him. Even in his drowsy state, he knew that the end was fast approaching. He imagined what sound *he* would make after being punctured through in such a way, a human keg with much less value than a pint of lewpetal juice.

Loxrin stepped closer, the tip of his sharp sword aiming straight towards Aran's clenching stomach. The boy closed his eyes and could hear little else but the gushing of liquid and the beating of his own heart.

Loxrin lifted up his sword and prepared himself for a satisfying execution. He was just about to take the final swing when he became distracted by a pair of enormous arms wrapped around his torso.

"Let go of me, you imbecile!" shouted the pirate.

Aran opened his eyes to see that Roaf was now hugged tight around his furious superior in a strange piggyback.

"No more hurting Duchess!" wailed the deckhand. "Leave Duchess alone!"

Loxrin flung him from side to side in an effort to get free, surprised by the man's unusual strength. "I said get off, you fool!"

He tilted his head forward and flung it back towards Roaf's nose. After a loud crack, and an even louder cry, the deckhand loosened his powerful grip. No longer restrained, a raging Loxrin came charging at him with flying fists. Several blows later, Roaf was lying in a sorry heap, whilst his aggressor mauled him down like a rabid dog.

"This is exactly what you deserve!" shouted Loxrin, whose heavy boot was digging into the edge of Roaf's stomach. "I'll teach you the meaning of respect!"

Aran could no longer bear to watch. He knew that the leftenant had no intention of stopping until his victim was beaten to a pulp.

"Stop it!" Aran called out. "You're going to kill him!" His words had become slurred, coming out in one continuous groan.

Exhausted from the barrage of kicks and strikes, Loxrin paused for a moment to catch his breath. Roaf had become still and quiet, albeit the occasional twitch.

The pirate stepped back to admire his destruction. This brutal attack on the helpless deckhand had not been his original intention, and yet somehow he had become overwhelmed in the moment. He strolled back towards the fountains of cascading purple liquid and doused his entire body, like a duck playing in the rain.

Aran crawled across the floor to the sound of manic laughter and placed his hand on top of Roaf's battered body. He felt a tremble of rage.

"You think I'm finished?" asked Loxrin. "At least he was too stupid to know what he was doing." He raised his arms in the air, as if baptising himself in the most unlikely of holy water. "I am not like your precious Wettman; soft, merciful, weak... I will rule this vessel with an iron fist and there's nothing a puny boy like you can do about it!"

Aran's lip began to quiver. He took one look at the glowing lantern beside him and grabbed it. Its solid glass chamber contained a burning white candle that had all but melted away. In a burst of uncontrollable fury, he chucked the lantern high into the air and watched it shatter against his target with an almighty smash.

Loxrin cried out as his drenched uniform lit up like a human torch. Flames flowed out across his entire body and shot down towards the floor, creating a puddle of hot fire beneath his feet.

The sound of his high-pitched screams carried out through the entire ship. The boy shielded his eyes from the burning light. Loxrin ripped off his flaming jacket as the fire continued to spread. He patted down his burning hair, which was now singed into a black mess. With his torso safely extinguished, he threw himself to the ground and rolled along the floor in a bid to put out his legs.

Aran made a dash for the discarded coat and rustled through every pocket he could find. His heart fluttered from the feeling of warm iron against his excited fingers. He pulled out a large set of keys and went running for the nearest staircase.

His dash for freedom was halted by a wall of rising flames that reached all the way up to the ceiling above. Fuelled by the pools of spilled lewpetal juice, the raging fire had already begun eating its way through every corner of the narrow storage space.

Aran backed away from the scorching heat, sending him straight into the arms of a vengeful Loxrin.

"You think you can escape me that easily, boy?" cried the pirate, who was now stripped down to his burnt underwear. He wrapped his arm around Aran's neck and pulled him to the ground in a vicious chokehold.

The sound of a deafening blast shook them both. The roaring fire had devoured its first barrel, and the floorboards beneath them were being eaten through like singed paper. Aran braced himself as he felt the ground beneath his feet open up, sending half the deck crashing down to the level below.

He landed with a heavy thud, accompanied swiftly by an avalanche of falling debris. Another eruption followed, as the remaining barrels continued to ignite at a dramatic rate. The fire raged on, creating numerous gaping holes across both sides of the great hull. Seawater poured through into the flaming deck, creating clouds of steam that hissed like a mountain of angry snakes.

Aran looked up to see Simlee lying there in his square cage. With Loxrin nowhere to be seen, he crawled across the burning cargo until he reached the steel frames.

"Is this your idea of getting us out of here?" asked Simlee, who was surprisingly calm considering the situation. Aran lifted up the set of keys and scrambled for the lock. With the first key inside, his heart sank as it jolted against him. "You'd better try them quicker than that. Or we'll be here all day."

Flustered and shaking, Aran went for the second key and rattled it inside the hole. After a series of desperate shakes, his third attempt was sabotaged by a mighty blow to the side of his waist. After a humongous tackle out of nowhere, the boy went flying to the ground. Loxrin was now lying on top of him, digging his crusted fingers into the base of his throat.

Simlee stretched out his arm towards the set of keys still

dangling from their narrow hole. He wrestled with each one, until the sweet sound he had been waiting for clanked inside his ears. On the other side of the bars, Aran was still embroiled in a hopeless struggle with a much larger opponent. Loxrin continued to mount him, determined to choke out every last breath from his tired lungs.

"You did this to yourself, boy!" he cried out.

Aran looked back at him with a purple complexion and two bulging eyes. Tears of frustration streamed down the side of his cheeks and created long lines through the layer of black soot. The incoming water trickled against his cold feet, and the lack of oxygen caused him to start losing consciousness.

Loxrin glared back at him with a cruel smile. His expression of pure hatred could still be made out through the layer of sweat and black powder, until it morphed into a look of sheer horror.

Aran felt the weight on top of him lift up at great speed. Loxrin was suddenly hoisted up to the tips of his toes and bashed in the head by something hard and solid. The pirate went falling backwards into the steel bars and landed with a hollow *clang*. The culprit merely dusted off his raw fist whilst cracking out his knuckles, almost disappointed by such an easy victory.

With two slaps to the face and a thorough shake, Aran burst back into life with a gasp.

"Are you coming or what?" asked Simlee, stretching out his tight muscles after the discomfort of his tiny cell.

The floor above had been completely opened up by the blazing fire. Simlee offered out a helping hand. They both looked up to see an entire wall cave-in from the enormous pressure. Water crashed through at a dramatic speed, smothering everything in its path with an unstoppable force. It swirled around the hold in a great wave, pushing both Aran and Simlee away from the wooden staircase and back up against the opposing wall.

"Keep your head above water!" shouted Simlee. The floor below was now an ocean beneath their feet, and within seconds, they both began floating upwards from the rising water levels. Aran looked up to see the deck above come hurling towards him.

"We're going to get trapped!" he cried. The incoming ceiling filled him with panic; surely, they were now doomed to be dragged down into the unknown depths of the sea, never to be seen again. Being trapped in a tank full of water, with nowhere left to escape, was a worst nightmare brought to life.

"Grab my shoulders!" said Simlee, who began swimming towards the far side of the hull. Aran clung to his human lifeboat. The force of the man's enormous strokes sent them cruising towards the square hole leading up to the deck above, which was now only inches above water level.

"Kick your legs boy!" called Simlee, thrusting them forward with his powerful arms. Aran tried his best to contribute, the gap of air becoming narrower by the second, until, eventually, both of their gaping mouths were swamped by an influx of freezing cold water.

They held their breaths.

Simlee continued to crawl, his legs kicking with the confidence of a giant frog. Now fully underwater, and with the help of this experienced diver, both went shooting along at an incredible rate. Aran held on for dear life, riding the old pirate like a great seahorse. Just as his lungs were about to burst, they came rising up in an explosion of foaming water and splashed against the higher deck with a squelching bellyflop.

With little time to catch his breath, Aran was yanked towards the safety of the next staircase. They made their way across the next deck, slipping and sliding with each stride.

"No time for a rest!" shouted Simlee, pulling him along as if he were a dog on a lead. Water had already begun to rise up through the small opening, and it wouldn't be long before this level would share the same fate as the last.

Lined up on the deck above were rows of sleeping pirates, dangling from their hammocks, oblivious to the carnage that was taking place below.

"Wake up, lads!" cried Simlee, as he passed through in a desperate sprint. "Are you lot deaf? This old lady's sinking!"

A stir of panic followed, and by the time the confused men had shot themselves upright, Simlee and Aran were half way up the next staircase.

The air outside was crisp and icy. Aran's small feet went sliding across the frosted surface of the main deck.

"We need to move quickly!" called Simlee. The two went skidding along the floorboards as fast as their soaking wet clothes would allow. "There are only *two* lifeboats — and a whole load of pirates."

"How do you know there are only two?" asked Aran, trying not to go flat on his backside.

"First thing I do when boarding a ship: always check the lifeboats." Simlee charged towards a longboat covered in frozen tarp. He looked up at the rickety pulley system. "We need to get her in the water."

"Wait — the gauntlet!" Aran looked back towards the great cabin and went running across the main deck.

"Sod the flaming gauntlet!" Simlee called out. He was just about to prepare the ropes, when a hoard of flustered pirates came swarming towards him. "This'll be a tricky one..."

Over in the main cabin, Captain Wettman was fast asleep across his table of maps. The sound of Aran bursting through the thin doors sent his paperwork flying across the entire room.

He shook away the grogginess and looked up at the small intruder.

"Aran..." he said with a faint smile. "You could have waited until morning."

"The ship is sinking!" cried the boy, barely able to catch his breath.

"It's... what?" Wettman's face went pale.

Before Aran could continue, the edge of a large blade slid carefully underneath his chin. Standing behind him was a stern Dewin.

"Who allowed you to be away from the lower decks, boy?" asked the enormous pirate. His hand clenched the handle of his sword with enough power to crush a small boy's skull.

"The ship..." Aran croaked, trying not to lower his jaw any further than it had to. "I came here to warn you."

The sword grazed his delicate skin with its cold edge. Even with its razor-sharp blade only a hair away from a fatal cut, he couldn't keep his eyes away from the piece of armour on Wettman's desk. Sat there, in all its green glory, was the emlon gauntlet. The captain readjusted his hat and went running towards the door.

"It can't be true," he said. "This vessel has survived eight of the worst storms known to man."

He signalled for his bodyguard to lower the weapon. Dewin never took his oaths lightly. He had sworn to protect his captain, at all costs, and he would do so until the very end.

By the time Wettman came running out from the great cabin, his entire crew had erupted into chaos and panic. A lifeboat was already half way overboard, whilst the second was being fought over like a chest of priceless treasure. Groups of pirates clashed in vicious skirmishes, all over their right to abandon ship without drowning in the process.

It was clear that one side of the divided crew far outnumbered the other, and, by the concerned look on Wettman's face, the odds were stacked well against him. He drew his sword and prepared to rush in.

Aran stood behind him, his eyes fixated on the emlon gauntlet. It was now dangling in the captain's other hand; he saw his opportunity.

A snatch later, Wettman looked down to see that the gauntlet had not only disappeared, but was now darting away from him in the boy's possession.

"Aran!" he cried. "Get back here!"

The boy ducked and weaved through the brawl of pirates. The deck below was already rising up on a steep incline. He dodged a few more flying swords until he reached a flustered looking Simlee, who, by this point, was fending off attackers from every direction.

"Aran!" he called. "We need to get off this thing before it takes us under."

They heard a loud splash as the first lifeboat went flying overboard. Simlee climbed up to a ledge and catapulted himself into the air. Had gravity not taken over, Aran could have sworn that the man was about to fly away. He plummeted downwards, crashing into the sea with an explosion of water. Other members of the crew decided to do the same, plummeting into the waves like human cannonballs.

Simlee looked up to see a tiny face peering back at him.

"Jump, you fool!" he called. "Before it's too late!"

Aran felt a shudder in his knees. The infinite drop that now awaited him was far from appealing — not that the situation onboard was any better. His body stiffened as he talked himself into taking one giant leap into the endless void. His hands froze against the side of the ship.

"I can't do it..." he said to himself.

As he remained glued to the deck, for what felt like an eternity, a familiar voice cried out to him from behind. He turned around to see a furious Wettman running towards him, his sword raised.

"Give it back, you thief!" roared the captain, his wild eyes honing straight in on the gauntlet underneath the boy's arm.

This was all the motivation Aran needed. Within seconds he was leaping into the air, his treasured possession held tight against his small chest. The fall took even longer than he had first feared, and he braced himself for the pain of a thousand icicles against his body.

He let out a short gasp as the life was sucked out of him in one foul burst. The water was as cold and unbearable as he'd remembered. After a few short breaths, he began kicking to stay afloat.

Through the splutters of water he could see that the first lifeboat had already capsized and was now bobbing up and down with its backside facing the air. Like everybody else, he swam towards it with a desperate crawl. Simlee was nowhere to be seen, and, with every rotation of his weakening arms, the floating hull grew further and further away. He battled against the tide with everything he had left, only to be thrown backwards with each attempt.

In an effort to rest his failing body, he swung onto his back and let the sea carry him from side to side, like an aimless piece of driftwood. Unlike the panic of the surrounding waters, the sky above was calm and tranquil. A star twinkled at him in support. As calming as the view was, the starry night was soon eclipsed by an enormous falling object. Aran's eyes widened. The second lifeboat had been released, and, unluckily for the boy, it was now plummeting towards him at a frightening speed.

He held out his hands, knowing full well it wouldn't make the slightest bit of difference. The longboat landed with a devastating smash and sent shock waves out from every side.

Aran opened his eyes to see a bulging arm had narrowly pulled him out of the way. He looked over at the familiar tattoos.

"This is no time to take a nap," said Simlee.

The longboat had barely touched the water before it was swarmed by half a dozen pirates. They fought and bickered over their right to board the vessel, resulting in a series of messy fist-fights and brutal scuffles. Simlee leapt out of the water and joined them in their fierce battle for limited territory. As one group began to settle, another barged their way onboard. The boat jerked from side to side, edging its way ever closer to another capsize.

"Simlee!" called Aran, who was watching his struggle from the tranquility of the water. He could see that his berserk associate was already losing this hopeless battle. With the second lifeboat fully submerged, more and more pirates were swiftly beginning to descend.

Aran lifted up the gauntlet and threw it as hard as he could. A puzzled Simlee caught the familiar looking object, pulled it across his hand and wore it like an armoured glove. With a clenched fist and a mighty swing, he struck the nearest marauder clean across the chin. The force of this reinforced punch sent his baffled opponent flying backwards into the water.

Simlee felt a rush of excitement. He prepared himself for a wave of incoming attackers and began knocking them all down, a pirate at a time. Each blow from his glowing right hand sent a new unlucky victim hurling from the boat at an incredible speed.

After another handful of well-timed shots, Simlee had completely cleared the entire lifeboat of all its inhabitants. The last man standing roared out in celebration at his newfound strength.

Aran looked on in horror. Even after all this time, it

appeared he was still yet to witness the true potential of his precious gauntlet. Simlee lifted up his covered hand and embraced his newfound power.

"What a marvellous little thing you are..." he said, before reaching into the water and pulling Aran onboard. The boy landed with a hollow *squelch*.

More pirates went flying backwards into the water, as Simlee slipped in a few more shots at the few soles still brave enough to climb on board. He then grabbed the oars and began rowing them away from the swarm of desperate crew members. Aran watched as the men called out to them for help. They splashed and paddled in the freezing cold sea, like ants scattered in a bowl of water.

"Don't give me that look," said Simlee, who had caught sight of the boy's guilty stare. He continued to launch the boat forward with a flurry of large strokes. "They would have swamped the whole boat and drowned us all. They were more than happy to leave *me* for dead. Locked in that cage like some dirty animal... If it weren't for you, I'd still be going down with *that* thing."

They cruised past the sinking ship as it descended into the dark waters, its long nose pointed upwards towards the moon. Aran couldn't help but feel responsible. The last thing he ever expected was to single-handedly sink an entire pirate ship. As they prepared to push away from the doomed vessel, Aran caught sight of a peculiar shadow.

"Look out!" he cried, as the darkened figure came falling down from the ship above. The warning was too late, and, with a shake of the entire boat, he was crushed by the weight of their hostile new passenger. A furious Simlee leapt up from his rowing bench and engaged in a manic scuffle with their uninvited passenger.

The attacker twisted and wriggled until he had secured

himself a more dominant position on top, his sword raised high. With one lift of his right arm, Simlee deflected the man's strike with a loud clash. The unexpected impact from the emlon gauntlet sent his opponent's weapon spinning through the air and down into the greedy clutches of the sea.

Simlee saw his chance, and he tackled the unarmed intruder before pinning him down to the floor.

"No!" Aran cried. The armoured fist was ready to make its fatal blow when, all of a sudden, the boy leapt across the man's body. Simlee halted his punch in midair.

"What are you doing, boy?" growled Simlee. "Get out of the way!"

Aran remained still.

"No more," he said. "No more killing. I saved *your* life. Now I'm asking you to spare this one."

Simlee shook his head and released a small chuckle. "You really know how to ruin all the fun, don't you, boy?" He lowered his fist and sat back down on his bench. "Your foolish mercy will be the death of you one day."

Aran climbed to his knees and moved to the other side of the boat. Lying on the small deck was a relieved Captain Wettman. He gave the boy an appreciative nod.

"Of all the people I really wanted to smash to pieces..." Simlee continued, the disappointment quite clear. He removed the gauntlet and grabbed Wettman by the scruff of the neck. After careful consideration, he struck him square in the jaw with his bare knuckles. The solid punch was still enough to render the former captain unconscious.

"That's better," he said. "I prefer him like that."

Aran reached out his hand. "Can I have it back now, please?"

Simlee looked down at the gauntlet. He saw the serious expression on Aran's face and chuckled.

"This thing is wasted on you, lad."

He chucked him back the gauntlet and picked up the oars. Aran took a deep breath and lied back against the inside curve of the hull.

"Oh, and by the way," said Simlee, "I think you'll find that *I* was the one that saved *your* life — a few times, in fact."

They sat in silence for a while. Behind them, the sinking Duchess was now a triangular peak. It stuck out from the depths of the sea, its long snout getting smaller with each splash of Simlee's perfectly timed oars.

Aran pressed down his exhausted body against the hard floor of their new vessel. The distant cries of the abandoned seamen sent a chill down his already frozen spine. He did his best to block them out until all that remained were the deep sloshes of the two paddles.

17

THE EYES OF THE SOUTH ISLAND

A fter hours of steady rowing, the eerie silence of the open sea offered very little comfort to the three inhabitants of a single, stray lifeboat.

Simlee heaved his solid chest backwards and forwards, the repetitive motion melting his mind into a hypnotic trance. Every so often, he would break into song for his own amusement. The ballad of choice was surprisingly gentle for a man of his ferocity, and it poured out from his dry, crusted lips like it had done from the moment he first heard it. This simple melody was a soothing addition to what had been quite the traumatic evening on board the Blue Duchess.

Aran had remained awake for most of the night. He listened to the comforting music whilst twirling the precious armour through his cold hands. His small fingertips worked their way around the gauntlet's distinct markings with careful fascination. He looked up at the scattering of stars and thought about what the captain had told him. Hours later, this maze of twinkling constellations was scorched away by the burning rays of the morning sun.

Wettman slowly opened his eyes. The sight of Simlee's harsh stare sent him stumbling backwards in fright.

"Morning, sunshine," said Simlee, who was still throwing his weight back and forth with that same, controlled rhythm.

Wettman stood up to find himself surrounded by miles of clear seawater. The only sign of life were his two new crew members, one of them being a sworn enemy he had never expected to ever see again. He jumped into a guarded position and searched for his weapon.

"Looking for this?" asked the smug looking rower. He reached backwards and pulled out a long dagger.

Wettman slumped into a disappointed hunch; he should have known better. Had he been able to leap from the boat and swim for the nearest shore he would have done so in a heartbeat.

"Now sit down and shut up," continued Simlee. "*I'm* the captain of this here ship."

Wettman didn't say a word. He merely responded with a reluctant scowl before dropping himself to the floor.

Simlee chuckled and continued to row. He was enjoying every moment of the captain's discomfort.

"You're lucky," he said. "I was half tempted to throw you overboard. The extra weight is slowing us down. Course, we could still use you for fish bait. I'm absolutely famished."

Wettman ignored him and looked around at the empty scenery. "Where are we?"

"Where do you think?" asked Simlee. "We're nowhere."

"You should be weary of the company you keep, boy," said Wettman. Aran caught him looking down at the gauntlet. "This man will cause you nothing but trouble."

"Says the man who lost his entire crew in one night," snapped Simlee.

"Well you'd know all about losing crew members, shiprat..."

The oars went crashing to the floor. Aran jumped up in front of a raging Simlee, only seconds before the dagger was just about to make contact with Wettman's chin.

"Try calling me that name again, Wettytoes!" called Simlee. "See what happens to your insides!"

"Stop!" cried Aran. He pushed them both apart with all his strength. "Both of you! Or we'll never get anywhere."

Simlee hesitated for a moment before letting go of Wettman's throat. The two men locked eyes until they had both made it to separate ends of the boat. They all sulked for a while, until the sound of splashing paddles continued once more.

Before long, the midday sun was well upon them, scorching their dry faces and heating up the small deck. Wettman removed his wide hat and wiped off the sweat from his sore head. It wasn't until now that he had truly begun to mourn the loss of his doomed ship. The plans he had prepared to put in motion would never see the light of day.

"This is not how it was supposed to go," he said eventually. He shook his head whilst staring at the bright sparkles on the reflective surface up ahead. The ocean glistened against the bright sunlight like a pane of infinite glass.

"You think this was my plan?" asked Simlee. He heaved his tired body against the stubborn pull of the tide. It was as if the water below had now become a sea of thick tar. "There's no use crying over your precious Duchess now. It's buried at the bottom of the sea where it belongs."

"Unlike you, I still have my crew," said Wettman. "In fact, that second lifeboat will probably be making its way in this direction as we speak."

Simlee sniggered. "Whatever brings you comfort. But if I didn't know any better, I'd say your days onboard that ship were numbered already."

Wettman looked towards Aran.

"You told this treacherous liar everything, boy?" he asked in disappointment. "I shared my plan with you in confidence."

"I haven't told him anything," said Aran.

"He didn't need to!" cried Simlee. "I've been on enough ships to know when a crew is divided. Half of those men were about to turn on you like a pack of dogs. It was as clear as day."

"And some of them would have followed me to the ends of the earth," replied Wettman.

"Shame they weren't the majority," said Simlee.

"I wouldn't expect you to understand the value of loyalty. Nobody ever risked their life for a washed-up Sharkskin. And they never will."

"No? And how else do you think I escaped that cage? By magic?"

Simlee pointed towards Aran.

"He will discover your true colours soon enough," said Wettman. "Then you'll be all alone, once again."

"Which is exactly how I prefer it. You always were too soft to be a pirate."

"I'm a man of ambition!"

"You're a hopeless dreamer — and you always were. When I look at you, all I see is that foolish young lad with his head in the clouds."

"Your father didn't seem to think so."

For the first time in a while, the boat went quiet.

"Ah, yes, the old man..." Simlee's face grew serious. "His judgment was always questionable."

Aran turned to face the captain. "You know his father?"

"What pirate doesn't?" Wettman let out a smug grin at Simlee's discomfort. "Ever hear of a man called Razor Blade Pete?" Aran shook his head. "Poor old Razor *Junior*, over here, grew up in quite the shadow."

"I never gave a damn about my father's reputation," muttered Simlee.

"Razor Blade was the last of the great pirates," continued the captain. "There aren't many who reach a ripe old age like his, not in this line of work. He was as shocked as anyone when his downfall came at the hands of his own son." He could see the boy's horror. "That's right, Aran. You've aligned yourself with someone cold-blooded enough to betray his own flesh and blood. What chance do you think *you* have?"

"You don't know what you're talking about," said a furious Simlee. He lifted up the oars and began rowing. His eyes were deep in thought. He pulled at the resisting waters with short, sharp strokes, burying his emotions in a hardened expression.

Nobody said anything for the next few hours.

Eventually, the awkward silence was disrupted by the appearance of a black dot on the northern horizon.

"What's that?" asked Aran. The unexpected cry of his voice snapped the other two men into life.

They all turned to see a dark shape coming towards them. It moved slowly and steadily, growing in size with every splash of the gentle waves.

"Looks like another rowing boat," said Wettman with a squint.

"Don't talk daft," snapped Simlee. "We're in the middle of the ocean."

Wettman lit up at the sight of a familiar figure. As the vessel grew closer, the blurred shape cleared into focus.

"Aha!" he called, leaping to his feet with a raise of his arm.

The long watercraft flowed through the water with strong jerks from its powerful rower. Manning the oars was a mighty Dewin, his bulking chest glowing in the sunshine. The two pirates on either side of him pulled out their swords with defensive stances.

"I told you!" cried the captain with a proud face. "My three most loyal crew members. They would follow me to the dungeons of hell!"

Simlee cringed as the second lifeboat pulled up beside them. The armed pirates leapt on board and thrusted their weapons straight towards his throat. Their target merely shrugged in amusement.

"You think you can intimidate me? You'd be putting a tired, old man out of his misery. I had more chance of dying before you lot arrived."

Wettman turned to Aran and pointed towards the piece of armour.

"Hand it over," he said. Aran reached his arm over the side of the boat and held it above the water. "No!! What are you doing?!"

The gauntlet was now dangling above the Balog Sea's murky abyss.

"Lower your swords, or I'll let it go," Aran instructed.

Simlee unleashed an excited laugh.

"That a boy, lad!" he said. "Do it now! Get rid of it forever."

Wettman was fairly certain the boy was bluffing. His suspicions may well have been correct but he could not afford to risk it. That gauntlet was the only proof he had left to justify everything he had worked towards. Years of searching were about to be dropped into the very ocean he had been foraging.

"Lower your swords," he said.

The two pirates reluctantly obliged. Simlee smiled, taunting them with his playful grin.

"Very well." Wettman let out a frustrated sigh and shook his head. "Let's settle this with our heads." The weary captain propped his boot up against the rim of the hull and stared out at the calm waters. "It's not like any of us want to be out here."

"You can say that again," agreed Simlee. He spat out a large stream of saliva across the deck.

"We are all here for a reason," the captain continued. He turned to the boy. "You get me what I need, and I'll get you what you need."

"What I need will chop you into tiny pieces," said Simlee, his eyes focused on their sharp swords. "What you need is a damn good hiding."

"The letter," Aran said, reaching out his hand. "I need the letter."

Wettman ignored the pirate hunter's piercing stare and turned his full attention to the boy.

"I see you're clearly the brains of this ridiculous partnership," said the captain. "I'm glad one of you is at least reasonable." He propped up his other foot and slipped his fingers through the tongue of the heavy boot. Out popped a rolled up sheet of paper. "You may have it, by all means. But first you must tell me who it's intended for."

"It's the same man we are searching for," said Aran.

Simlee shook his head and cringed.

"You want to tell him everything, boy?" he barked. "Knowledge is worthless if everybody knows it. A magician without his secrets is nothing but a performing monkey — a fool!"

"Quiet!" roared Wettman. "A deal is nothing without trust. Something a traitor like you would never understand. You would do well to learn from this, boy."

Simlee rose to his feet and thrusted his forehead up against the captain's. They were like two rams about to engage. Within a matter of seconds, the blades were once again grazing the hairs of Simlee's raw neck.

"I can smell the fear inside you," hissed the bounty hunter.

"Enough!" Aran cried. "Or we'll be out here forever."

Simlee sat himself down again. "It seems like the boy has more courage than you have, *Captain*."

"I say we leave them out here to roast," said Dewin. His deep, commanding voice caused everyone to look over. He was still sat upright in the other boat, his posture composed and strong.

"Here," said Aran, handing over the gauntlet. Wettman accepted it with a raised eyebrow. He studied the boy's trusting face. "Call it an act of faith." The captain gave him an appreciative nod. "The man we're searching for might be the same person who can help you get to Emlon."

"And how can you be so sure?" asked Wettman.

"Because he's been there before." Everywhere went silent for a moment. Aran's words had baffled them all, especially the captain. "The person we seek is a man called Wyn Drathion."

"The outlaw?" asked Dewin. "Any man who searches for Drathion, searches for an early grave. He is not a man who wishes to be found."

"You two are either brave or stupid," said Wettman. "What would an outlaw like him know about the Kingdom of Emlon?"

"Because he is the owner of that gauntlet," the boy continued. "And you know as well as I do that people who wear armour like that are known by another name."

Wettman's hands began to tremble. He muttered under his short breath: "You think he's an Emlon Rider."

Simlee rolled his eyes. "Oh, please..."

"And where do you expect to find this Drathion?" asked the captain.

"On the South Island," said Aran.

"What reliable source, if any, told you this?"

The boy paused. "His brother."

The captain let out a giddy laugh. "My, my..." He turned to Simlee. "You really *have* found an interesting companion." He knelt down beside Aran and handed him the letter. The boy took hold of it with great caution. "I have no idea whether your facts are correct or not. But I do know one thing — that gauntlet is as real as you or I." He placed a hand on the boy's shoulder. "You need help finding this man? I know every bay of the South Island like the back of my hand. I grew up on that coastline. If your Drathion is indeed still on the island, then we will find him."

"We were doing just fine on our own." The entire crew, as small as it had now become, turned to look at Simlee. His body was hunched over into a sweaty ball, like a bad-tempered toddler in a sulk.

"And what exactly did you intend to do once you found this man?" Wettman asked. "Have a talk with him? Most outlaws would strike you down in an instant."

"It hasn't stopped me in the past," said Simlee. "Besides, this man is not like other outlaws."

"Well, that's even *more* reason to have us on board. We have the numbers. We might have just saved you from a brutal beheading."

"I'd rather take my chances."

"And you will end up dead before you even get near him. No mortal man has ever spoken to an Emlon Rider and lived to tell the tale."

"He's right," said a small voice beside them. Aran looked down at Gwail's letter. The mysterious writing was an unpleasant reminder of how little he understood about the man they were trying to find. For all he knew, this feared individual could quite easily slit his throat before he even had a chance to speak. He stood up in the middle of the boat. "We could do with the numbers."

Wettman punched the air. "Then what are we all waiting for?" His finger pointed south. "To the South Island! To the town of Kolwith Bay!"

The sun began to descend as the two boats set off on their new journey. The two pirates had returned to their own vessel and were now leading the way with the help of Dewin's monstrous strokes.

Much to Simlee's disappointment, Wettman had decided to remain with them. The captain was not prepared to let these new crew members out of his sight, especially with everything that was now at stake. He had taken plenty of chances before, and he knew that he would be taking many more if he were to ever achieve his ultimate goal. Something kept telling him that he had been presented with the exact opportunity he had been waiting for. This strange boy from the North Island had already given him far more than he had achieved on his own; to hold a piece of that mysterious kingdom in the palm of his own hand was a feeling like no other. Surely, the whole encounter had been more than an act of chance.

Simlee was, once again, maintaining a steady rhythm on the oars and had almost grown to enjoy the constant pain. Anything that distracted him from the passenger in front would be a blessing. The younger man was peering out towards the horizon. Simlee felt his stomach tighten up at the thought of his famous father, the same man who resented his own wishes as a young man, and yet, had still gone on to mentor the development of some snivelling deckhand.

"That's a big bloke you have there," he said after a few hours. Wettman turned around and looked over at the giant silhouette in the boat ahead. Dewin's broad shoulders almost eclipsed the orange sunlight. "You sure he can be trusted? If a man like that were to get a little upset... It could be the end for all of us."

Wettman scoffed. "That man there, is the most loyal friend you could ever hope for."

"A pirate doesn't have *friends*."

"A pirate needs all the friends he can get. Especially ones with strength like his."

"And what does some hulking brute and a weak-minded captain have in common?"

"I saved his life," said the captain. He gave Dewin a fond stare. "Now he lives to save mine. We have known each other for many years. He's the oldest companion I have."

It was now Simlee's turn to scoff.

"You think that such a favour will last?" he asked him. "It's a miracle you're still alive in the first place."

"It must be hard for a man like you to comprehend qualities such as honour and dignity."

Simlee ignored his piercing scowl and turned his attention back to the oars. The boat fell silent, once again, as the blackness of night had began to fall.

When Aran next opened his eyelids, he was shrouded in the shadow of bright moonlight. He sat up to find that the two boats were still moving. Dewin had barely slowed his pace the entire night, and a tired, yet stubborn, Simlee was determined not to fall behind.

Over towards the south, a line of flickering specs littered the darkened skyline. A layer of thick mist was gradually moving its way towards them, as they approached what appeared to be a great coastline. Aran's stomach fluttered at the thought of dry land.

"Is that what I think it is?" he asked.

Wettman was slouched back against the stern of the small boat. He nodded.

"Those there, are the twinkling lights of Kolwith Bay," said the captain. "They call them *the Eyes of the South Island*."

18

THE OLD MULE

Aran couldn't help but smile. He could even have shed a tear. It had been a long time since he'd first heard the name Kolwith Bay, a destination he never thought he would ever get to see. This port at the edge of the South Island may not have been as glamorous as the great spires of Calon, but it was the first real indication of how far he'd come.

He watched in wonder as the yellow dots of light grew larger with every moment. He knelt up against the bow so he could witness every moment of their imminent arrival. Dozens of wooden piers reached out to greet them like fingers grasping out towards the sea. Ships much larger than their own came and went with remarkable ease, their sails a deep shade of blue from the ever-present moonlight. As each one unloaded their precious cargo, merchants and hagglers were already bartering like greedy vultures in a mad feeding frenzy. Makeshift market stalls stretched out all the way towards the towering wharfs. Deals were being made and promises were being broken.

Beyond the enormous docking areas was a lively seafront full of taverns and gambling establishments. The bustling atmosphere of the wide bay was a stark contrast to the sleepy quietness of the sea. Hundreds of fiery torches lit up the many corners of this animated coastline; an orange glow of life and soul.

It was a town that refused to sleep, a place unwilling to let the mere darkness of the night disrupt its screaming thirst for opportunity and pleasure. It was a place unlike anything Aran had seen before.

"We must stick to the eastern dock," said Wettman. "We can't afford any unwanted attention. If we are to find your man, we must do it carefully. There are soldiers everywhere. And most of them are as corrupt as we are."

He waved towards the second boat and pointed eastward. Dewin needed no further explanation. He swung his body to one side and immediately changed course. Both vessels steered away from the main harbour. They lurked through the mist like ghosts in the night, their whereabouts oblivious to anyone but themselves. To the occupants of Kolwith Bay they were merely shadows passing through.

Aran looked on, as they reached a much quieter part of the cove. On this side, the piers were bare and disused. Many of the raised storage buildings were old and decrepit, with some having been abandoned altogether. Dark figures wandered along the edges with their glowing lanterns.

Aran wondered whether these suspicious characters were waiting for other nighttime arrivals such as himself. He felt a nervous chill. If the main port had been a hive of corruption and villainy, he dreaded to think what went on in these quieter regions.

Once their boats had safely moored with little fuss or detection, both groups of pirates joined together in a single unit. Stood on the fringes of the great harbour was the most unlikely crew it had ever encountered. Aran looked around at his newly assembled team; they were certainly an unusual group. Each person had very little in common, and the only interest they shared was an individual they had never even met. The tension was at an all time high.

"So what now?" asked Simlee.

"We head to the Old Mule," said Wettman. "It's a tavern not far from here."

"A tavern? Finally something we can agree on. I could murder a few petals, that's for sure."

"We will meet with an old friend of mine who owns the place," continued Wettman. "If the docks of Kolwith Bay are the eyes of the South Island, then she is most certainly the ears. She will have heard more than her fair share about the whereabouts of your famous friend."

Simlee rolled back his head and let out a long groan.

"Do you ever take a night off?" he asked.

Wettman ignored the remark and led the way. The others followed in single file. They snaked their way around the misty shore like a confused centipede.

"I don't know about you, boys," said Simlee whilst tapping on his large belly. "But I intend to drink my bodyweight in fluids this fine evening."

Larson and Phen, the last of Wettman's loyal crew members, cried out in agreement. The two pirates flanked their new associate as if he were a god. Their shared interest in Simlee's passion for drinking could well have been the foundations of a newfound friendship.

Larson, the shortest of the two men, began sharing a story of how he once drank an entire barrel full of lewpetal juice in one sitting. The bodily repercussions were so dramatic, even a nervous Aran was forced to laugh. The small feeling of camaraderie was a new one to him. A growing sense of anticipation was burning through his stomach, as they wove through the rowdy backstreets in their united pack of six. All of a sudden, he felt safe. Despite the many dangers lurking around each and every corner of these forgotten passageways, he knew that the group would always have his back (or at least, they would for the time being).

Buried in a deep corner of Kolwith's neglected north side was a crooked tavern. The Old Mule was not unlike many of the other popular watering holes scattered amongst the coastal town's seedy night spots. But what made this particular venue even more frequented than all the others, was the fact that it opened its doors at all hours of the day. This had made it a hotspot for every type of customer imaginable; some were there to drink, some were there for trouble and others were merely passing through. By the time Aran and his weary travellers had walked through the main doors, most of the punters were doing all three.

"Mr. Tinky!" cried a voice as they entered.

Standing behind the long bar was a flamboyant woman with strong, fiery hair. She lifted up her arms in praise and shimmied over to greet them.

Wettman was devoured by a hearty hug and smacked on the cheek by a heavily planted kiss.

"Hello, Syannah," he said, with a blushing smile.

"It's been far too long!" she said. "Come! Pull up a stool and we'll get you all watered up."

Syannah marched straight back towards the bar. She stepped over an unconscious customer as if he were invisible. Bottles of purple liquid were soon thrusted across the table, before returning to her packed cupboard to rummage for something even stronger.

"I like this woman already," said Larson. He licked his lips and rubbed his hands together.

Simlee turned to the captain and muttered in his ear. "Mr... *Tinky*?"

Wettman rolled his eyes.

"It's an old nickname," he said.

"You're not short of those," said Simlee. "*Wettytoes.*"

"The name is from..." he looked back at the raised eyebrow and sighed. "Never mind."

"Come!" called Syannah. "Gather your friends, Mr. Tinky."

The entire group looked at each other and shrugged. They swarmed towards the line of drinks quicker than wasps to an open picnic.

Aran did his best to ignore the prying eyes. Walking through this den of mischief was like strolling across a stage with an audience of hungry bears. Strangers always peaked a lot of interest, and this was the strangest ensemble of misfits to have haunted this establishment in quite some time. The group was received with a mixture of both suspicion and intrigue.

What was a rabble like this doing in here? Where were they heading? What was a small boy doing with a bunch of old pirates?

Aran had asked the last question himself on a number of occasions, but these were just a few of the curious thoughts that hovered around the Old Mule that night — not that it seemed to bother Syannah.

"And who is *this* strapping young man?" asked the high-spirited landlord. She placed a hand on either side of Simlee's grizzled cheeks, patting them with her assortment of colourful rings. Aran had yet to see Simlee experience fear, but the affectionate advances of this feisty woman had been enough to instil terror into his very soul.

Wettman gave an awkward twist of his body.

"This..." he said with a grind of his teeth. "This is Captain Simlee."

"Is that so?" asked Syannah, with a wide-open mouth.

An unsuspecting Simlee was swiftly pelted by an enormous

slap. The impact from Syannah's metal-encrusted fingers left a bright red mark across his face. The rest of the party winced.

"I've been waiting to give you that for years!" she snapped.

Simlee rubbed his cheek after the unexpected blow.

"Well if that's your best chat-up move then you must be very lonely," he said.

"You don't even remember me, do you?" Her question was met with a confused shrug. "My Uncle Teron — you tricked me into giving you his location."

The memory came flooding back. Simlee nodded. "Ah, yes... Your uncle was quite the scoundrel."

"He was only providing for his family."

"His family must have eaten very well indeed." He looked the woman up and down. "If I remember rightly, you were his little helper. Goodness, how you have blossomed."

He shook off the slap and consumed his entire drink in one mouthful. The landlord shook her head in disgust and placed an arm around Wettman.

"Now, tell me, lad," she said, stroking his unwashed hair. "What brings the great Captain Wettman back to a hole like this one?"

"We are looking for a man who can help me with my next voyage," he replied.

"What a shame." She swallowed her drink as if it were water. "Every time we get the honour of your return, you're already getting ready to leave again."

"I can assure you that, if all goes well, this journey will be my last."

"Bah! You say that every time. And each time you disappoint. Not still chasing magical creatures and fairytale kingdoms, are you?"

"Something like that," he said with a smile. "Only this time, the treasure I'm looking for might actually exist."

Syannah slapped her own thigh and laughed.

"Hah, hah! I love your enthusiasm, lad." She poured them all another drink and leant herself against the bar. "So... Who is this special man you seek?"

Wettman took a gulp of his strong beverage.

"We are looking for a man named Wyn Drathion."

The entire bar went silent. Syannah gave him a long, hard stare. The gulps from his fellow pirates' heavy drinking could be heard with unusual clarity.

"That's a very brave name to mention around these parts," said Syannah, eventually, after the quietness had returned to its usual rowdy levels. "He has gained quite the reputation over the years."

"So it would appear," said Wettman. He looked around the room to see the punters had now gone back to their rambling conversations.

"Some say he only comes out at night these days," said Syannah.

"So do rabbits," interrupted Simlee. He necked his drink and scoffed. The landlord frowned at his disrespectful remark before continuing with her tale.

"A rabbit does not go around murdering soldiers. This man roams the island like a ghost, hunting down his next victim like death himself. Some believe he may even be a ghost."

Simlee shook his head. "Ghost!" he snorted.

"How many men has he killed?" asked Aran.

"Hundreds," said Syannah. "Thousands, probably. Word has it he's recently started targeting Brenin knights. Put you right at the top of the wanted list, that will."

"Sounds like a hero to me," said Larson. "Any man of title should be setting an example — not abusing their power like so many of them do."

"That's rich coming from a pirate," said Simlee.

"At least we don't pretend to be people we're not," snapped Larson. "There was once a time when being a member of the royal army actually meant something. Now they are just minions of the crown. Many of us became pirates because we never had a choice."

"Excuse me if I don't shed a few tears," said Simlee.

"Larson's right," said Phen. "When I was a boy I used to look up to my queen. Then, one day, her men burned my house to the ground. I had no idea why, at the time. But I do remember the way one of those soldiers interrogated my older brothers until they cried. I never did find out why those men came to the house that day. But I'd have been quite happy if Drathion had killed *those* soldiers."

The young pirate stared into the bottom of his glass, whilst the rest of his company remained quiet.

"Well I think you're all just a bunch of traitors," said Simlee. "She is our queen as much as anybody else's. Just because we're pirates doesn't mean we're not loyal to our own kingdom, unlike this Drathion."

"What do you know about loyalty?" asked Wettman.

"I know more about serving my kingdom than any of you lot do."

He rolled up his right sleeve to reveal a distinct cross on the side of his arm. Painted against his tough skin was a tattoo unlike any of the others.

"You see that?" he asked.

The men gathered around.

"That's the mark of the Royal Sharkskins," said Larson, without a doubt in his mind.

"The finest fleet in the entire navy," said Simlee. "That's ten years of service to the queen herself."

"Did you ever meet her?" asked Phen, struggling to contain his excitement.

"I met her personally," replied Simlee. He lifted up his middle finger to show off a thick ring with an engraved mark. "She was the same woman who gave me this. There was a time I would have given her my life."

"And look what you have to show for it now," said Wettman. "A piece of metal around your finger and a name that nobody will remember."

Hardly anyone spoke for at least another round. Wettman polished off his third drink and stretched out across the bar to face Syannah.

"So do you know anyone who has actually *seen* this Drathion?" he asked her. "Surely *someone* must have."

Syannah gave the answer a careful consideration.

"Anyone who has ever had the misfortune of meeting this man has not lived to tell the tale," she said. "They say he wears a mask, a green one, just like his skin. For all I know Drathion could be walking among us as we speak. It's why everyone is so afraid to talk about him. For all you know, you could be having a conversation with Drathion at any moment."

"I think I'd know if I met anyone with green skin," muttered Simlee into his drink.

Aran looked around at the medley of unpleasant clientele who were gathered around the various tables, all chatting above their metal pint glasses and laughing at the occasional joke. The thought that any one of these strangers could be the man himself was terrifying.

"But there must have been *someone* who survived his blade," said Wettman. He was normally a patient man, but the struggle to get at least one piece of useful information out of his old friend was proving too much. Syannah had met more people passing through her doors than most individuals would ever come across in an entire lifetime. If anyone could connect him with a person it was her. Worst of all, he knew she was holding something back.

Syannah sighed. "Well," she said, "There is one person. Or at least... so he claims."

Wettman glared at her and leant forward. Even the others were now shuffling their stools closer.

"He is a retired army officer," she continued. "A well-to-do type. Made a tiny fortune serving as a senior member of the queen's army back in his heyday. He comes in here for a drink every once in a while. Makes him feel like a man of the people. But, if you ask me, he's just a rambling, old codger with a passion for lewpetal. He's no more a man of the people than I am a woman of high society."

She wrapped an old rag around her neck and posed like a queen. The men sniggered.

"And he claims to have *seen* Drathion?" asked Wettman, his face urging her to continue.

"Claims?" she said. "He insists he has survived a whole encounter. The man is missing a hand. Says it was taken by Drathion, just like his fellow officers. Personally, I think he just lost it from talking too much down the harbour. But he describes the moment quite vividly. Whenever I get someone trying to find Drathion, he's the first person they go to. Then they realise he's just a mad, old war veteran who likes the attention."

Wettman gave a disappointed nod. It hadn't quite been the lead he had hoped for. But it was better than nothing.

"Where does this crazy old man live?" he asked.

"He owns a vineyard up in the hills," said Syannah. "Not too far from here. He'll be more than happy to show you around. But I warn you now — he may never let you leave once he gets talking."

"I suppose we'd better pay him a visit," said Wettman, with a reluctant frown.

"A vineyard sounds pretty good to me," said Larson. "He'd better give us some samples."

"Good luck with that," said Syannah. "He's a stingy old man."

"Then maybe we'll just take some," said Phen with a sly grin.

Wettman stood up and grabbed his jacket. "Everyone ready to depart?"

The men groaned.

"For goodness sake, Mr. Tinky!" cried Syannah. "At least wait until morning. You really have become a right boring, old fish since you left for sea."

"You can say that again," said Simlee with a toast.

Syannah marched around the bar and grabbed Wettman as if they were about to dance.

"You are my welcome guests for the evening," she said. "And believe me, there aren't many I would call that. Especially with the type of people who drink in here."

Larson and Phen leapt up from their stools with a loud cheer. They threw each other into a merry jig and began circling around the room.

Syannah reached behind the bar and pulled out an old harpsichord. Many of the slightly more sober members of the tavern began bashing their tables with a steady beat. An upbeat melody soon followed; it chimed out from her bulky instrument with a swinging rhythm.

Wettman let slip an amused smile and watched, as the jolly landlord began fluctuating her harpsichord and tapping her foot. A drunken Simlee recognised the song, almost immediately, and began singing the words at the top of his lungs (much to Syannah's surprise).

Aran couldn't help but grin. He clapped along, as the entire room burst into a chaotic mixture of song and dance.

Hours later, Aran found himself slumped against the side of a bench whilst trying to stay awake. Simlee sat beside him, leaning his suffering body against their small table. He'd had more than enough to drink but was still swigging away at some unknown liquid. Alone in the corner, they both gazed out at the remaining punters, many of whom were still determined to continue on the party.

The party, however, had long finished. A few stragglers were passed out across the floor, whilst the rest of their group continued to drink over at the bar. Simlee stared at the young captain, who was propped up on a stool, trying not to fall off, whilst he listened intently to one of Syannah's riveting stories.

"This is where I leave you, Aran," Simlee said.

Aran turned to look at him. The serious tone in the man's slurred voice filled him with an unexpected sadness.

"What do you mean?" he asked. "You can't leave us now."

"I prefer to work alone. Always have, always will."

The boy studied his cold gaze. "Captain Wettman... You really don't like him, do you?"

Simlee took a long, hard gulp of his drink.

"I don't particularly like *anyone*," he said. "But that man has brought back a sea of memories I had hoped to forget."

Aran thought more about the discussions on the lifeboat. "Was your father really a famous pirate?"

"Razor Blade Pete was as famous as they come. My father, on the other hand, was just a man. A man who made a few too many bad choices. Like raising your children on a ship full of thieves. Now *that* was always a questionable decision right there."

"Is that why you betrayed him?"

Simlee nearly choked on his mouthful of lewpetal juice. He wiped off the excess liquid from his chin and laughed.

"I betrayed him the moment I joined the queen's navy. It was all I ever wanted — to live an honourable life — a life I could be proud of. And I did, for a while. Until the curse of my father's name came calling. I remember his face the day I led my squadron of Sharkskins to his cabin door. I had expected to see pride, or even shame — even some anger would have been nice. Instead, I got nothing. He really was as cold as his reputation."

"But what about Drathion?" asked Aran.

"I've spent more years chasing people than I can remember," replied Simlee. "Sometimes their faces all blend into one. Along the way, you end up searching for the wrong person. You might as well be looking for the dead."

Aran didn't quite understand what he meant, but he had uttered the words with such pain and distance.

"This is a young man's game," he continued. "And I have grown tired."

Aran was beginning to accept that there would be no changing the man's mind. Simlee had not been the same since they had left the Blue Duchess. Ever since Wettman had first mentioned his father's name, the words had touched a nerve so deep that it continued to plague him.

He finished the last of his drink and stumbled off towards his room.

"I hope you find what you're looking for, Aran," he said, before turning his back and walking away.

19

THE MAJOR

A ran woke up to find Simlee had long gone. The morning sun had barely found its way through the draping curtains when he found the empty bed. His sheets had hardly been touched, and the smell of lewpetal hung around in the air. Aran wondered whether he would ever see the man again.

Wettman and his men were already prepared to set off by the time Aran had walked outside.

"So it would appear your friend has abandoned us," said the captain. "That's hardly a surprise."

Still disappointed by the sudden departure, Aran refused to satisfy him with a response. Instead, he merely followed the group of pirates onwards through the empty streets.

Up on the rolling hills of Kolwith Bay was a walled property. Bathing in the orange sunlight, the impressive home was far prettier than any of the clustered buildings down below. Its sandy brickwork was a stark contrast to the luscious vineyards that surrounded it.

Wettman and his group of followers made a steady climb up the curling path leading to the main gates. Aran looked back at what was the first clear view he had seen of the whole town. From this great height, and at such an early hour of the day, the ferocious atmosphere of the seafront was mellowed by a view worthy of any landscape painting. Up here, the air was calm and peaceful.

At the front of the vineyard was a wooden sign. It read: *The White Gower*.

A group of labourers turned their heads at the passing visitors, whilst a suspicious old woman stood behind the main gate with an unwelcoming frown. The property was larger than it had appeared from down below, and its mysterious owner was worth more than Syannah had let on. Larson looked up at the grand exterior and sneered.

"So who lives here?" he asked in amusement. "The queen herself?"

"Not quite," said Wettman. "According to Syannah, the man stumbled on a stroke good fortune."

"And how did he do that?"

"Nobody quite knows," replied the captain. "The owner gives a different story each time. Some say he was an army general, others claim he's nothing but a low-ranking member of the infantry. But the most popular opinion is that he's just a mad, old soldier who tripped over a treasure chest."

"Lucky devil," said Larson. "Isn't that what we all are? Mad, old soldiers?"

"Except, without the treasure," added Phen.

They looked up and feasted their eyes on the enormous front door. Across its surface were carved patterns that flowed outwards, like a dancing bird warning off its enemies.

The woman at the gate greeted them with a cold silence.

"We're here to see the owner of this establishment," said Wettman, in his most commanding voice.

The woman stared at him. Her face hung low as if it were being stretched by a dangling weight.

"My master rarely accepts visitors," she croaked.

"We need to speak with him about an extremely important matter," said Wettman.

They waited for a reply.

"My master will not see anyone today."

The captain tried not to lose his composure.

"Tell him we are here to ask him about a man named Wyn Drathion."

After a long, uncomfortable pause, the woman eventually gave a solemn nod.

Taken back by her sudden willingness to cooperate, the entire group watched as she swiftly headed inside, almost floating with her long, drooping attire.

Aran watched as the great door opened up with a loud thud. It moved in a slow and controlled motion, unveiling a smooth marble flooring that continued into the grand porch. The interior was as quiet as the outside; not a sole in sight for as far as the eye could see.

The pirates looked at each other with a careless shrug. Aran followed them with great trepidation. He prepared himself, once again, for yet another reluctant step into the unknown.

Once they had all gathered inside, each member of the group raised a curious head to admire the most impressive ceiling any of them had ever come across. It curved up above them in a symmetrical dome, a great sky of painstakingly constructed artwork that bounced light into every corner of the room.

It wasn't until they lowered their awestruck faces that they realised the old woman had returned.

"The master will see you now," she said.

Larson bent his knee and gave her an exaggerated curtsy.

Phen giggled like a schoolboy, until a scowl from Wettman caused him to cover up his mouth.

Aran found himself leading the way into a large drawing room. Rows of towering bookcases lined the walls on opposite sides, whilst a central window overlooked the sprawling fields outside. A dark figure sat with his back turned and admired the rows of carefully planted fruit. He turned around to reveal a head of thick, grey hair.

"Well, I say..." said the man. "What is a gabble of pirates doing so far inland? It's as though a school of fish has just walked into my home."

Wettman and his crew were huddled together in a small cluster. They looked at each other with awkward glances.

"We are here to see Major Golwin," said Wettman.

The old man opened up his wild eyes until they were bursting from their sockets. "Then you boys are very much in luck."

Major Golwin rose to his feet and spread out his arms. For a moment, they could have sworn he was about to take a bow.

"Major Golwin, I take it," said Wettman.

"The very same," confirmed Golwin. He swanned over to a nearby table and poured himself a glass of red wine. "Come! You must all celebrate with the finest wine this side of Morwallia. A drink such as this takes a very long time to prepare. You could spend your entire life waiting for it to be ready and it would be a life well spent."

He lifted up the glass and inspected its beauty.

"What exactly are we celebrating?" asked Wettman.

"Why, the chance to share a glass of wine with Major Golwin of course," replied the old man. "Not everyone can lay claim to that. You are very fortunate people, indeed."

The captain rolled his eyes whilst an eager Larson and Phen rushed over to be handed their own glasses.

"So I hear you're in search of a man who took this from me," said Golwin. He lifted up his right arm to reveal a missing hand.

"Then the story is true," said Wettman. "You *have* met Wyn Drathion."

"Met him?" asked the major. "My boy, I did battle with the man!"

He handed the captain his drink and looked up at a stern Dewin.

"Won't you be having one?" he asked. Dewin crossed his arms and shook his head. "My, my! You *are* a big lad. You know, I once fought a man like you back in my prime. He was twice your size. By the time I was finished with him he was squealing like a pig."

He danced backwards and forwards in a bid to initiate a duel with the larger opponent. Dewin remained still without moving a muscle. His refusal to be intimidated caused a playful Golwin to laugh and pat him on the back.

"Don't be afraid!" said the major. "I won't be doing the same to you — I promise."

Wettman clutched his own forehead and contained his frustration.

"So, your battle with Drathion..."

Golwin turned to him sharply.

"My what?" he asked. "Ah, yes — the great battle!"

They watched, as the old man began bouncing around on the spot, ducking and weaving against his imaginary opponent. He stuck out the arm with his missing hand and thrusted it forward in a bizarre reenactment.

"So there I was..." he said. "Myself and the monstrous Drathion — face-to-face — in a fight to the death." Aran looked on, captivated by the tall tale. The others merely raised their eyebrows whilst sipping on wine. "He was the tallest man I had ever seen. His eyes were cold, as cold as the air had been that night. The fog was thick, and my blade was frosty..."

"He seems to remember more about the weather than he does about anything else," said Larson, after a cynical gulp of his drink.

"It was the officer's sleeping quarters," Golwin continued. "All the other men had been slaughtered in their beds — but not me! I sleep with one eye open, you see."

"Course he does..." said Phen.

"The ground shook with every clash of our swords. His devilish eyes burned like fire."

Golwin spoke with the conviction of a man who had told this story a thousand times before. He hissed out a series of exaggerated sound effects. With a "swish" and a "swoosh", he darted across the room and stopped just in front of Aran's horrified face. The major looked at him with wide eyes and slapped him on the arm in an effort to make him jump. The slap worked.

"Just as I was about to move in for the killer blow, he sliced me with his rusty blade."

Aran leapt again at the sight of Golwin's chopped-off hand. The small stump popped its way out from his sleeve like a jack-in-the-box.

"And what happened *then*?" asked Wettman, who had grown tired of this theatrical performance.

Golwin paused as if not quite remembering. He turned to face him and sensed the cynicism in his voice.

"Why, he let me go, of course," he replied in a defiant tone. "Nobody locks swords with Drathion and lives to tell the tale. Not unless he allows it."

"He let you go?" asked Larson. "Just like that?"

"What makes *you* so special?" asked Phen.

The major locked his arms together and smiled.

"My dear boy..." he said. "I have been asking that same ques-

tion every morning since that very day. It has truly been a gift —
a blessing, even."

"Did he not say anything?" asked Wettman.

"Drathion speaks only in actions," said Golwin. "Which is
why I now worship the man as if he were a god. Bah! He *is* a god!
Only *he* can choose who lives and dies. He wanders the night
like a moonlight executioner."

Wettman gave a heavy sigh; this had not been the outcome
he had hoped for.

"Let me show you something!" said the major.

He hurried over to a corner of the room where something
was covered in a layer of expensive fabric. The men gathered to
watch him pull off the material in a dramatic reveal. Underneath
was a glass cabinet. Aran clasped his mouth in shock.

"Every day I kneel before it," said Golwin. "And everyday I
pay homage to the spirit of Drathion. Thanking him for giving
me such a symbolic reminder of life's true worth."

The pirates continued to stare at the glass case. Inside was a
hand. Its white, skeletal fingers reached out, frozen in motion.

Aran wasn't the only person who felt uncomfortable. Larson
leaned over towards Wettman.

"I think the old man's lost his marbles," he whispered. "Let's
get out of here."

Golwin rubbed his remaining fingers against the glass case
in a bid to comfort his former hand.

"Come!" he said, and turned to his guests with an excited
grin. "Let me show you the fruits of our labour. I can assure you
it's the most beautiful sight you have ever seen."

The pirates turned to each other with unconvinced frowns.
Golwin would not take no for an answer, and he led them
outside before they had a chance to object.

They stepped out into the back courtyard. Up ahead was a
great vineyard that stretched out as far as Aran could see. Miles

of dangling grapes were all lined up in carefully prepared rows. Golwin took in a deep breath and admired the scenery.

"You know, when I first arrived on this plot of land it was nothing more than a patch of dirt," he said. "And it all starts with a single seed."

Before they knew it, the bored pirates were following him through the crops, until most of them had completely lost their bearings. Golwin continued his tour, chatting away on a subject they had very little interest in.

"This is the most important stage of the entire process," he said. "If you mess anything up at the beginning, you will never achieve true greatness." He clutched a handful of grapes and took a big sniff. "If it weren't for Drathion, not a single one of these grapes would be here today. For I would not be here to grow them."

Wettman rolled his eyes.

"Is there nothing else you can tell us about him?" he asked, taking off his hat and wiping off the sweat.

"What more do you need to know?" asked Golwin.

"An idea of what he looks like would help," grumbled Larson.

The major laughed and shook his head.

"My dear boys..." he said. "I have grown fond of you people. Which is why I will offer you this friendly piece of advice: people who go around asking after Wyn Drathion have a very limited life span."

The group were taken by surprise. This jovial old man had not shown a serious side in all the time they had been there. But now his face had turned cold.

"If you look for Drathion, you will have no trouble finding him," he said. "For he will always find you first."

They all fell silent for a moment. Larson brushed him off with a careless shrug.

"Well it will certainly make our lives a lot easier," he said. "I'd rather he came to us first anyway. Saves us traipsing around in a field all day."

The major ignored him and turned to Wettman.

"And what possible madness could bring you men to seek an audience with the devil himself?" asked the major.

"Drathion is just a man," said Wettman, with an assured face. "And we have reason to believe that this man will give us the location of somewhere we hope to visit."

"I assume there's a spot of treasure involved, no doubt?" asked the major.

"The greatest treasure you could ever hope to find."

Golwin scratched his head and nodded in amusement. "So you need his help? Only a truly brave man would ask Wyn Drathion for help."

"We have something for him," said Wettman.

"*Do* you now?" asked Golwin. He was suddenly very intrigued.

Wettman pointed towards Aran, whose presence had almost been forgotten.

"This boy has a letter," said the captain. "It's a letter we know will mean a lot to him."

Aran placed a hand on his satchel and held it tight. He had grown weary of the sudden attention, especially with a stranger he did not trust.

"So you are a glorified postman?" Golwin asked him. Aran looked back and refused to say a word. This eccentric landlord made him uneasy. There was something about the major's demeanour that had disturbed him since the moment they first arrived. Now this strange old man had taken a particular interest in him.

"You think a letter will be enough to earn the trust of Drathion?" asked Golwin.

"Like I said," Wettman assured him. "He is just a man. And he will help us whether he wants to or not. I have come too far to allow any other outcome."

The captain gave him a cold stare. His ruthless tone was a glimmer of what Wettman was determined to do in order to achieve his goal. There were plenty of ways to get people to do things, and he was willing to do whatever it would take.

"I see," said Golwin. He gave the captain a grave, yet understanding, nod. "Well I wish you boys all the luck in the world."

The major continued the rest of his tour speaking only of wine and its endless complexities. Aran was surprised how long a man could talk about a substance he personally had very little taste for. The miles of endless grapes had very quickly lost their novelty, and his drifting attention was soon struck by an unexpected presence in the corner of his eye.

Lurking, deep in the valley of everlasting fruit, was the outline of a hooded figure. Aran had long suspected they were being watched from the moment they had first approached the main house. In a darkened window there had been a ghostly face staring back at him. Or had there? He had already begun to doubt the hooded stranger, until, once again, it slithered into view. A second later, it vanished into the heavy camouflage of the creeping vines, as if it were merely a figment of the boy's increasing paranoia.

"So what is your secret to finding buried treasure?" asked Larson, as the major walked them back towards his impressive house.

"It's quite simple, my dear boy," said Golwin. "Never assume it's buried. Most of life's great treasures are hidden in plain sight."

Larson raised his nose and scoffed.

"Not the ones I'm looking for," he said.

The men had already bid their farewells before the sun had

even reached its full height. Wettman had decided that their strange host would get them little further in their quest for the outlaw. His personal accounts, however dramatic they may have sounded, were as vague as any of the drunken stories down at the Old Mule. They may as well have asked the average local on the streets of Kolwith Bay. For everyone knew someone with a Drathion story.

The trail was still as cold as it had been the night before, and Wettman was now clinging to his hopes on a new plan. Rather than chase his creature into the deep unknown, they would lure him out into plain sight.

According to the ramblings of their new watering hole, the last Drathion sighting had only been a few nights before. As far as Wettman could work out, many of the outlaw's recent victims had been claimed in a similar part of town. Deep in the heart of Kolwith's eastern borough was a series of narrow side streets, known by most as the Barking Lanes.

"They say he haunts those lanes like a restless demon," said one of the more sober punters that night.

Wettman and his crew had decided that the Old Mule would serve as the perfect base of operations for the next few nights. The regular flow of lewpetal juice on offer was certainly an added bonus, and the pirate captain knew full well that there was never a tongue so slippery as one that had been soaked in the purple drink.

"They say you don't even see him coming," continued the drunken man at Wettman's table. "He just rides in and slices you down like a joint of beef. Brutal if you ask me. He needs to be hung, drawn and quartered."

"But his victims have never been innocent," said an older man. "They were mostly crooked soldiers. We could do with someone like him to clean up the filth in this town. It's getting worse all the time. Even the law enforcers have stopped going down some of those lanes."

"We'll have a scout of those streets tomorrow," Wettman said to his only sober crew member.

Dewin sat beside him, looking extremely bored and uncomfortable. If there was one place he couldn't stand, it was a room full of slurring drunks with their meaningless conversations. A life at sea had always suited him more.

The rest of the men were scattered throughout the tavern. Wettman had reminded them all that the purpose of their visit was to gather information. Larson agreed, but he had also decided that there was no reason not to have a little fun in the process. The man was already on his sixth glass and had succumbed to a hopeless arm wrestle with one of the larger members of his table.

"Stop squeezing my wrist!" he cried. "You're a slimy cheat!"

Phen shook his head in embarrassment. His fellow pirate had always enjoyed a drink, a trait that had also made him extremely unpleasant company — after the tenth drink he would become unbearable. It was at that point that Larson's life-long collection of inner demons would rear their ugly heads. His old friend would morph into a man he no longer recognised, a man he no longer wanted to be around.

"Cheer up, you old goat!" Larson spat out. He turned to the stranger beside him. "Don't you think he has a face like an old goat?"

Phen scrunched up his body and clenched his fists. He hated being called an old goat, and now an entire table was laughing at him.

Upstairs, Aran sat on the side of his bed listening to the drunken laughter beneath the floorboards. He had not been in the mood to socialise, but couldn't bring himself to sleep, either.

He leant forward and peered out the window overlooking

the street. Down below, the cobbled road was covered in a layer of thick fog. The fog seemed to be a permanent feature of this lively cove. When the night drew in across Kolwith Bay, the fog would soon follow. It rose up from the sea, like an aquatic monster, and flowed through the dingy streets until the entire town was engulfed in its misty haze.

Aran stared out into the fog. Suddenly, before his very eyes, a dark figure melted into view. The boy rubbed his tired eyes before taking a second glance — and then a third — until, eventually, he had to accept that a hooded stranger was indeed standing there in the street below. Whether it was flesh and blood was another question. For in that very moment, he could have sworn he was witnessing a ghost.

Aran jumped up and threw himself down the flight of stairs leading to the busy bar. After charging out into the room of drunken pirates, he felt his entire body freeze into place. Stood in the middle of the main entrance was the hooded figure.

"Aran!" cried a volatile Larson. "Isn't it way past your bedtime?"

The boy looked around at the groups of rowdy drinkers. Not one person in the entire room had batted an eyelid. The hooded figure was already making its way into a darkened corner of the bar — and none of the other customers were any the wiser.

Aran went tense, as a large arm wrapped itself around him. The smell of lewpetal polluted his nostrils as Larson's sour breath was now pouring across his face.

"Glad you could join us," he said. "Trying to have fun with this lot is like scraping out your eyeballs. Now let me show you how an adult is *supposed* to drink."

He lifted up a half drunk bottle and pointed its long spout towards the boy's mouth.

"No, thank you," said Aran, pulling away. His attention was still firmly rooted on the hooded figure.

"Come on!" said Larson. "You're as bad as this lot. I need someone who can keep up with me."

"I'd say you've had enough," said Wettman. The captain gave his crew member a threatening stare.

Larson nearly lost his balance from the rush of frustration.

"You people don't know the meaning of enough!" he wailed, swinging his bottle in the air and thrusting it in Aran's face. "Come on, Aran. We'll show them."

The boy squirmed as he grabbed him by the neck. Larson looked down to see Aran's focus was aimed solely towards the stranger in the corner of the room.

"What on earth are you looking at, boy?" he asked. The pirate lowered his head until it was leaning hard against Aran's. Larson looked over towards the mysterious figure and chuckled.

"What's the matter?" he asked. "Is that man over there scaring you?"

The faceless stranger remained still, and silent.

"Hey!" he called out. "Is your face so ugly that you need to hide it?"

Larson took a swig of his bottle and cackled. He looked back to see that his words had made no effect. The drunken pirate stumbled across the room towards the figure.

"Do you think your silence intimidates me?" he continued. "Show me your face and prepare to be beaten within an inch of your life!"

Larson yanked out his sword, almost dropping it in the process.

The figure merely tilted its head and slowly lifted off the hood. Every punter silenced their conversation. The entire tavern turned their attention towards the darkened corner.

Larson's jaw dropped down a few notches. Beneath the mysterious hood was the face of a young woman. Her jet-black hair was cut short and featured a white streak that ran along the entire length of her scalp.

Aran couldn't help but admire the beauty in her strong, piercing gaze and watched as she stared at the man in front of her with a perfectly straightened posture. Her composure was strong, as if her spine were made of iron.

"What have we here?" asked Larson, with a lick of his lips. He pulled up a stool and sat himself down in front of her. "This place is far too rough for the likes of a pretty girl like you. What's your name there, sweetheart?"

She remained silent, her eyes shooting straight through him. He shuffled closer, his own eyes slanted, whilst his drooping tongue slithered like a hungry lizard.

"Leave the girl alone," called Syannah. "She doesn't want you slobbering all over her."

"Don't be afraid, my dear," said Larson. "I'll look after you."

He lifted up his fat fingers and placed them firmly around her hand.

Within seconds of him touching her, the woman slipped out a dagger and stuck it straight through his large hand.

Larson unleashed a deafening scream. Even in his intoxicated state, he could feel every inch of that razor sharp blade, gnawing and twisting against his intricate joints.

The young woman yanked the knife back out again, which only resulted in a second cry of pain. The sound of crunching flesh sent a wave of sympathy throughout the horrified onlookers.

A furious Larson fell backwards against the floor, nursing his hand like a wounded animal. He looked up at the woman, who seemed unfazed by the entire incident. She remained in the comfort of her chair, watching him with a hint of pleasure in her face. Little did the pirate know that she was simply an amused cat playing with her doomed mouse.

Larson charged towards her in a vengeful rage.

"Larson!" barked Wettman, whose warning had already fallen on deaf ears.

The screaming pirate dived towards the table with his great sword. By the time he made impact, the woman was already safely out of the way. Larson had struck nothing but a gust of air and went tumbling over against the empty chair.

Lying on his belly full of lewpetal juice, he looked up to see that his sword had not only been pried away from him, but was now aimed straight at his gulping chin. His neck muscles quivered as the woman shuffled in her solid stance. She gave him a merciless stare and prepared herself for a final blow.

Her blade shot up with expert precision, only to then clash against a solid, opposing force. What could have easily been a fatal blow to Larson's throat had been halted by a second sword.

The young woman turned around in search of the culprit. Standing beside her was Wettman, his stern face willing her to stand down. She took a long, hard look before turning her attention to the small bag that was dangling beside his waist. Their two weapons were still at loggerheads, with both swords trembling in a delicate standoff. The woman relaxed her blade for a moment, before slicing the strap on Wettman's body.

The bag slid open and out dropped the gauntlet. Before the armour could even reach the floor, the woman had already swiped it clean away.

"Hey!" called Wettman, as she darted across the room. Her agility was that of a wild feline, and she moved with the grace of a soaring bird. Every person she passed reached out to grab her, but were left with nothing more than an empty hug. She ducked and weaved, leaping onto tables until she reached the back exit.

The last person in her way was also the smallest. A nervous Aran placed his hands on either side of the doorframe, blocking her path with his tiny frame. He braced for the heavy impact, only to see her vault over him as if he were a short hurdle. He looked over to see Wettman and his men charging towards him with their swords raised.

"After that thief!" roared the captain.

Aran turned around and felt a horde of angry pirates bulldozing him forward. The young woman had already kicked open the back door and was now sprinting down the cobbled passageway outside. She glided through the mist with a lightness that almost defied gravity.

Wettman burst out from the back of the tavern and caught sight of her thin silhouette sliding itself around the first corner up ahead. He chased after it, his men only a couple of yards behind him, tripping and stumbling after their recent drinking binge. After the second corner, the group had splintered into multiple side streets.

"We can't let her get away!" cried the captain. "Cover all of her options. She can't run forever!"

By the time Aran had made his way outside, the rest of his party were streets ahead of him. He scurried around the first corner, realising it was pointless. The young woman was long gone and with her was the emlon gauntlet. Nobody was more frustrated than he was. He had come close to losing the gauntlet on many an occasion, but this was the first time it had truly felt gone.

He strolled through the fog in a hopeless state. His cold feet walked the empty streets, until he had lost any sense of where he was.

An icy chill fluttered across the surface of his skin. The air was heavy, and despite the sudden isolation, he did not feel alone. Something was wrong. The mist had silenced any hint of outside noise, and yet, somewhere, in his mind, he could hear the faint echo of footsteps. Although the sound was strangely familiar, it was not the noise of a human being.

He kept walking. The unknown presence felt stronger with every step, until, eventually, he felt a multiple set of eyes looking down on him.

After a loud whooshing sound that nearly knocked him off his feet, something flew past him at a tremendous speed. Whatever this passing creature of the night was, it had been extremely large.

Aran trembled on the spot, rotating his body to catch a glimpse. A thunderous noise began shaking the very ground beneath his small soles. Something was once again heading his way, and this time it was coming directly for him. The surrounding mist was still swirling around in a twisting dance. With the crashing of stone, and a pummelling of heavy footsteps, the dreaded monster finally reared its ugly head.

20

THE EMLON RIDER

O ut of the darkness came a large snout. Its pointed ears and oversized bite gave Aran a familiar shudder. The head above was more human than animal, although its face was concealed behind a green visor.

"Are you... *him*?" asked Aran. His entire body was quivering, so much so that the words were little more than a faint mumble.

The two-headed creature came floating out from the mist to reveal its true form. Standing there before him was an animal that Aran had spent most of his life in fear of. Its four legs were those of a dark stallion, lean and powerful — like four pistons, ready to spring into action at any given moment.

Above the tall animal was a masked horseman. His two glaring eyes shot through the fog like a pair of sharp daggers.

Aran waited for an answer but received little more than a cold silence. The rider manoeuvred forward, circling him in one continuous loop, until the boy became dizzier and more disorientated than he already was.

"I come to you with a message!" the boy cried. The words burst out of him in a mad desperation. He didn't know why, but something in that moment told him that this was the man he had been searching for.

Once again, there was no reply. The restless horseman continued to close the gap, until all Aran could smell was the odour of damp fur. Dazed and off-balance, the boy took a few steps back. Stumbling away from the towering figure, he felt something sharp and pointed rise up against the crux of his spine.

"Don't move," said a voice in his ear.

Aran froze. A lump the size of an apple began throbbing inside his throat. Standing there behind him was the hooded young woman.

"Hold still!" she said, as something damp and cold wrapped itself across the boy's eyes; the world plummeted into darkness.

For a moment, he was certain that his life had ended, right there and then. As his other senses began to heighten, it became clear that he was in fact blindfolded. A firm hand grabbed him by the shoulder, raised him into the air and placed him down on something very hard and very uncomfortable.

His guts tightened as the animal in between his legs jerked forward into an instant gallop. Within a matter of seconds, he felt a cold breeze, which calmed the surface of his damp skin, his cheeks still glazed with a layer of nervous sweat.

The sound of beating hooves reminded him of his epic journey across the Northern Heights, only now there were the added echoes of thumping cobbles. All other noises were drowned out by the steady rhythm, until eventually it merged with the crashes of angry waves. His cold nose was soon struck by the smell of sea salt, as it became clear he was heading far away from the shelter of the streets.

Despite not having any idea of where he was being taken, he had begun to feel strangely at peace. For what he could no longer see, could no longer scare him. Without the distraction of his eyesight, the sounds of the outside world were now heightened into a burst of loud noise. He had once asked Corwel what a life of eternal darkness had actually felt like. She had told him that the word *darkness* was a poor description and he was now beginning to understand why.

The crashing of waves grew louder with each second, as the clanking of cobbles became the crunching of gravel. The mugginess of the streets had been melted away into an icy gale.

Aran was soon struck by an atmosphere that was damp with moisture and hollow in sound. Its unique acoustics could highlight even the tiniest of noises, creating a series of distinct sounds that seemed to go on forever.

As he was laid firmly on his back, he felt the comfort of his internal world shatter by the sudden invasion of a bright light; his blindfold had been removed.

Gazing up at the rough shell of leaking rock, he discovered that the ceiling above him was actually the roof of a small cave. The swirling waves of the shore outside had been muted into faint splashes, and the blinding rays had now become tranquil pools of blue moonlight. He sat up as his eyes slowly began to adjust.

Standing in the opening of the dark cave was a tall figure. His back was straight, his posture firm. The quiet stranger gazed out at the rough sea as if it were calling to him.

"I hear you've been looking for me," said a deep voice.

Aran felt his hands begin to tremble against the surface of the cold rock. He had imagined this conversation many times over, and yet, still, he struggled to find the words.

"I am looking for a man named Wyn Drathion," he spluttered out.

The man lowered his head and turned himself around.

"Then I congratulate you," said the man. "For you have achieved your foolish goal." His pupils glistened in the pale light, whilst a layer of green metal covered the lower part of his face.

Aran glanced behind him to find the hooded young woman crouched in the shadows. Two pairs of eyes were now burning through him.

"*I* am Wyn Drathion," continued the dark figure. "And there aren't many people who come looking for *me*, at least, not with any good intentions."

He reached into his cloak and pulled out the emlon gauntlet.

"Where did you find this?" he asked.

Aran watched him inspect his most treasured possession with sad, reflective eyes, as if it were igniting a trail of painful memories.

"It belonged to my uncle," replied Aran.

"Then that man is a thief," said Drathion. "I know this because it was forged for my own brother."

"The man who raised me *was* your brother," said Aran. "It was he who told me to find you, to give you this letter."

He reached into his worn-out satchel and pulled out the crumpled envelope. Drathion reached out his hand. The moment of handing him this piece of paper felt like the exchange of a flaming torch, a moment of slow motion. The thought of handing over this sacred baton was a fuel that had driven Aran across half of Morwallia. It had kept him alive through every peril that had come his way. He had built up the moment so much in his mind that it felt like it would last forever.

Drathion rubbed his fingertips against the broken seal.

"What was your uncle's name?" he asked. His eyes had become solemn, and grave.

"Gwail," said Aran. "Gwail Saddler of Galamere."

"Gwail..." Drathion let out an amused grunt. "That was my grandfather's name."

He slipped open the envelope and glared at the letter inside. The scribblings that had been so alien and indecipherable were now being read with remarkable ease. The further down the paper his eyes went, the more his body began to tighten. He read every written word with tender care and fascination.

Aran felt like he had been waiting an eternity. Eventually, Drathion turned to him with a newfound appreciation. The man stared as if he were witnessing this boy for the first time.

"Where is your uncle now, boy?" he asked. A dark tone in his voice implied that he already knew the answer.

"He has been arrested," said Aran. "An army of men came to our house in the middle of the night."

Drathion nodded. The paper in his hand had already begun to shake. He scrunched it into the rough surface of his palm and slipped on the gauntlet like he had done so every day of his life. The outlaw brushed his fingers across its emlon surface before pulverising it into a nearby wall.

Aran jumped with fright, as he witnessed a composed man lose all sense of control, thrusting his clenched fist into the solid rock. Pieces of the cave went flying over the boy's head, as the robust metal continued to chomp away through the wall. Drathion grunted with every punch, the speed of his blows increasing with every breath.

Aran had also been distressed at the arrest of his uncle, but he had not expressed it in a blind and physical rage.

Drathion finished his assault with a final blow that almost shook the entire cave. Aran pressed back against a wall of rock, still shaken by the unexpected outburst. The young woman to his side hadn't even flinched.

Having exhausted every ounce of energy he had left, Drathion took a moment to catch his breath. He inhaled deeply with his eyes still closed. His soul had been wounded, but it wasn't long before he had returned his focus back towards the boy.

Aran became tense. The attention of this unpredictable outlaw was now firmly fixated on his own face. He leant back as the masked man climbed up from his knees. Drathion stretched out his aching limbs and immediately began heading towards him. The boy began to shake, as the horseman lifted up his armoured hand and placed it up against Aran's jittery chin.

"You have your father's face," said Drathion.

Aran relaxed for a moment. His terror of sharing the same fate as the cave wall had subsided by the mere mention of a single person, a man he had never even met.

"How do you know my father?" he asked.

Drathion's face went cold. "He was probably the same age as you when I taught him the way of the sword," he said. "I was a younger man back then — stupid and naive."

He released Aran's jaw and stepped away. At the back of the cave was a small pool beneath a wall of rock. Water dripped down through a stream of blue moonlight. Drathion headed over to the pool and lowered his mask for a splash of cold water. His face was still covered in the darkness. He rested the weight of his weary body against the hard rock, before staring into the reflection below. Aran watched, curious about the appearance of his hidden face.

"There was a time I would do anything to protect my homeland," said Drathion. "Even if it meant never seeing the place again."

"Is it true that you and my uncle were Emlon Riders?" asked Aran. "That you were... *assassins*?"

"Where I come from we were known as protectors," continued the outlaw. "Our purpose was to defend our kingdom by any means necessary. And we have done so for hundreds of years." The gauntlet was now rotating in his fingertips, his eyes honed in on the emlon's hypnotic colour. "To wear this armour means to swear an oath, and a person is bound by this oath for the rest of their lives." His eyes melted with sorrow at the thought of his homeland. "The people of Emlon are a peaceful race. But in order to have peace, there must also be bloodshed. There must be those who are willing to fight for it. We were part of the Emlon Circle. We would perform tasks that most Emlonians would never be willing to do."

"You mean, killing people?" asked Aran.

Drathion could feel his judgement from the other side of the cave. "If the emperor of Emlon deemed it necessary for a life to be taken, then it was our duty to execute those wishes. And we would do so without question."

"Did my uncle, Gwail, take this oath?"

"We both did," Drathion replied. "My brother and I were the finest assassins in the entire Circle. Within our first year we had killed more people than a soldier could manage in an entire life. We were young men in the prime of our lives. Then, one night, we were summoned by the emperor himself. Little did we know we were about to receive the most important mission we would ever take. It all feels like yesterday."

Aran tried his best not to look shocked. He knew he was in the presence of a killer, but he could never imagine his uncle as an assassin.

"The emperor of Emlon had received news of a betrayal," continued Drathion. "That year, we had received some visitors to our quiet shores. They were led by a knight in red-plated armour. He called himself Vangarn. The emperor had welcomed these visitors with open arms, whilst taking the rare opportunity to learn more about this far distant land that they called Morwallia. The knight's true motives, however, were only really made clear when he had left our island, carrying with him a boat full of our most precious resource. The emperor was furious, and it was shortly afterwards that my brother and I set sail to find these thieves and assassinate their leader."

Aran listened to every word with a heart in his throat. Never in a million years did he imagine he would be told such a story, let alone by the main protagonist himself. It was a better narration than any *book* had ever provided.

"Once we had reached the shores of Morwallia, we tracked down each member of the Brenin's crew and, one by one, we executed them all — including Vangarn himself. When it came time to set our targets on the Brenin king, we knew there were only a handful of people who would ever get close enough. It was then we came across the famous Brenin Tourney; what better chance to slay a king than to become one of his closest guardians. My brother had always been the better fighter. He was younger, faster and stronger. I'd taught him everything I knew. After a gruelling series of matches, he went on to become one of the most dominant victors the tournament had ever seen."

Drathion took a long and heartfelt sigh.

"Then, shortly afterwards, something truly terrible happened. It was the worst thing that could possibly happen to any assassin." The masked man turned around and lowered his head. "My brother fell in love."

Aran gave him a confused frown. This was not the outcome he had expected.

"You see, the king of Morwallia had a daughter. My brother had described her as the most beautiful woman he had ever seen. After being assigned as her own personal guard, he grew closer to her every day. By the time the moment had come to complete our mission, the damage had already been done. My brother had become weak. He could no longer do what was necessary for his duty."

The man squeezed the gauntlet as if he could crack it into tiny pieces.

"I was furious, of course." Drathion said. "When it came time to do the job myself, my brother got in my way. He challenged me to a duel, and we participated in a fight that was supposed to be to the death; I lost my hand and he gained a limp. My brother proved, once again, that the Emlon Rider inside of him had long gone. He won the duel and spared my life. As an act of mercy, he sentenced me to a life of exile, a life I begrudgingly accepted. We parted ways — never to see each other again. I went into hiding, and he returned to his post. With the head of state still alive we would never be able to return home."

Drathion lifted up Gwail's letter, which was now crumpled from its recipient's frustration.

"I warned my brother that no good would ever come of his new relationship. A princess could never marry a knight of the Brenin Guard. And my brother knew it." He lowered his head and squatted down into the blackness of the shadows. "Worst of all, this future queen was destined to marry another man, someone she had been expected to marry since she was a child."

Aran was captivated by every word.

"According to this letter," said Drathion, "he left the Guard the moment he found out about her arranged marriage. A broken heart had sent him fleeing to the North Island for a life of solitude and isolation."

"What else does the letter say?" asked Aran. He knew there had to be more.

"It was nine months later that he found a newborn child on his doorstep, a newborn carrying the famous royal birthmark." Drathion lifted his head to look up at the narrow opening in the rock above. Outside was a constellation of stars. "That child was you, Aran."

A feeling of sickness brewed up from the pit of the boy's

stomach. He had never met his mother, but there had always been the faint hope that one day he might. He tried to hold back the tears.

"But — *how*?" he cried.

"My brother asked the same question for many years, I'm sure. He writes that it was only recently that he discovered you had been dropped on him by a Brenin called Falworth, one of the king's most trusted soldier. It turns out that his daughter's unexpected pregnancy had come as quite the shock. The public knowledge of such a scandal would jeopardise the entire family's future. And so, the princess was hidden away for months on end, her unborn child kept secret from everyone but a select few. It was like it never happened."

The lump in Aran's throat was growing larger by the second. The image of those horrific last moments back on Penarth Farm clouded his mind. He had lost both an uncle and a father, all in one night. Only now did he know the truth.

"Your mother had seen to it that you were taken somewhere safe," Drathion continued. "As the years passed, it had become clear to my brother that the child was indeed his own. It would forever serve as a cruel reminder of his lost love."

The news of his parents' unlikely identities had left Aran in quite the state of depression. He knew very little about Morwallian royalty.

If the blood of this great ruler also flowed through his own veins, what did it all mean? Did that make him a prince?

"So the queen is my mother," Aran said. It had felt strange to even say the words. Still, somehow, he knew it to be true.

Drathion paused for a moment. He saw the look of dread on the boy's face.

"A man is defined by his intentions," said Drathion. He stood up and headed back towards the middle of the cave. "When my brother became a Brenin, I was left with very little purpose. I created a new identity, and, for years, I have followed the movements of the Brenin very closely."

Drathion turned to him and lifted up his hand. He lowered his green visor.

Aran looked up to see the face of a man he had previously known as Major Golwin. Only this was no longer the wide-eyed madman who had guided him through the great vineyards. This person was calm and deadly serious. Even the depth of his voice was different. The person he had buried, deep beneath his public performance, was now fully exposed. A man who, less than a day ago, had appeared friendly and harmless was now emanating the presence of a trained killer.

"I kept my real name hidden for many years," Drathian said. "It was only recently, the day that they announced Wyn Drathion as the most wanted man in all of Morwallia, that I knew something had happened." He lifted up the piece of paper in his hand and shook it. "This letter has confirmed my greatest fear: our cover is finally blown. My brother has reason to believe that, somehow, the Brenin Guard have discovered who we really are."

His attention was drawn back to the emlon gauntlet. He stared into its hypnotic engravings.

"With my brother already in shackles, I must move quickly. It is clear that his sympathy for these Morwallian people has been a grave mistake. Unlike him, I will do what should have been done a long time ago. The time has come for me to return home, to complete my mission."

"But..." Aran could barely speak. "The king you were trying to assassinate is no longer on the throne."

Drathion nodded. "You are smarter than you look, boy. The ruler I now seek is the same person who caused my brother's downfall in the first place. She deserves no pity."

"But, you can't —"

"I have no other choice," snapped Drathion. He began pacing the rough floor, working himself up into a restless frenzy. "Fortunately, I have been preparing for this moment for many years."

He turned to the young woman kneeling in the dark.

"This is Miel," he announced. "When I first found her, she was running around the streets of Calon, stealing to survive — an orphan with no direction. Now she is skilled in the way of the Emlon Rider, the same fighting style that my father taught me."

Miel stared at him and bowed her head.

"In three days she will enter the Brenin Tourney and achieve the greatest victory a soldier could ever hope for. When the time comes for her to kneel in front of Her Royal Majesty, on that great Ogofinia podium, she will do something my brother was never capable of."

Aran felt a streak of perspiration trickle down his neck. There was no doubt that Drathion believed in every word of what he said, but the thought of having his own mother assassinated over the beliefs of an Emlon emperor made him sick to his stomach.

"There must be another way." Aran spluttered out his words in an uncontrollable slur. "Surely you can return home without murdering a queen."

"There is no other way," said Drathion. "And as you are technically my nephew, I will allow you a simple choice: either you can join us, and honour the blood of your Emlon forefathers, or you can stay behind, like your traitor of a father. If you decide on the latter, you must be gone from here by sunrise. For I never wish to see you again."

Aran scrunched up his face in disgust.

"But the queen has done nothing wrong," he said.

Drathion turned around and gave him a surprised look. This was not a man who appreciated having his actions questioned.

"And how would you know?" he asked. "You would spare the

life of a person you have never met? A person born into power and wealth — without ever having earned it?"

"No person deserves to die," Aran replied.

Drathion let out an impressed chuckle.

"You are very much your father's son," said Drathion. "He also had a distaste for bloodshed. But it didn't make him right."

He took one last look at the gauntlet before handing it back to Aran.

"You have done well to keep this safe," he said. "It's only right that it remains with you."

He headed over to his horse and lifted down a bag of supplies.

"Now we must sleep," he said. "I have held up the first part of my brother's wishes. In the letter he asked me to tell you the truth about who you are. Whether it will change who you *become* is another matter. He also asked me to protect you, and that is not a promise I am able to keep. For tonight you may sleep without fear, but in the morning, Miel and I will head to Calon. From then on your fate will lie in your own hands; you are either with me or against me."

Drathion flung the boy his own blanket and Aran wrapped it tightly around his shoulders. It was the first time he had felt wool so comfortable since he had left Penarth. He huddled underneath it whilst watching Drathion moving around the cave. He could barely take his eyes off him. In the man's physicality he saw the resemblance of Gwail, but, in presence, he was a different person altogether. He felt a nervous unease in the man's company, something he had never felt around Gwail.

The boy had hoped he could trust this man. Instead, he had witnessed a hatred and cruelty unlike anything he could have anticipated.

The thought of aiding in his own mother's assassination, a woman he had never even met, had sent Aran into a confused frenzy. The only certainty he had left was that he would have no part in any of it. He had longed to visit the great capital his entire life, but not under these circumstances. If there was anything he had learnt so far on his great journey, it was that everyone has their own path to follow (whether they are aware of it, or not). Drathion clearly believed he was doing the right thing. Aran, on the other hand, was not so sure.

A good night's sleep had become the least of his priorities on *that* evening. Whilst the other two cave dwellers slept soundly into the early hours of the morning, Aran lied there awake, restless, his back throbbing from the uneven dirt.

It had been a meeting he would not forget.

21

THE PRINCE OF MORWALLIA

By the time dawn had broken across the sleeping coastline, Aran was already clambering across a stretch of rocky cliff tops. The fact that he stood a better chance of survival on these treacherous edges than he did with Drathion gave him at least a slither of confidence.

He knew that they'd be in no rush to find him. The boy's presence would only have jeopardised Drathion's mission, and there was no doubt that his decision to slip off in the early hours of the morning had done them all a favour. Aran had seen the way Drathion had looked at him back in the cave; the boy was just another member of the royal bloodline that the assassin had yet to dispose of.

As he caught a glimpse of Kolwith's great harbour in the far distance, a slither of hope fluttered its way back into his chest. There was only one group of people he could now trust; they also happened to be some of the most thieving, double-crossing rabble of individuals to have ever graced the shores of the South Island.

When it came time for Aran to once again step foot outside the looming sign of the Old Mule, the skies had already grown dark. The sound of heavy drinking and heated conversations rumbled from inside.

The noise levels jumped up a few notches, as he pushed open the heavy door and walked in on a scrappy bar fight in mid-scuffle. The two men embroiled in this violent dispute were none other than Larson and Phen, who were now rolling around on the wet floor. As the door flew open, the small fight came to an abrupt stop. Both pirates, along with the rest of their fellow drunks, looked over towards the main entrance. A short silence hit the entire tavern, as the sight of this small boy in the doorway caused a wave of excitement.

"Aran!" cried Wettman at the top of his lungs. "We thought we'd lost you!"

He ran across the room to greet him with open arms. The warm welcome had ignited a rare feeling of joy in Aran's heart. He couldn't help but smile, as the captain and his crew swung him up into the air before dancing around in a merry celebration.

"We were certain you had been a victim of that wretched sorceress," said Larson. He rubbed his injured hand, which had been wrapped in a lewpetal-stained bandage.

"She was no sorceress," said Phen.

"How else do you explain what she did to my hand?" asked Larson. "Nobody I know could ever move like that."

"I'll bet I could take you!" said Syannah. "I'd have no trouble knocking you around this here tavern."

The men burst into laughter, much to the resentment of a bitter Larson.

"So what happened?" asked Wettman. "Decided to take a midnight stroll, did we?"

His question wiped away the smile on the boy's face. The events of the night before came flooding back in an instant.

"I had a meeting with Drathion," he replied.

The gravity of Aran's words shook the entire room. The men stared at him in disbelief.

"Nonsense!" said Larson. "If you had, you wouldn't be standing here now. You'd be lying in a ditch somewhere."

"I managed to escape," said Aran.

As much as he wanted to believe it, even Wettman was struggling to take him seriously.

"Are you sure it was *him*?" he asked.

Aran nodded. "He knew everything — about the gauntlet, the letter — even the man who gave it to me. *Everything.*"

A ripple of excitement spread out across the captain's face.

"Did you see his face?" asked Wettman. The boy nodded. "Would you recognise him again?"

"I even know where he's heading at this very moment," Aran said.

Eyebrows were raised as the intrigued men circled around him.

"And where is that?"

"He's going to Calon," the boy answered. "He plans to take part in the Brenin Tourney."

A flash of commotion lit up amongst his captivated audience.

"The child is a liar!" cried a drunken punter, who hadn't even bothered to turn away from the seclusion of his pint. Many others groaned in agreement.

"It's all true," said Aran. "He's planning an assassination. That hooded woman is his apprentice."

"I knew she had the devil in her!" cried Larson.

"And who, exactly, are they supposed to be assassinating?" asked Wettman.

Aran took a deep breath before answering: "The Queen."

Laughter erupted once again, only this time it was louder than ever.

"I think the boy has been sleeping in a gutter somewhere!" cried Phen. "Probably been helping himself to your cellar, Syannah."

The landlord raised her glass. Wettman gave Aran a sympathetic grin and placed a hand on his shoulder.

"You must have had a bad dream, Aran." said the captain. "Very few people have even met this outlaw, let alone been privy to his plans."

"It's all true!" cried Aran. He clenched his fists and tightened his body.

"Then you are simply mistaken," said Wettman. "Whoever you saw was just a conman. There are many to be found in this town, I promise you. He was probably an old drunk. There are many of those, too."

Aran let out a sigh of frustration. He knew it was pointless to argue. They were always going to be unlikely to believe the words of a small boy, especially without proof.

"If the boy is right, he will have made fools out of each and every one of you," announced a familiar voice.

The entire room turned around. Standing in the doorway was Simlee. He puffed on a small pipe whilst trying to contain his amusement.

"I thought we were rid of you," said Wettman. His jovial expression was now a harsh frown.

"Not quite yet," said Simlee. "You think I'd leave this lad with a sorry bunch like you lot for too long?" He exhaled a large cloud of smoke into the air. "From what I heard, you lost the boy already."

Aran struggled to contain his excitement. He hadn't realised how much he had already begun to miss that man's wild heart and carefree attitude. Simlee's self-assured manner and indestructible confidence were a strange comfort. He was half-cynic, half-optimist. The perfect combination for anyone in a town like Kolwith Bay.

"The boy lost *us*," said Wettman.

"Don't blame him," said Simlee. "I would lose you all in a heartbeat. You call yourselves a crew? A captain who instantly dismisses the advice of his crew member should hang up his hat."

"He claims to have spent the evening with Wyn Drathion," Wettman added, with a smug grin. "The boy's not thinking straight."

"Maybe not," said Simlee. "And maybe he is. Still, he seems to believe this man is a threat to our kingdom, and I'll be damned if I'm going to let some Emlon Rider assassinate my queen."

"We are pirates," said the captain. "Our allegiance is to the sea, not to the crown. Your father taught me that. Not that a royalist like you would understand."

"I'd say your allegiance is to yourselves. Either that, or you're all a bunch of cowards."

"And since when did you ever care about anyone other than yourself?" asked Wettman. He marched over and placed his nose firmly up against Simlee's. "You think you're still in the navy now? You think you're still better than us, you snitch?"

Simlee merely smiled at him in return. "If it means winding you up, I'll do anything."

"You have to trust me, captain," said Aran. "If we don't do something, the queen will die."

Wettman turned around to find Aran was now directly behind him.

"And why should that be any business of yours?" asked the captain. "Even if what you say is true, why should *you* care about the welfare of someone you've never even met?"

The boy froze. He knew that revealing the truth would be a risk that could cost him his life.

"Yes, do tell us, Aran," said Simlee with a grin. "Or why don't you show him that mark on the back of your neck?"

Aran scowled. He had forgotten about the mark. In fact, he had barely come to terms with the truth himself.

"That's right, fellas," continued Simlee. "This boy is not quite what he seems. We have a dose of royal blood on our hands." He turned to a confused Wettman and glared at him, enjoying the upper hand. "Don't tell me you didn't know? Go on, Aran. Show them."

They all turned to look at the boy, who was shaking his head in dismay; there was no avoiding it now. He lifted up the back of his long hair and exposed the dark pattern engraved in the surface of his skin.

The room gasped.

"It can't be..." said Wettman. His mouth dropped open as his knees began to crumble.

"Looks like a bad case of rash to me," said Larson.

"It's the royal birthmark, you idiot," Phen snapped.

Even though he knew what he was about to say was the truth, Aran struggled to form the words: "The queen... she's... she's my mother."

Phen dropped down on one knee. The others remained frozen.

"A member of the royal family!" cried Syannah. "In my own bar!"

The tavern had never been so quiet, and Wettman had never been so lost for words. They all hung on the boy's every word.

Aran took a deep breath and stood tall.

"The rest of the emlon armour lies at the bottom of a lake. I know this, because I threw it in there myself. If you help me stop Drathion, I will show you where that lake is. You have my word."

Wettman stared at him. It was as if the boy he had known

previously had grown wings and was about to fly away. He turned to his crew members with an impressed smile.

"Well... if there was ever the word of a person I had to trust... Then the word of a prince is good enough for me."

Aran smiled back at him.

"Well? What are we all waiting for?" Wettman cried. "We have a queen to save!"

He pulled out his sword and raised it into the air. The pirates cheered in unison, their swords bashing together in one almighty clank. Aran peered through the line of blades to see Simlee giving him a cheeky wink.

22

THE OGOFINIA

The city of Calon stood tall on the bank of the River Aran. Its circular streets spiralled down from its rising centre, stretching all the way out until they reached the surrounding walls. According to legend, it had all started with a single chamber, a formation of rocks built upon the great base of a prehistoric volcano. This chamber, which had since become a pile of rubble, could now be found at the heart of the city's famous amphitheatre: the Ogofinia.

Aran had envisioned this mighty capital for as long as he could remember; those tall spires, that white brick, the great palace at the very top overlooking its swarms of busy citizens.

His high expectations had not been disappointed. One aspect he hadn't anticipated was the sheer volume of people. It seemed that every corner of this bustling melting pot was bursting with life and soul, the likes of which he had never seen, or imagined.

When Aran and his pack of unlikely followers had finally reached the city gates, he felt an onset of nervous jitters. These uncomfortable tingles rose up inside of him like a plague of hungry insects. His actions over the coming days would have the potential to change the entire course of history. Beyond those gigantic walls was a hive of activity that would soon be disrupted by the greatest event in all of Morwallia.

Horses and carts flowed through the hole of Calon's main entrance like a stream of fresh blood. People came and went with little or no care for their fellow travellers. Passing through that gate meant accepting their place as an insignificant shrimp in a sea of countless other inhabitants.

Simlee gazed through the crowds with a honed instinct for observation. With only a few glances, he knew every position of every patrolling soldier within a square mile radius. Deliveries were inspected and visitors were questioned.

"After you, *Your Highness*," said a cocky Larson, as they entered through the gates. He held out his hand to allow the boy aside. Aran cringed and looked around to see if anyone had heard. He turned to Simlee who was now walking beside him.

"Why did you have to tell them?" he whispered.

"Did you think these idiots would ever help you otherwise?".

"But if word gets out that —"

"You see that man over there?" Simlee interrupted, pointing towards a figure nestled against the edge of the wall. The old man's loud rambling could be heard from metres away, and yet, every passerby simply ignored his shaking hands. "That man claims to be a reincarnated god. I don't see anyone paying much attention to him."

Aran stared at the homeless individual, who had been so easily cast aside. They both made eye contact for a moment, before Aran felt a towering presence blocking his path.

"Stop right there," said a husky voice.

Standing in front of him was a frowning soldier. His armour glimmered in the scorching sun. The burning heat, along with both layers of his heavy uniform, had clearly made him very irritable. The soldier scanned across the medley of unusual characters standing there before him.

"What is the purpose of your visit?" he asked, for what must have been the umpteenth time that day.

"We are here for the Tourney," said Wettman, in his politest of voices.

The soldier nodded. "So are half the people heading through this gate. But that does not mean everyone is welcome. Something tells me that you are more than just a bunch of idle spectators."

Aran looked back at his party with a worried expression. Larson turned to a sweating Phen and whispered to him.

"I'd better not get locked up for this," he muttered. "I became a pirate for the freedom."

Phen silenced him, as Wettman took a step forward.

"As a matter of fact, we do have another purpose," said the captain. "We have come here to aid our new competitor."

The captain pointed towards Dewin, who stood behind him like a hulking beast. The soldier had to crank his head back just to take a better look.

"Your man is competing?" asked the soldier, with a slight change of tune.

"Our fighter has battled to the death on many occasions," Wettman continued. "As you can see, he has not yet lost."

"Well of course he didn't lose," said the soldier in a snarky voice. "If he had lost then... well... he'd be dead, wouldn't he?"

"Goodness, you're smarter than you look," said the captain. "I am his manager and these good fellows are our helping hands."

Dewin took a step forward. The soldier leapt backwards after the great thud of the giant's boot. "Is there a problem?" he asked, in a booming voice.

The soldier took a long gulp and looked straight ahead at his bulging chest.

"I see no problem here," he replied.

Aran let out a sigh of relief. The soldier moved aside and let them all pass.

"Wait!"

The entire group froze in mid-step.

"What the devil is it now?" asked Simlee, who did not take kindly to acts of authority.

The soldier took his time with the response and walked over to face Dewin. Out of the serious expression came an unexpected grin. "I wish to be the first man to shake hands with our future Brenin."

He extended out his hand like a starstruck fan. Dewin stared him down for a moment and engaged in a reluctant, yet firm, handshake. The pirates winced at the sound of crushing finger bones. The soldier looked up at his new hero with a tension in his jaw muscles. Blood drained away from his pale cheeks as he prayed for a sudden release.

Dewin gave him one of his rare and terrifying smiles in return, until he eventually decided to disengage. The soldier took back his hand as if it had been swallowed up by a large snake. Having nearly lost all of his fingers forever, he clutched them with a delicate tenderness. His throat grew dry, as he forced out some final words before continuing on his way: "I think your man will do very well."

THE OGOFINA WAS by far the largest open air venue in the entire kingdom. The arena played host to only the most important of events — and there was no event more important than The Brenin Tourney. To ride upon its dry, yellow sands was an honour very few had ever accomplished. The Ogofinia was the grandest stage in the entire land, and its most prestigious event would enable only the most skilled and courageous to perform on her. No amount of wealth or power could ever guarantee a person's success. Instead, it would require a relentless thirst for victory and a will to defy the odds. The end goal was simple: fight until there was no one left to fight. It was a straightforward solution to the most difficult of tasks.

The eve of the great tournament had brought an excitement to the entire city. Every man, woman and child were all welcome to attend — provided they could first attain a seat, of course. The sheer level of demand had caused many of the population to set up camps several days before the event. Flimsy tents and makeshift huts lined the narrow streets, until they curved around the edges of this enormous structure.

Located in the heart of the city centre, the Ogofina was a symbol of hope and glory. It was a reminder to the people of Calon that, with enough will and determination, any one person, large or small, could someday rise up above the rest.

Beyond the main arena were clusters of smaller venues known as the Shodan Pits. These circular chambers normally served as the stomping ground for meaningless bouts with unknown fighters. They were often the second homes of blood-thirsty crowds or low-rolling gamblers and served as small pavil-ions for the casual entertainment of local peasants.

Today, these dusty pits were as prestigious as any amphithe-atre in the entire kingdom. Now they would host the opening battles to the greatest tournament of them all. To qualify for the main arena, a challenger had to first make their way through a series of initial heats. Every willing fighter who walked their horse through the sweat-induced fumes of the Shodan Pits had as much chance as anyone else of proceeding to the final rounds. Provided that they walked out of those pits as the final victor, anything was still possible.

Each pit had their own champion. And each champion dreamed of becoming *The Champion*.

"How can you tell who wins?" asked Aran.

"You look for the fighter who still has a horse between his legs," answered Simlee.

The group had already found their spot in the pit of choice, and Aran's face had soon been reduced to a mere speck in a pool of bouncing dots. The crowd circled the pit like a moat of raging heads. The wooden barrier that held them back had seen much better days and was now buckling under the immense pressure.

Clouds of dust rose up towards the dome shaped ceiling, as every eager spectator pounded their feet in anticipation. They booed and heckled the previous unsuccessful challenger, who was now being dragged away in a crumpled heap.

"You're going to need some armour," said Wettman to his old friend. Dewin turned to him and shrugged.

"He's going to need a bleeding miracle if you ask me," said Larson.

"Armour will only make him slower than he already is," said Simlee.

"And what makes you such an expert?" Wettman snapped. He could barely look the man in the eye.

"I'm just stating the obvious," said Simlee. "I've seen more of these matches than you have. The laws of physics are not kind to a moving, great lump."

"Next you'll be saying he doesn't need a horse," muttered Wettman.

"Don't get me started on *those* things."

They looked on as the victorious horseman began circling his newly gained territory, calling out for his next opponent.

"The winner stays on," said Simlee, just as Aran was about to ask the question.

The next challenger entered with quite a different reception to the previous challengers. A chorus of whistles erupted into the hot and humid atmosphere.

Aran recognised the face immediately. "There she is."

The gate to the pit flew open to reveal a composed Miel on the back of a restless stallion. She laced up the last of her thin body armour and flung a helmet over her long, black hair.

A scruffy pit attendant showed her the way.

"Don't come crying to me if you get hurt, little girl," he said. "This ain't no tea party."

Miel grabbed hold of the reins and booted her left foot into the man's face. Her kick sent him flying backwards into the barrier, causing the entire arena to roar with laughter. The front line bashed their palms against the shaking barrier, until it rocked and swayed in a steady build up.

"I say she won't even last a minute," said Larson.

They all watched, as the reigning champion continued to circle the pit. His upper body was heavy, and his shoulders were broad. Even the quality of his well-maintained helmet implied that he had been haunting these pits for many years and had taken very little falls in the process.

"That, there, is Zolowich," said Simlee. "He's been tipped to reach the quarter-finals. There aren't many who can withstand a sword like his."

Miel manoeuvred her horse into the centre of the pit. She followed her opponent's every move, keeping her distance until the time was right.

Zolowich stared her down with his beady eyes, kicking up the sand into a small whirlwind. He waited for his moment to strike, knowing full well that it was only a matter of time before he would claim his next victim.

With a kick of his back heels, he moved in for the attack. He flung his sword and ripped through the dust with all the might his right arm could muster. The slice of his lethal blade was met with so little resistance that it caused him to fly forwards. After the enormous swing, a confident looking Zolowich turned himself around to admire the destruction.

Much to his disappointment, there was nothing behind him but a gust of flying dirt. The confused fighter looked around for his missing opponent and yanked his reigns in a flustered rage.

Meanwhile, Miel was galloping along the inside barrier, circling her prey, until the dust clouds blinded him. With a series of sharp and precise movements, she lunged at her opponent, bashing against his thick armour with her thin sword. Zolowich swung around in a state of panic whilst doing his best to deflect her relentless strikes.

The crowd gasped at the sight of their beloved champion being humiliated by the smaller fighter. Miel had found her opponent's weakness and continued to take advantage of his short temper.

A furious Zolowich swiped in all directions, as if swatting away an irritating fly who would not stop hovering. He sliced through the clouds of dirt with the hope that at least one of his powerful swings would surely make contact.

Exhausted from the intense blitz of heavy striking, he began quickly losing control of his own horse. It was in that very same moment that a second horse came charging out of the dust. With a last-minute jolt of the reins, Miel's stallion reared up his front legs and crashed them down into the large metallic head.

The sound of Zolowich's steel body hitting the ground caused a chilling echo throughout the entire pit.

Wettman let out a weary sigh. "Still don't think he needs any armour?" he asked the man beside him.

Simlee shook his head in disgust. In an eerie silence, the crowd turned their attention to Miel. She had flattened their excitement within a matter of seconds, and the only gesture of celebration was a gentle nod towards her defeated opponent's groaning face.

By the time this new champion had prepared herself for the next opponent, Aran and his small team had seen enough.

They wandered out from the Shodan Pit's daunting exterior with pale faces and squinting eyes. The sunlight blazed against the warm stone of the streets outside. Passers-by went about their daily business with no idea of the commotion taking place only a stone's throw away. The world inside this rounded structure had a life of its own.

The sheer enormity of the task ahead had now dawned on the party of six. They strolled down the busy street, side by side, deep in thought.

"Well..." said Simlee. "Rather you than me."

He patted Dewin on the back before quickening his pace.

"This queen had better be worth it," said Dewin to his captain.

"It'll be worth it when you get your reward," reassured Wettman.

The other man shook his giant head. "Rewards mean nothing to a man with a second chance. If winning this tournament will help give someone else the same gift that you gave me, then that is what I must do."

Wettman nodded back in appreciation.

"And win you shall," said the captain. "I have no doubt about that. You are stronger than the rest of us all put together. All we need now is to find you a horse."

"I can think of one man who won't be needing *his* horse anymore," said Dewin.

They both turned around to see a bruised and battered Zolowich limping his way down the street.

Aran and Simlee increased their walking pace so that they were ahead of the others. The boy's mind had been swirling with a hundred different thoughts ever since they had left Kolwith Bay.

"What made you come back?" he asked the man walking alongside him.

Simlee considered his answer for a moment. "When I left the inn I headed to a cemetery further along the coast. When I got there I found a grave I had not seen in many years." A sadness washed over Simlee's tired face. "It belongs to my wife."

Aran looked up at him as if a veil had been lifted to reveal a different person altogether. "You never told me you were married."

Simlee forced out a playful smile through his overwhelming grief.

"Hard to believe, isn't it?" he said with a chuckle. "Believe it or not, there was a woman out there who actually loved this crusty, old man you see here before you. I was a decorated naval officer back then — not that my wife ever cared about the medals. She was the only person who ever saw the good in me. The *real* me."

"What happened to her?" asked Aran, who had struggled to bring up the question.

"She became ill," said Simlee. "Very ill." The man spoke as if he was reliving the last moments of his marriage. The scars still hurt.

The moment she drew her last breath was when Commander Simlee of the Royal Sharkskins died away, never to be seen again. Nothing was ever the same after that day."

He looked over at a sleeping homeless man with a flash of empathy.

"I sat at that grave until the sun went down. Seeing it again reminded me why I had spent so much time at sea. The ocean holds few memories and little regret. Out there, a person is washed free from past actions that they might otherwise rather forget; free of guilt, free of consequence. It is always the harsh reality of dry land that will stir up bad memories."

Simlee looked up at the blue sky, an everlasting ocean of its own.

"I was born into a world of corruption and greed," he continued. "Once a pirate, always a pirate — that's what people have always told me. I had tried so hard to escape that world. When my wife passed, I started to revert back. She always had the purest heart I had ever come across. And then you came along..."

Aran looked up to catch his warm gaze.

"I thought more about those markings on the back of your neck. They had to be a sign. It was then I heard my wife's voice again, talking to me, like she had never left. I had been given a second chance; a chance to become the man my wife always saw in me — a man of honour, and dignity."

Aran stroked the back of his hair. Even the mere mention of his newfound secret made him extremely uncomfortable. Simlee chuckled.

"You really have got yourself rolled up in a right messy situation here, haven't you, lad? Even I couldn't resist being involved in this one."

He slapped the boy hard against his fragile back.

"You are destined for great things, boy," the man said. "And if anyone can save our queen, it's her own flesh and blood." Simlee felt the scars against his grazed hands. "I have taken many lives over the years. We'll see how it feels to save one for a change."

It then occurred to him that Aran had said very little. He looked down at the sorrow in the boy's face and gave it a playful slap.

"Cheer up lad!" he said. "We've got an entire kingdom to save!"

23

THE CHALLENGER

Quork, the pit keeper, was not best pleased to find a group of suspicious looking characters outside his back door. The sun had long turned in for the night by the time he had finished the last of his closing-up tasks. The crowds had all departed, and the dust of the last fallen warrior had finally settled.

"I've already told you — we don't give out weapons, armour or horses," said the tired keeper. His long robe drooped over his feet, causing him to trip and stumble, as he pushed his way through the wall of men. He continued on with his chores and emptied an entire bucket of sweaty, red water against a nearby wall. Prancing beside it was a tied up stallion. Its back was bare, the saddle having been sold off to the highest bidder.

"What about him?" asked Wettman.

He trailed behind the grumpy looking man, determined to keep his attention. Quork grabbed the stallion by the reins and began pulling him away from the stubborn pirate.

"He's not for sale," he snapped. "And even if he was, I'd hardly sell him to the likes of you."

Simlee had listened to the captain's reasonable pleading for long enough. He stormed over and shoved the surprised pit keeper hard against the wall.

"How about we take this horse by force, instead?" asked Simlie, lodging his thumbs up the startled man's nostrils.

"Get your hands off me!" cried Quork, whose face had gone from red to blue within a few seconds.

Simlee nodded towards Larson and Phen, who immediately began untying the horse.

"You walk away with that horse, and I swear I'll have you all arrested," croaked the pit keeper.

"Fair enough," said Simlee, who shrugged a little before dragging him through the dirt. "Then we should probably make sure you don't say anything."

Quork soon found his large mouth choking on the unpleasant contents of an overused water trough. Every so often, Simlee let him back up again for air, if only to let him squeal.

Aran was horrified by the whole display. Wettman folded his arms, irritated by the fact that the former Sharkskin had once again taken control.

"Stop, please!" cried Quork. His face was covered in a layer of something thick and brown. "Take the horse — he's all yours! I'll say you bought him fair and square!"

Simlee lifted him up from the water and patted his snivelling head.

"How very kind of you," he said, before knocking the grovelling man straight back to the floor with a cheap slap. He strolled past the captain with a smug grin.

"I thought you were supposed to be a pirate?" he said. "Pirates don't ask for things — they take them."

Wettman shook his head and walked away.

"Come on lads," called Simlee. "We should probably use a different pit from now on. This one stinks."

Dewin placed a hand on Wettman's tightened shoulder. The giant observed his leader's livid expression and tried to offer him some words of solace: "You really don't like that man, do you, captain?"

24

THE ASSASSIN

The second Shodan Pit was as noisy as the last, only this time, Aran and his group of pirates were blessed with the finest view in the house.

Dewin was rocking away on the top of his new horse, swaying from side to side, in an effort to control his new set of legs. Never had Aran seen a man look so unstable on the back of an animal (unless that person happened to be himself).

"Control him, man!" cried Larson. He looked up at the struggling giant, who had now doubled in height thanks to the whopping great beast beneath his bulking thighs.

The stallion had clearly never been burdened with such a weight, and he had now begun kicking back his hind legs in an effort to rid himself of this new master.

"Steady, boy!" said Dewin. "Steady..."

His words of caution did little to keep the frazzled horse at bay, and they soon began fighting each other for control, twirling in all directions, until they crashed violently against the wooden barrier. The crowd roared at the sound of smashing timber.

Simlee turned to Wettman and grabbed him by the scruff of the neck.

"You chose to nominate *this* man to enter the tournament?" he hissed. "How is he supposed to knock another man off his horse when he can't even control his own?"

Wettman shoved him away.

"Touch me again and I'll —"

"You'll do *what*?"

The captain twisted back his waist and swiped him with a solid punch to the jaw. Simlee stepped back and felt a smear of blood underneath his lip. He was almost impressed.

"So," he said with a grin, "you *do* have a spine, after all."

Aran charged between them before the older man could retaliate.

"Stop it!" he said to them. "We don't have time for any more of this squabbling."

He ran towards the jerking stallion. Dewin was holding on for dear life. The reins were pulled tight to his chest, as he hugged down against the animal's twisting neck. Down below, he could see a small boy calling back at him.

"Lean back!" called Aran. His voice fought hard against the roaring levels of the crowd. "Use the stirrups, and push your heels back!"

He could hear the familiar words of his Uncle Gwail crying out from his own mouth. Even with his limited knowledge on the subject of horses, he could still remember those stern orders and angry barks. What had previously been a slew of painful memories were now coming in useful. Those early experiences of learning how to ride had somehow remained with him.

With nothing left to lose but a broken back, Dewin followed the boy's advice with some remarkable results. He pushed back his weight and pulled down his giant heels, until the horse slowly began to steady his frantic movements.

"Now keep your back straight and loosen the reins!"

Aran's second set of instructions proved just as effective. With a few more basic pointers, Dewin had finally managed to get his horse into somewhat of a stationary position.

"Great..." muttered Simlee. "So as long as the horse doesn't move, the man might just have a chance of not coming off. That's some challenger we've got there."

On the opposite side of the pit, a second competitor rode in with a confident swagger of his horse. His armour was as rusted and battered as his blade. He was certainly no stranger to taking a few hits.

"If he decides to charge, our man is a sitting duck," said Simlee. He struggled to watch.

The pirates gathered behind the barrier. As Aran observed the nervous footing of Dewin's troubled horse, it had become clear to him that his friend was in grave danger; it would take a lot more than a size advantage to survive this next encounter.

Aran leant over the barrier and waved his arms in the air.

"Give your horse a firm kick!" he called out. "Swing your boot against the side of his body — show him who's boss!"

Dewin, who, in a desperate bid to move forward, was now yanking on the reins and listening out for the boy's calls. He lifted up his right foot and bashed it hard against the horse's ribs. The horse shrieked in protest and sent both of them jolting forwards. Dewin went hurling across the pit in a rapid charge. Barely able to fathom what was happening, he lifted up his sword and went crashing into his smaller opponent.

The combination of his great weight and newfound speed had sent the lighter challenger flying backwards like a helpless dummy. An entire mushroom cloud of dust rose up from the horizontal fall. The audience cheered; a winner had been decided.

As for a confused Dewin, there was no time to celebrate. The harsh impact had stirred his horse into a violent fit of leaps and jerks. Aran closed his eyes in despair, as the unbalanced giant was propelled into the smoking dust. The men on either side of him cringed.

"For a bloke who's just won, he's probably the worst horseman I've ever seen!" said Larson.

With a fragile victory under his belt, a bruised Dewin spent the next few duels safely behind the wooden barrier of the front row. Amongst him was his band of concerned pirates, who observed the standard of competition with great intrigue.

By the time Aran had found his way outside to get some much needed fresh air, it was already midday, and the rays of the sun were burning into his sandy hair. He sat down against the wall of the rumbling pit and watched the variety of passing strangers.

Up in the distance he could see the back of Simlee's large head making its way over through the crowd of people.

"Where have you been?" asked Aran, when the man finally arrived.

"Thought I'd see if I could find that little witch," he said. "At this rate, I might as well try ringing her neck myself with the chances that big lump has of stopping her. But she's a slippery fish, that one. Nobody knows anything about her. She shows up for her duels and then disappears without a trace."

"But Dewin just won," said Aran. "He's getting better with every fight. If he can just control his horse he should be fine."

Simlee shook his head with a smile. The boy's optimism had never ceased to amuse him.

"He's a strong fighter, sure," he replied. "There's no doubt about that. But the odds of him making it to the final rounds are about as high as they are of him winning a dancing competition."

Aran watched him walk off towards the pit. He knew the

pirate hunter had a very good point. One could even say that their chances of victory were about as likely as stumbling upon a suit of pure emlon.

By the time Aran had returned to ringside, Dewin was back in the saddle with a brand new opponent. This time, the man he faced was taller than he was. Unlike the previous bout, the two fighters were more than equally matched in both size and strength. They circled each other like bitter enemies, lashing out with giant swipes and vicious attacks.

Aran could barely watch.

"I think our friend has finally met his match," said Larson. "I never thought I'd see a bigger bloke than our Dewin. But I was wrong."

He pointed to the great monstrosity heading in Dewin's direction. The horse-bound pirate did his best to fend off the charge, but there would only be so many of them he could withstand.

Aran watched the frustrated giant shake himself off and prepare for another attempt.

"This'll be it now," said Larson. "One more knock like that and it's over."

The pirate turned to his left to see Aran leaping over the barrier before scurrying around the edge of the pit.

"Dewin!" Aran cried, waving out his arms to grab the giant's attention.

Dewin looked down to see what appeared to be an emerald-coloured gauntlet flying towards him. He caught the object in mid-air, almost slipping off the edge of his saddle in the process.

"Put it on!" Aran called. "Quickly!"

A confused Dewin glanced at the peculiar object with a cynical raise of his eyebrow.

The horseman on the other side of the pit had already kicked his animal into yet another aggressive charge. He galloped through the dirt to the sound of excited cheers, building up his speed at a dramatic rate.

Dewin was still frozen in place in an effort to keep his horse steady. He looked up to see his formidable opponent fast approaching.

With the gauntlet tightly fastened and his sword in the same hand, he sent both of them crashing down against his attacker's blade. The reinforced blow sent the other fighter flying backwards with an unnatural force. The impact was so great that it almost broke the two swords in half. The jaws of the crowd dropped in unison, as Dewin's opponent went soaring across the pit. Having been hit with the power of a runaway boulder, the unprepared horseman went plummeting to the ground like a bag of heavy cannonballs.

The crowd winced, until the brief silence was followed by a wave of riotous applause. Aran rejoined his companions with a sheepish look on his face.

"That thing certainly comes in handy," Simlee told him.

Aran nodded with a relieved smile. The fallen rider had been knocked out cold, and it would be quite some time before he ever got up again.

Dewin was still the reigning champion. His next opponent was knocked down even quicker than the last, and it wouldn't be long before many others would soon be sharing a similar fate.

A satisfied Dewin embraced his fortified hand with a joyous laugh. He raised it into the air and admired its great beauty. The longer he remained on the horse, the more confident he became. Soon he was knocking down men as if they were children on the back of ponies. The crowd could hardly believe their eyes. They relished in their new champion's winning streak more and more with every fight. With each new challenger that was flung across the pit, they chanted Dewin's name as if he were a king.

The group of pirates cheered on their fighter long into the evening, until, eventually, there was no one left to fight. An ecstatic Larson revelled in a string of successful bets, much to the annoyance of his willing participants.

Wettman watched his old friend circle the empty pit in a victorious celebration. He had certainly come a long way since his first bout.

"Let's hope all this winning doesn't go to his head," said Wettman, with a concerned frown.

"At least he's still *got* a head!" said Simlee. "You old stick in the mud." He clapped his hands together as the captain pushed past him.

"Come on you lot," he said to the rest of his crew. "Time to go. We're done here."

Larson and Phen groaned in protest, as they were still keen to bask in their fighter's new fame. The group followed the captain out to the sound of an important announcement; Dewin, it had turned out, had progressed to the final rounds. The news was met with a rapturous applause, and the pit was soon invaded by a swarm of adoring new fans. Each one gathered around their hero whilst chanting out his name.

That evening, Aran and his entourage of pirates found it very difficult to keep a low profile. They wandered the streets of Calon and were greeted at every corner; people pointed as they passed, and lines of children began trailing behind them, as women blew kisses from overlooking windows — all for the enormous man who strolled alongside them.

Dewin was no stranger to being gawked at in the street. His great height had always attracted unwanted attention, but to have fellow pedestrians shake his hand at every opportunity was a new sensation altogether. He was now a person who people wanted to be associated with. News of his dominating performance in the pit that day had spread like wildfire, and every member of the local neighbourhood was keen to meet the kingdom's next Brenin.

Larson led the champion's new steed along with great pride; for every stroke of that dusty mane he would charge a hefty price.

"I never expected any of this," said Aran. He watched as a woman ran over to them and wrapped a silk scarf around Dewin's thick neck.

"Neither did I," agreed Wettman. He looked towards Dewin's beaming face as it suddenly got planted with a wet kiss. "And neither did he."

They were soon escorted to a grand establishment with some of the finest food and drink any of them had ever come across. With its comfortable seating, carefully designed layout, and an array of wealthy clientele, it was a far cry from the dingy corners of the Old Mule.

Dewin was happily waited on with bottomless cups of fine wine and luxurious platters. Wettman sat beside him, sipping on a glass of something as mysterious to him as it was expensive. He cringed at the frequent visits from upper class well-wishers and flattering socialites.

"Shouldn't you be practicing your riding skills?" asked the captain. "I seem to remember they were pretty rusty."

Dewin looked at him with a surprised chortle.

"You think I need riding skills with a right arm like this?" He raised his emlon covered hand. "With this, I am unstoppable. I will destroy anything that comes my way."

Wettman continued to sip his drink. His grave expression said it all.

Dewin slapped his old friend on the back. The impact almost catapulted him forwards off his seat.

"You worry too much," he continued with a laugh. "I am a champion now, remember?"

Aran gazed around at the groups of adults, with their fine clothes and merry faces. They drank and socialised as if they hadn't a care or worry in the world. Amongst the crowds of unusual people, he spotted one person who appeared to stand out. This individual was a lot smaller, a young girl his age, with a likeness that struck his heart rate into a speeding frenzy. She looked bored and out of place, much like himself. Suddenly, their eyes caught one another, causing both of them to stand up at exactly the same time.

Aran weaved through the crowd of oblivious partygoers. When he reached the small table, she looked at him with a horrified disbelief.

"Aran?" she gasped. Aran's response was stalled by a tight hug. "They told me you had been locked away, just like your uncle."

She released her grip and looked down at his dishevelled clothes. It had only just occurred to the boy that he hadn't changed them since he had left the farm. Her disapproving frown hit Aran with a wave of self-consciousness that only she could ever create.

Sarwen's concerned look soon morphed into one of great anger.

"Where have you been?" she asked.

"It's a long story," Aran replied.

"They say your uncle was a traitor."

"*Who* says he was a traitor?"

"My father, for one," she said. "He says he was an enemy of the queen."

Aran grabbed her by the shoulders and held her in close.

"It's all lies, Sarwen," he said. "You can't believe anything people say about him — you just can't. There is a lot you don't understand."

Sarwen felt herself being squeezed like a dry lemon. This

wild and delirious person in front of her did not sound like the Aran she once knew. She pushed him away.

"What's the matter with you?" she cried. "Are you calling my father a liar?"

Aran looked around at the people nearby. He scanned their faces in a paranoid burst.

"Is your father *here*?" he asked.

"No, he had to leave. I'm here with my brother." She looked around. "Aran, who are *you* here with?"

"Aran!" cried a rough voice from the other side of the hall. "Leave that poor girl alone, you old dog!"

Aran cringed. They both turned around to see a drunken Larson balancing himself on a tabletop, waving at them.

"I'm here with... *them*," said Aran.

Sarwen looked over at the group of rowdy pirates who had taken over their corner of the room. She looked back at her childhood friend and took a step back.

"*Those* people are your friends?" she asked.

"A lot has changed since I last saw you," said Aran. "But you can't tell anyone you saw me here — promise me."

He took her by the arms.

"Aran, you're scaring me," she said.

His heart sank. He could see the look of fear in her eyes, as if she were staring at a complete stranger — and maybe she was. He was certainly no longer the naive, innocent child she once used to boss around the fields of Penarth Farm and, in some ways, he wished he *were*.

"Whatever happens, you must know that it's for the good of the entire kingdom," Aran told her.

"Is that what your uncle used to tell you?" she asked, pulling herself away. "You're beginning to sound like a criminal yourself, Aran."

She struggled to hide her disappointment, which came out

in a look of pure disgust. Aran could barely bring himself to respond.

"Sarwen!" said a voice from above.

They both looked up to see a tall, young man with dashing good looks and a full head of long, bright hair. His distinct features were the spitting image of his sister's, and he held himself with a remarkable air of confidence.

"Come and let me show you my future opponent," he said. "He's the biggest brute you've ever seen!"

Aran stared at him as he escorted Sarwen to the other side of the hall. It became clear that this was the same man he had heard so much about (whether he had wanted to or not).

If there was one person who Sarwen looked up to the most in her small world, it was her older brother, Tarin. He had been described as the most perfect human being who ever existed. Having now witnessed him in person, for the very first time, he could finally see why; Tarin was quite the specimen. Had he been born a horse, he would have quite easily given young Meaden a run for his money.

Aran followed them over towards the group of pirates — his new dysfunctional family. Dewin was sitting beside a sulking Wettman, who was still chugging on his jugs of unlimited wine.

"Here he is!" said Tarin. "The big man himself. My fellow pit champion."

Dewin watched him approach and raised up one of his thick eyebrows. Even as Dewin sat there, slouched on his expensive array of cushions, he was still quite close in matching him in height.

"*You* are the champion of your pit?" asked Dewin. "You are merely a boy."

Tarin ignored his casual observation and presented his perfectly white teeth through a jovial smile.

"I am a champion, nonetheless," he said. "Which makes you

my future opponent. You have quite the reputation, big man. I hear you can strike people down with a single blow. That must be quite a right hand you have."

Sarwen's eyes fell down on the emlon gauntlet. Her face went pale. She turned to look at Aran, who knew exactly what she was thinking.

Dewin stroked his right forearm in a defensive manner.

"They call you — the Fortress," declared Tarin.

"And what do they call you?" asked Dewin.

"Why, the Gentleman, of course."

The other pirates sniggered.

"The dusty circle is hardly a place for manners," said Dewin. "Not when you're up against the likes of me."

Tarin smiled. He had an expression that seemed to be immune to insults of any kind. Nothing would ever break his spirit, especially when it came to harmless fighting banter.

"I have ridden horses since I was old enough to walk," he said. "I am more at home on a four-legged animal than I am on foot. It is not a question of brute strength, but a matter of skill and precision."

Aran listened with great admiration. He spoke like a true Brenin. If there was ever an ideal champion, it was the young man who stood before him (as opposed to the slurring giant who continued to mock him).

"Say that to the men I have buried this afternoon," said Dewin. "I'm sure many of them were equally as skilled. But when you bring a wooden stick to face a sword of steel, the odds are severely against you."

He flickered his thick fingers inside the gauntlet. Aran felt Sarwen's burning stare in the corner of his eye.

"I look forward to our little encounter," said Tarin. "In the meantime, I thought I would show my dear sister over here the man I will knock off his saddle come this time tomorrow."

He placed an arm around a concerned Sarwen.

"For her sake, I would sit this one out, lad," warned Dewin. "It will not end well for you."

"I appreciate your concern," said Tarin. "May the best man win."

He reached over to offer up a sporting handshake. Dewin grabbed the young man's hand, and Tarin's eyes widened. The gauntlet was now crushing the bones in his fingers with a loud crunch.

"Argh!" he cried, before dropping to his knees in agony. "He's just — he's broken my hand!"

The entire hall gasped. Aran and Sarwen cupped their mouths in shock as Dewin smiled.

"That's what happens when you meddle with power beyond your own," he said.

The young horseman did his best to contain the pain. He tried to shake it off with a shudder of his long hair, although it was hard to hide his fury.

"It's a good job I'm left handed," he growled. "I look forward to wiping that smug smile off your face."

He leapt to his feet and pulled his sister with the other hand.

"Come, Sarwen," he said. "Let us leave this savage to enjoy his last victory — whilst he still can!"

Sarwen was pulled away. Her eyes were still fixated on Aran's concerned face, until she was dragged out of sight.

"Was that entirely necessary?" asked Wettman. He rose to his feet and towered above his amused friend. Dewin took a long gulp of wine.

"I'm looking forward to breaking that man's perfectly formed face," said the giant.

The rest of his entourage did not say a word.

25

THE REUNION

fter the party had gradually died down (which wasn't too long after the unpleasant incident with Tarin's hand), Dewin and his small support team made their way to the Champion's Quarters. Reserved specially for the tournament's prestigious finalists, the Champion's Quarters was a grand accommodation in the shadow of the Ogofinia. It had always served as a welcome reminder of how far each challenger had come from their dusty bouts in the Shodan Pits.

The competitors were now in the company of true greatness. Brenin knights had walked these marble halls for many centuries, sharing in the same honour of a night in their luxurious bedrooms. It was a taste of a lifestyle that, provided they were successful enough in battle, many of them could hope to achieve for themselves.

A Brenin was treated like a person of high society and the mighty Dewin enjoyed this treatment very much indeed. The giant man had been born in a climate much harsher than this one, a land far more unforgiving than the luscious terrains of Morwallia. Where he came from, the deserts stretched out for thousands of miles, with sand so hot it could burn through toes.

Born into a life of gruelling manual labour, he had escaped his homeland for an equally troubled life on the high seas.

He was now on the verge of reinventing himself as a legendary figure, and a hero amongst the people — an opportunity he was not prepared to hand over in a hurry, especially to some spoilt, young aristocrat born into a life of privilege. He intended to make an example of this person and he would do so in front of an audience of thousands.

"It seems your little helper has done well for himself," said Simlee. He looked around at the impressive line of giant pillars leading the way forward.

"He is not my *helper*," said Wettman. "The man has served me well."

"Better watch out he doesn't bite the hand that feeds him," replied Simlee. "For he seems to have a giant appetite — especially for fame and fortune."

"Don't we all..."

It turned out that the Champion's Quarters boasted a room for each person in Dewin's group, a luxury many of them had not anticipated.

Aran placed his troubled face into a sink of cold water and held his breath. As he lied on the feather-filled mattress, it occurred to him that this was the comfiest bed he had ever slept in. It was typical, therefore, that on this particular night, he could not sleep a wink.

He slipped out of his room and took to wandering the endless hallways of this ancient structure. If he couldn't stop the unreasonable force that was Dewin and his deadly right hand, he could at least try and warn off his doomed opponent.

Torches flickered along the spacious passageways, creating a series of dancing shadows along the pale walls.

Aran peered through each hole on the chamber doors. Most of his crew were fast asleep, exhausted after their long day standing in the pits. Loud snores trailed out into the hallway, like a chorus of chesty hogs. Even the giant was deep in a heavy slumber, unfazed by the challenging confrontations that awaited him the following day.

Aran crept past more chambers, until he reached a darkened corner with nowhere left to turn. Even with nobody in sight, the unshakable feeling that someone was watching him plagued his every move. He turned around; the shapes of the night were taunting him now. On the previous turn he could have sworn he heard footsteps.

It was only when gazing into the darkness that he felt a small hand wrap itself around his mouth.

"Don't scream," said a voice.

The figure behind him was more slender than he had expected and similar in height to his own. He pushed himself forward and turned around.

Standing there, beneath a flaming lantern, was Sarwen.

"Who said I was going to scream?" asked Aran, pretending not to be startled. "What are you doing out here?"

"What are *you* doing out here?" she asked back.

"I came to find your brother," he said. "He's in grave danger."

"I think my brother is more than capable of handling himself," snapped Sarwen. "He's much tougher than you are — and far braver!"

"Have you seen what that gauntlet is capable of?"

She paused, trying hard to hide her uncertainty. "It's just a stupid piece of old armour."

The boy grabbed her by the shoulders.

"Do you still have yours?" he asked. "Is it here with you now?"

She pushed him away.

"What do *you* think? That I go around carrying around pieces of old junk? It's back home in Gala."

"Sarwen, that gauntlet has strength and power unlike anything I've ever come across." His eyes pleaded with her. "It can break through... well — anything!"

"So you gave it to some monster with half a brain?"

Aran nodded, fully aware of his questionable actions.

"I had to," he said. "There's a lot at stake. If the wrong person wins that Tourney then..." He looked around and lowered his voice. "A queen's life is at stake. And so is your brother's if he rides against this man."

"Tarin could beat up a lump like that with his eyes closed," she insisted.

"That lump has the power to break through walls with just his right fist — he'll have no trouble with your brother's head."

Sarwen's expression soon changed.

"There's nothing we can do," she said. "Tarin's the bravest person I know. He'd fight him even if he were a dragon."

Aran felt a rush of guilt. He hadn't meant to upset her, and her scared eyes were making him sick. He reached forward and grabbed her by the shoulders again.

"I'll find a way to help your brother," he said. "I promise you that much."

Sarwen nodded. His determined tone gave her a feeling of warmth. She had first felt it back at the old ruins of Lanbar Castle, which now felt like a lifetime ago.

Aran headed back to his room with a reinvigorated feeling of hope. The truth was, he had no idea what he was going to do. He had failed to convince Sarwen about the dangers of the gauntlet, and she would never believe him until it was too late. There were now even more lives at stake. If he didn't act now, he would regret it forever.

26

THE CHAMPION

The great walk into the Ogofinia's main arena was an experience like no other. Its open roof and raised seating rose up beyond the clouds, into the heavens high up above, where the ghosts of champions-past would gather around and take their seats.

Aran approached the front barrier of the lower stands with a stomach full of dancing grasshoppers. He had imagined this moment since he was old enough to first read about it. So far, it had not disappointed.

The morning sun lit up the yellow sands of the inner circle like a gigantic spotlight. Aran lent over the raised edge to get a proper look at the gates below. He knew that in a matter of minutes, the first pair of worthy competitors would emerge from those darkened tunnels and become worshiped like returning heroes.

"That's quite a view, eh?" said Simlee. "These are some of the best seats in the house."

He had seen many impressive pieces of architecture over the course of his travels, but even Simlee couldn't help but marvel at this incredible feat of human engineering. The Ogofina had a life of its own, and its heart was the thumping cheers of the people inside.

Up on the northern side of the arena, high up in the stands, was a designated space with a large, empty throne. Its polished back overlooked the main pit as soldiers lined up in front. Aran knew exactly who that seat was intended for, and so did the crowd.

After taking a few moments to fully soak in all the atmosphere, his eyes fell down on a familiar looking girl. Sat far closer to the royal seating than he was, with her father and a team of servants, was Sarwen.

The rumble of a gigantic horn sent a trail of goosebumps down his entire body. Everyone in the entire arena went silent and turned their attention to the vacant throne. Having thousands of people go quiet, all at the same time, was quite something to behold.

All eyes were now on a distant figure with a large crown. She strolled into the arena as if it were her own home, before addressing the people who occupied it like passing visitors.

"Say hello to mummy," muttered Simlee.

Aran turned to him with a frown. Overwhelmed by the excitement of this great spectacle, he had almost forgotten. He watched as the queen of Morwallia approached her private chair and raised up her hand to a wave of applause. This small gesture had signalled the beginning of the quarter-finals, and the anticipation was at an all time high.

The crowd roared as an entire regiment of Brenin knights circled around the pit. They marched in perfect formation, until they reached their final position with a confident halt. Facing the centre of the pit, they raised their swords like a series of sharp flags, before rotating back towards the Royal Stand. The queen kneeled, and both sides acknowledged each other with a bow of the head and a salute of the fist. Within a matter of seconds, they had all cleared the entire pit in preparation for the first match.

"And so it begins..." said a nervous Wettman. He turned to Aran and gave him a gentle nod.

The first of the eight finalists rode out at the speed of a fierce hurricane. Aran couldn't help but smile as he watched a confident Tarin perform an enormous lap around the entire pit. He held up his arm and touched the hand of every spectator lucky enough to have a front row seat. His skill with a horse was certainly something to behold. The young horseman dazzled the arena with an impressive display of elaborate sword tricks and advanced riding techniques.

Another cheer shook the surrounding stands, as Tarin's opponent thundered through the gates at great speed. This rider was covered in a layer of bright steel, with a blue coat-of-arms that filled his entire chest. His face was concealed with a solid looking grate that folded down from his large helmet.

"Who is he?" asked Aran.

"That is Rupan, the son of Sir Ruegon of Delre," said Simlee. "They call him the *Thunderstorm*. His father is a Brenin himself."

They watched as the two competitors circled the pit like a pair of hungry alpha wolves. These young men were no amateurs, and they were far more than a couple of budding jousting enthusiasts, hoping for a lucky win. Instead, they were tactical, calculated and extremely well-trained. On paper, they were both evenly matched, but on the field, it was Tarin, the young man from Gallamere, who was the most gifted.

Aran marvelled at, what had turned out to be, a masterclass in hand-to-hand combat. Tarin remained patient, keeping himself back within a safe distance, waiting for his opponent to make the first move (or as he preferred to call it — the first *mistake*). When the time was right, he deflected the incoming strike with an effortless counter-attack. Rupan slid backwards, his torso now hanging from the edge of his galloping horse. Another similar blow would have sent the young man head-first into the moving ground, a fatal landing that could have quite easily paralysed him for the rest of his life. Fortunately, and in what the crowd had deemed as a remarkable display of sportsmanship, a noble Tarin allowed his opponent to sit back up again and readjust himself.

Such chivalrous behaviour had filled Aran with a boost of inspiration. If there was ever a manner in which a Brenin knight should conduct himself, it was surely in the way that young Tarin had just done.

Both men were now moving around the pit like two chariots in a furious race. Clouds of dust trailed behind them, as the surrounding audience pounded their feet to build up the already mounting tension. After a series of enormous circles, both champions braced themselves for their inevitable second collision. Tarin met his attacker head on — manoeuvring his body in such a way that it forced Rupan straight from his saddle at a gravity-defying speed. Without even having to draw a single sword, Tarin had successfully managed to knock the other fighter clean off his animal. A frazzled Rupan soon found himself lying amongst the sand, without a clue where he was or what had just happened.

Aran cheered at the top of his lungs, which surprised even his fellow pirates. He had become as invested in the outcome of this match as everyone else in that great arena, who joined him in an explosion of praise and celebration. They marvelled at the victorious Tarin and his incredible show of skill and restraint.

"He did it!" cried Aran. "I knew he would!"

"You sound like one of that lot," said Simlee. He pointed to a group of young girls on the tier above. They called out their new hero's name with adoring squeals.

"I really think he could win this whole tournament," Aran admitted. "I really do! We may not need Dewin, after all."

"What does it matter who wins?" asked Simlee. "As long as that little witch doesn't."

Aran wasn't as convinced. He looked towards an ecstatic Sarwen, who was now greeting her victorious brother with open arms.

"Besides, I think our man will flatten him," continued Simlee. "If he shows any of that sporting rubbish again he's a dead man — Dewin takes no prisoners. As far as I'm concerned your little hero's dead already." Simlee watched the boy's gaze with great intrigue, before turning to see what he was looking at. "And if I didn't know any better, I'd say someone's taken a fancy to his little sister..."

Aran looked up at him with a defensive frown.

Simlee smiled. "You've barely taken your eyes off her since we got here."

"I've known that girl my whole life," said Aran. "She used to come and visit back on the farm."

"A childhood sweetheart? Even *more* dangerous. You wouldn't be thinking of jeopardising our entire plan over a girl now, would you?"

Simlee laughed and slapped the boy hard on the back.

Whilst Tarin and his family continued to celebrate, a defeated Rupan hauled his bruised body up from the dirt. Still overwhelmed by the feeling of shame and frustration, he hobbled towards the stands in search of his disappointed father.

It was whilst watching this sorry sight that Aran experienced a sudden chill down the base of his spine. He looked over towards the stands on the other side of the pit. Sat there, greeting his defeated son, was a man he had seen before — on two separate occasions. A hand covered the man's disappointed face, as he could barely look his own offspring in the eye. When the hand came down, it revealed a face that had haunted Aran's dreams ever since that dreadful last night on Penarth Farm.

Sir Ruegon of Delre, it had turned out, was also the name of the first Brenin knight he had ever seen. The same man who had come to arrest his Uncle Gwail in the dead of night.

The boy felt his knees weaken, as he lowered himself down from the overlooking barrier.

"You look like you've just seen a ghost," said Simlee, who had caught a glimpse of his pale complexion.

"I wish it *was* a ghost," said Aran.

The boy jumped, as the great horn let out a booming call; it was time for the next match.

An armoured horseman came charging into the arena. This was Count Huxphrey, an experienced swordsman who had fought more skirmishes in his time than any of the other competitor's track records put together. A well respected war veteran, he had swapped the brutality of the battlefield for a more civilised way of life as a skilled blacksmith. After years of boredom during his early military retirement, the Tourney had provided the perfect opportunity to quench his thirst for some much needed action. To Huxphrey, these one-on-one duels were just a meaningless sport — a sport he also happened to excel in.

The older generation in the crowd paid their respects with a burst of applause.

"This one's been tipped as a favourite to win," said Simlee.

"Why him?" asked Aran.

"Because they don't know who they're dealing with this year," said Simlee.

The cheering eventually died down, and the crowd turned their attention to the black gates. A nervous energy swept over the arena, as an armour-less Dewin strolled out from the imposing darkness. His horse heaved along its heavy passenger, with an entrance so underwhelming that you could hear a coin drop. Dewin lifted up his hand to reveal the unique looking gauntlet covering his forearm. Like a cold executioner, he limbered up for what he predicted would be a short bout.

His horse groaned at the feeling of a vicious heel to the ribs. Dewin had no pity or care for the struggling animal beneath his great thighs, and as far as the horse was concerned, the feeling was mutual. After another painful boot, they trotted across the pit.

Huxphrey lifted up his shield and braced himself for a powerful encounter.

Dewin picked up speed and raised his sword. The sound of clashing steel shot out across the pit like a horrified scream. Thousands of mouths dropped open, as Dewin's emlon-assisted blow shattered the heavy shield as if it were a shard of glass. Huxphrey could feel the resulting vibrations coursing through his armour, shaking him from head to toe like a human bell. Dazed from the thundering crash, his body froze into place, until he was hit with yet another right handed strike.

Dewin's sword smashed against his breast plate, denting it like a layer of tin foil. The blows continued to come, as Dewin battered his helpless opponent into submission. By the time the giant had finished his raging assault, Huxphrey's armour had been completely bashed out of shape, and the damage underneath was far greater.

Dewin moved away to watch him tumble downwards — a twisted lumberjack with his falling tree.

Many of the spectators could barely watch. The fallen veteran was now resting in a pile of sand and horse dung. Even the fearless Tarin was struggling to contain his horror. Sarwen turned away and covered her face. Had it not been for his curious mind, Aran would have done exactly the same thing. He couldn't help but envision a fallen Tarin in the other man's place and the unforgiving stare that Sarwen would forever give him.

Although it was Dewin who was responsible for this brutal victory, it felt as though he, himself, was equally to blame. Gwail was right — no good would ever come from the power of the emlon armour, a fact that was unlikely to change anytime soon.

During the night of Dewin's infamous victory against Count Huxphrey, Aran watched over the sleeping giant with a nervous sense of dread. This beast of a man was now helpless in his own private chamber, his oversized torso fluctuating up and down with every breath. Aran peered at him through the narrow crack in the chamber doorway.

He knew what had to be done, and it had to be done that very same night.

27

THE THIEF

Dewin woke up to a stream of morning sunshine. Rays of bright light shone down on him through the small window

It was going to be a big day. For on this day, he was just a single match away from that prestigious final — which meant he was only *two* matches away from the greatest achievement of them all. He was so close he could almost taste it.

As he lifted up his large body, he felt an unusual bareness across his right forearm. His breathing stopped; something was missing.

Dewin leapt out of bed and went scrambling around the room in search of his most precious asset. A burst of adrenaline gave his normally sluggish body the lightness of a small dancer. Feathers burst into the air, as he tossed up his soft mattress and tore it apart.

The other pirates were soon woken up by a series of violent slams. Their doors were flung open, and, one by one, their rooms were searched by a raging bull.

"Where is it?!" roared Dewin.

A terrified Phen was pinned against the wall by a pair of

gigantic hands. He could feel the hot breath against his pale skin.

"How should I know?" he cried. "I've been asleep all night."

"Well one of you rotten thieves wasn't," said Dewin. He chucked the quivering young pirate to the floor. Then, it struck him – he knew exactly who it was.

"That little rat!" he cried out. "I'll squash him!"

Dewin went stomping out into the long hallway and headed straight for the last chamber. A groggy Wettman stuck his head out, his eyelids drooping and his hair sticking up in all manner of directions.

"What's going on?" asked the captain.

"That lousy cockroach has taken it!" echoed the giant's booming voice.

"Taken *what*?"

By the time Wettman had dragged himself to the doorway of Aran's chamber, Dewin was already tossing up the empty bed. He pounded his huge fists against the crumbling walls.

"I knew it!" Dewin wailed. "I'll ring his scrawny little neck when I get my hands on him!"

Wettman looked over towards the bulging forearm of his furious crewmember. He shut his eyes in despair.

"I guess you'll just have to just win that match without any help," said Simlee.

The onlooking pirates, who were now gathered in the open doorway, all turned around. Simlee was very casually leaning against the doorframe with an amused expression.

Dewin looked up from his furious tantrum. He gave the floor one last pounding before charging at him like a determined ram. His eyes were locked in on Simlee's face. Before he could attempt to murder the man in a blinded rage, Wettman stepped out in front. Blocked by the concerned face of his old friend, Dewin halted within an inch of running him down.

"Out of my way!" called Dewin.

"You are not yourself, old friend," said Wettman, and placed a friendly hand on the man's broad shoulder. "Everything will be fine."

Dewin took in a long breath, which deflated his bursting neck muscles.

"Losing that gauntlet might well be for the best," he continued. "You have not been the same, ever since you first started wearing it. It could well be your undoing if you're not careful."

Dewin forced out an understanding nod and tried to contain his urge to kill someone. Instead, he went storming back into the room and fired off one last punch into the cracked wall. Wettman and his crew breathed out a sigh of relief.

Meanwhile, a nervous Aran was wandering around the stalls of Calon's bustling marketplace. The gauntlet was nestled safely in the bottom of his satchel, and he could hear the sound of Dewin's furious cries echoing deep in his mind.

He looked up at the looming castle over in the north. From this distance, it could quite easily have been the size of Lanbar's frail ruins, only with *real* guards and a *real* queen. With any luck, it might still have a queen that same time the next morning, Aran thought.

The streets had yet to come alive at such an early hour, and it wouldn't be long before they'd be swarmed again with thousands of people. This hive of activity was something Aran looked forward to, as being so exposed on the deserted pavements made him very anxious indeed. He much preferred to be one in a thousand faces than a single face with nowhere left to hide. He had made more than a few enemies who would have loved to come across him that morning. He had gone from being a faceless traveller, who nobody cared about, to someone who had upset more than his fair share of unsavoury characters. If a handful of dangerous criminals and a corrupt

Brenin hadn't been enough, he now had to worry about a giant pirate.

The final day of the Brenin Tourney had come around quickly. With only three matches left, the excitement levels had reached an all time high. Citizens descended on the Ogofinia in their droves. Aran joined the snaking trails as they flooded the arching gates.

By the time he had made it inside the great arena, the best seats were long taken — so much so that he had to make do with a view from the *Roosters*, the highest tier in the Ogofinia. Up there, in the heavens, the pit below was nothing more than a small circle. Each of the surrounding tiers were a descending layer of wide rings that became narrower with each inner circle.

The air was cooler up in the Roosters. With a careful squint of his watering eyes, Aran could just about make out the competitors entering in on their horses. Their sudden appearance sparked a loud cheer that rumbled beneath him.

Even from this great height, it was quite clear who was who. They circled each other like a pair of rivalling insects, the larger of the two dots moving a fair degree slower than the other.

Down in the pit below, Dewin was swinging his sword like an enraged madman. His powerful swipes hit nothing but dusty air and were executed with such force that they nearly caused him to topple over.

Tarin was as calm and collected as he always was, ducking and bobbing to avoid those telegraphed attacks. He made several pretend charges, lunging forward and then pulling back at the very last minute. The constant teasing only infuriated his opponent even more, until the giant man was slicing through the dust clouds in a wild frenzy.

Dewin's horse yelped out in pain as its reigns were yanked and its ribs were bashed.

"Move, you stupid creature!" growled Dewin, urging his animal forwards using brute force.

Tarin could see that the horse was buckling under the increased stress and backed off so that he could witness the inevitable consequences. His horse had become an extension of his own legs, and he knew that assaulting your own legs was never a good idea.

After several more boots to his animal's midsection, Dewin felt everything beneath him shudder like an impending earthquake. The horse kicked back its hind legs and sent his helpless passenger flying upwards into the air.

Having barely lifted his sword, Tarin sat back and enjoyed the entire show. Seeing a man of such great size being thrown into the sky was quite something to behold, and the only thing more impressive than watching a giant defy gravity was the sound he made when he came back down again.

The young man listened to the sound of several thousand people all cheering at once. A confused Dewin opened his eyes to find himself sitting in a pile of dirt. When it dawned on the man that his horse had now abandoned him in the middle of the pit, he unleashed a roar so loud it could be heard from high up in the Roosters.

Spectators laughed at the sight of a furious Dewin, charging around the pit in an attempt to catch the other fighter.

What had started as an honourable duel between two horsemen had descended into a comical bull fight. Tarin toyed with his bitter enemy, who had become so desperate in his pursuit of revenge that he had resorted to a public display of humiliation. Four legs would always be better than two, and the latter had put Dewin at a severe disadvantage.

Aran looked down at this humorous scene with great fascination. It was the perfect blend of bad sportsmanship and noble restraint. From high up in the Roosters, he witnessed this unusual ending with a guilty pleasure. This was how a good match *should* conclude — the noble warrior, overcoming a monstrous villain.

There was no doubt that Tarin had come out of this duel as the beloved hero. Even the grumpiest of spectators couldn't help but leap and cheer, as the young horseman galloped around the pit in a lap of celebration.

The second match, however, would not be nearly as comical.

Durienne Munwell was born in the hay bales of her father's stable. She was raised in the same manner as all six of her brothers — through hard graft and ruthless discipline. By the time she had reached the age of thirteen, she was already the strongest sibling on the entire farm. She ate twice as much as the youngest and could lift three times the weight of the eldest. But the area that she really excelled in the most was horse riding.

Durienne strode across the sandy pit with her head held high. She had worked hard to make it this far, and, until today, most of her opponents had been brutish looking males. It had, therefore, come as quite the surprise when it turned out that her next big challenge came in the form of a small young woman.

Miel flowed into the arena like a weightless ghost. She was once again covered in a layer of light body armour; not too heavy, and not too weak. Her long, dark hair trailed out from underneath her small helmet. The bottom half of her face was concealed by a metallic cover, which acted as both a shield for her mouth and a cover for her identity.

Although both women were more than formidable opponents, these two competitors could not have been any more different.

Whilst Durienne, the larger of the two, was bursting with emotion, Miel seemed like she was void of any feelings whatsoever. Her lifeless eyes scanned her opponent with a calculated stare. This was a dangerous predator on the verge of a hunt, and her prey, a civilised human being, was ready for the taking. A traumatic childhood on the streets of Calon had hardened away any sense of compassion or empathy that she might once have possessed. When it came time to deal with new strangers who stood in her way, this lack of natural emotion had always served her well. The following match would be an act of survival — just like it had been her entire life.

Durienne was also not prepared to go down without a fight, either. She had been raised in the security of a large family, but her journey to the Brenyn Tourney had been anything but easy. Unlike Miel, she had been preparing for this tournament her entire life.

Without fear or hesitation, Durienne fired up her horse and sent it exploding across the pit. By the time it was halfway across the great circle, her opponent had already vanished into a cloud of dust. Durienne turned her head to see a slender figure swooping up from behind her horse. Her body twitched as she was struck against her armour by an unusual looking sword. The thin, but lethal, blade slashed against her steel back with perfectly timed strokes. She batted away a second wave with a furious swing of her longer weapon.

Durienne was already in trouble, and the longer their match lasted the worse it became. She was now on the back foot, forced to defend herself whilst trying not to think about the increasing damage.

These steady blows were by no means an act of luck — Miel knew full well the impact of her well-executed lunges. The simplest strike was always the most effective, and she would much rather fend off a series of berserk attacks than a single, accurate one.

All Miel had to do was take her time. The drops of sweat from her opponent's brow were like grains of sand in a falling egg timer. For Durienne, the clock was ticking, and pretty soon, her body grew tired.

Miel could have finished her right there and then, but instead, she played with her new enemy a little while longer. Eventually, an exhausted Durienne collapsed from her horse in a lifeless fall, the sand below her feet scattering upon a heavy landing.

Miel had no care, or need, for any theatrics. Instead of celebrating her win, she merely galloped away to prepare for the next bout.

It had been quite the semi-final, and the crowd was more than ready for the impending climax. What followed next was a short interval, which Aran had decided would be the perfect time for him to locate Sarwen. Armed with a powerful advantage under his arm, he hoped that the added element of the gauntlet would provide her brother with an easy victory.

He climbed up across the rows of seating until he was scurrying along the back wall, keeping himself close to the edges of each tier, a strategy that enabled him to dodge the oncoming traffic of restless spectators as they came and went.

He continued down into the level below and came across a bottleneck of loiterers. He barged through them, twisting and turning his body through the endless forest of passing legs.

Each new group of people felt like having to wade through yet another river of thick weeds; they pulled him back, restricting his forward movement with every new step.

After what had felt like an eternity, he had made his way further down the Ogofinia's many levels. Having lost any sense of direction that he might once have had, the experience had given him unwanted flashbacks to the sinking Duchess.

It wasn't until he had reached an open space near an overlooking barrier that he realised he had somehow made it to the lower section of the arena. From there, the pit was virtually the same level. He could even make out footsteps on the surface of the sand.

He scanned the front rows, all the way along, until he reached the opposite side of the arena. To catch sight of one child in a pool of so many people was no easy task. Instead, he headed in the direction of the Royal Tier and weaved through the masses like a determined salmon. Pieces of clothing brushed past him, as he leapfrogged his way across the seats. Before long, he had completely lost himself in the northern section of the main stalls. A giant mass of taller bodies surrounded him from all sides, bumping and knocking him in every direction.

He persevered until he caught sight of a small opening and darted forwards before the gap could close. As his pace quickened, the stray leg of a clumsy passerby caught his small foot, tripping him upwards into a forward dive. Although he had still made it through the narrow opening, he came out through the other side crawling on his hands and knees.

When he looked up, the boy froze; within a couple of metres from his horrified face was a pair of cold, stern eyes. They stared him down like a hungry broncat, only this time there was nobody around to save him.

This was a man who Aran had once looked up on with a sense of awe and wonder. He remembered the tall silhouette, rising up through the mist of Skelbrei Forest. That chiselled face and dazzling, red body armour now sent a surge of terror throughout his entire body. *Surely it wasn't him.*

Sir Ruegon, the first Brenin Aran had ever come across, was as surprised as *he* was. The last person he had expected to see that day was the same boy who had foiled his plans back on the North Island. His amused stare was all it had taken for Aran to begin scrambling backwards.

The arena shook to the sound of a booming signalling horn; it was time for the final match.

Ruegon didn't move. He watched as the boy darted away into the safety of the crowd, burying himself in the protection of numbers. Armed soldiers began descending towards him from the outer regions of the stands.

Aran pushed and shoved his way through towards the nearest exit. The excitement of the crowd had made navigating the stands even more difficult than it had been before.

Fortunately, the droves of restless people made it equally as problematic for the soldiers. Their authority meant nothing to a selfish mob, and their layers of plated armour only slowed their progress even further.

Tarin stormed the pit whilst giving his fans the usual show of impressive riding skills. He waved his sword high into the air, its blade gleaming in the harsh, midday sun.

Aran kept himself low and crawled his way through the clouds of dirt. When he came back up for air, he could see that the soldiers were already closing in from every angle. He was soon pushed up against the front barrier — cornered — with no hope of reaching an exit.

He turned around to face the pit. In the far distance, he spotted a cluster of familiar looking pirates, all bunched up together on the opposite side of the arena. Up on the tiers behind them, he could see more soldiers looking down. They signalled to their fellow guards on the level below to head for the front rows.

In a final act of desperation, Aran jumped on top of the stone barrier, pulled himself up on the steep ledge, and went running along the narrow rim. In a mad dash for freedom, he followed the curving white wall, which circled the entire circumference of the great pit.

An approaching soldier leapt forwards to grab him, missing his ankle by only a thread. Aran continued his sprint along the circular path, which was all that stood between himself and certain capture. He scurried around the pit whilst reaching out his arms for balance. This ledge of white stone had now become a death-defying tightrope. From the corner of his left eye, he could see a second fighter entering the grand stage.

Miel adjusted her helmet and pulled out her sword. Unlike Tarin, she was in no mood to draw out the proceedings. In her mind, there were only two people who existed in that arena — herself and the opponent opposite.

Tarin could see her growing impatience and began his traditional first move of circling the pit.

Aran felt a gust of wind from Tarin's galloping horse, as it rushed past him on his way along the edge. Seconds later, he could hear the clash of steel ringing through his ears, as the two fighters engaged.

Just as he had made some steady progress around the arena, Aran felt a hard tug on his right leg. The sudden pull sent him flying downwards into a group of unfortunate spectators, before he crashed to the floor, face-first.

With his knees scraped and his mouth full of dirt, he looked up at the sight of a furious soldier. The burly man lifted him up by the scruff of the neck and turned to the other guards for confirmation. It was true: he had caught the person they were looking for — a brand new prisoner for an empty jail cell.

Just as the soldier had turned his head back to look at Aran, his large, grizzly face was met with an enormous fist. After a second thump to the chin, he went down like a sack of manure.

Aran looked up to see a grinning Simlee.

"Got yourself into a spot of bother, I see," he said. "Why am I not surprised?"

Simlee grabbed him by the arm and pulled him through the roaring crowd. The confused soldier stumbled to his feet and chased after them, his reinforcements not too far behind.

Aran peered over the stone barrier as he was dragged along

like a limp rag doll. He could see the match was in full swing. Unlike the last two bouts, these two warriors were quite evenly matched. Although Miel had been trained by an Emlon Rider, Tarin was as skilled with a blade as he was with a horse. He also possessed the finest genes a fighter could hope for — the blood-line of at least a dozen war heroes, all gifted in multiple styles of combat. Here, in the heat of battle, he was truly in his element (and his opponent could tell).

Miel chose her moves very carefully. So far, none of her Tourney opponents had posed much of a challenge. But Tarin was different. One of her first lessons from Drathion had been to never underestimate a person — especially if that person carried a sword. Today she had broken that rule.

A dangerous error in judgment had allowed Tarin to flank up alongside her, and he began barging against her horse with a series of aggressive shoves. Furious at her own carelessness, Miel glared at her opponent, the first hint of emotion she had so far revealed.

Tarin's techniques were strong but rigid. Miel, on the other hand, could adapt as she went along. An Emlon Rider fought with fluidity and focus. It was like comparing a piece of string to a rubber band; one was both strong and reliable, but the other would always reach further in the end.

Tarin deflected the next onslaught of vicious attacks and responded with a series of his own. The audience were engrossed in every move. This was a match for the ages and nobody wanted to miss a second.

"Looks like this'll be a close one," said Simlee, as he pulled Aran along. They could feel the pounding of hoofs rushing past them, as they continued along the bottom tier, pushing and shoving their way through.

Word amongst the arena guards had soon spread, and they

swarmed towards the two fugitives like white cells in a stream of blood.

Over in the pit, Miel and Tarin were going at each other with everything they had left. Each thrust of their weapons could well have been their last attempt. A fatal blow was just around the corner and contained the power to end the fierce battle in a single strike.

The Ogofina erupted into a unified roar. Tarin had begun dominating his opponent with a combination of ruthless charges. His strength and size had become too much of an advantage, and the stamina of his prized stallion was leagues above the other.

Although Miel was determined to fight on, her horse shared little of her spirit. Its tired legs could only withstand so many charges, and she could feel the immense strain her animal was now under. After yet another giant lap of the pit, Miel could feel the great body beneath her legs begin to crumble. Her heels gave one last push against the stirrups, and she vaulted her body upwards into the air. As her horse went disappearing into a cloud of dust, Miel landed herself directly behind her enemy's saddle.

"Hold on!" cried Tarin, who presumed the match was well and truly over. He lowered his sword and steadied his own horse, who by this point was still swaying from the shock of the crash.

Nestled safely behind her unsuspecting rival, Miel reached into her pocket and pulled out a handful of green-coloured powder.

Even amongst the chaos of his own situation, a horrified Aran couldn't help but turn his attention towards the pit. He gasped as Tarin rode by him with an eruption of green mist across his face.

"No!" cried Aran, at the top of his lungs.

The young man wailed, his eyes blinded by the mysterious potion. It burned his skin and clouded his mind, until his senses went numb, and he lost all feeling in his arms and legs.

Tarin toppled from his seat like a lifeless squid, and, without a single hint of remorse, Miel slid forward and snatched control of the horse. She grabbed the reins and hurled her new beast into the centre of the pit. As far as Miel was concerned, she had done what was necessary. She was now the only competitor who had yet to take a fall and, to her, that was all that mattered.

Tarin had been unconscious before he even hit the ground. Aran couldn't see Sarwen's face but he knew that it would be filled with a stream of tears. She had looked up to her brother for as long as he could remember. Now she was forced to watch his lifeless body roll through the dirt as many others had done before him.

The crowd was bursting with applause, praising their new champion with cries of admiration. To an arena full of strangers, Tarin was merely an unknown challenger, another hopeful fighter who had been forced to bite the dust, just like everyone else. It had all been at his own risk. All they cared about was the person still riding, for she would now become their new Brenin.

"Where have you two been?" asked an excited Larson. He jumped into a merry jig as Aran and Simlee appeared through the mass of people. "You boys missed a blinding final!"

Aran looked around. The guards were nowhere to be seen.

"Looks like we lost them," said Simlee. "Bunch of idiots."

They turned to face the pit. Miel was poised in the centre, waiting for the announcement of her great victory. Tarin was already being dragged away, his green face slowly coming back to life as he tried to work out where he was.

Aran's heart sank as he caught a glimpse of Lord Falworth kneeling down behind the barrier. The man could barely watch, as his son went hovering through the lower gates — cast aside, like an unwanted stage prop. Sarwen was nowhere to be seen, which only tormented Aran further.

The thundering vibrations of the signalling horn sent a chill down the boy's backbone. An iron gate on the north side of the pit was heaved open by a dozen soldiers. Through the gate was a steep, narrow staircase made of stone. It led the way in a straight, ascending line, up past the first three tiers and directly to the Royal Podium. Sat on this giant platform was Elissia, queen of Morwallia.

The queen slouched in her uncomfortable throne, gazing down at the last remaining fighter. She took her time standing up before stepping down onto the enormous staircase. Brenin knights were lined up either side of her, as she slowly made her way down towards the pit.

"We have to do something," said Aran.

Simlee turned to him with a shrug.

"Do we?" he asked. "If you want to go in there and stop her — be my guest!"

He pointed towards Miel who was now climbing down from her horse.

"Trust *you* to be too afraid to act," said Wettman.

"Afraid?" asked Simlee. "Not stupid, is what I am. Go in there, and you'll be joining the lad who just got carried out."

"We need to warn the queen before it's too late," said Aran.

Queen Ellisia had made it to the sandy floor of the pit. She marched towards the centre of the circle where a patient Miel awaited her with a cold stare. The queen prepared herself for a tradition that had been around since the days of the first Brenin. As an act of faith, a queen was required to surrender her sword and hand it over to her new protector. The new Brenin would prove their loyalty by taking the sword, raising it into the air and sticking it straight down, deep into the Ogofinia sand. The champion would finish this routine with a final bending of the knee, a symbol of their lifelong commitment to the crown.

Aran watched, as the queen, his alleged biological mother, pulled out her sword and prepared to hand it over. His hands quivered. In what could only be described as an out-of-body experience, he ran towards the pit and leapt over the barrier.

"Aran!" cried Wettman.

"Oh, for goodness sake," said Simlee, rolling his eyes before reluctantly chasing after him.

Wettman soon followed, and, within a matter of seconds, the entire gang of pirates were charging across the pit. Aran led the way, as an army of guards began storming after them.

"Stop them!" cried a senior member of the soldiers.

It wasn't until Aran was making his way across the great pit that he realised just how enormous this grand stage was. The queen and Miel were still but a pair of small dots in a wide, open space. The boy could see the twinkle of his mother's sword in the far distance, as it was slowly being passed from queen to Brenin.

Aran's cries of warning were drowned out by the roaring of spectators.

Just as Aran and his crew had almost reached their target, they were circled by a pack of mounted Brenin and herded together like a flock of sheep. Dozens of swords were pointed towards them; resistance was useless.

"You are all under arrest!" called the lead Brenin. The pirates looked back at each other and groaned.

"But she's going to kill him!" cried Aran, as his hands were bound with iron cuffs.

He looked on helplessly, as Miel took the queen's sword and knelt down before her. The monarch lowered her vulnerable head.

To Aran's horror, the new champion lifted the weapon high

into the air and slammed it straight back down with a powerful jolt.

The pirates' mouths all dropped open in shock.

The tip of the sword was now lodged into the dry sand, and Miel had lowered to her knees. She bowed her head, as the queen stood up to bless it.

Aran couldn't believe his eyes. Not only had she betrayed Drathion, but she had made a complete fool out of him in the process. As relieved as he was that his mother was still alive, the thought that this cold-blooded young woman was now her trusted soldier terrified him even more.

The Ogofinia burst into a wave of cheers. Their queen took back her sword and marched out towards the gate.

Miel turned to see Aran and his band of pirates. She let out an amused smile and wandered over.

Her fellow Brenin listened with great interest, as she made an announcement to them that would seal the group's fate: "I know these men. They are traitors and enemies of the crown. As you can see, they were attempting to assassinate the queen herself."

Cries of protest erupted from the group of pirates.

"She's talking nonsense!" cried Larson.

"Silence, traitor!" barked a nearby soldier, who lifted up the handle of his sword and bashed it against the back of Larson's head. "Who would you have us believe? The words of a thieving pirate — or the words of our new Brenin!"

The other pirates gulped.

"They are to be arrested for treason," continued Miel. "A life sentence would be far too kind."

Aran kicked and wriggled, as his heels were dragged along the sand.

"That's the future king you're mishandling!" cried Larson.

The guards laughed.

"And who might you be?" asked the soldier pushing him along. "His future queen?"

More chuckles followed.

"Tell them, Aran!" called Phen. "Tell them they're in the company of royalty."

But Aran didn't say a word. He knew it would make no difference. The queen had already returned to the seclusion of her royal podium. Aran was now a convicted criminal — and nobody listened to *them*.

Pushing him from behind was the guard who Simlee had punched in the face only moments earlier. Unsurprisingly, he was now taking an unusual amount of pleasure in the performance of his duties. He joined in the laughter and made a brief announcement before they made their way out from the Ogofinia: "The only future this boy will ever have is darkness."

28

THE SIXTH PRISONER

T he word darkness had been correct; the cells of Calon Prison had brought little hope of sunlight.

Aran sat against the damp wall of his new accommodation. Through the iron bars, he could see a line of holding cells up ahead. Each pirate had their own share of minimal space, and he could hear their grumblings from the other side of the hallway.

"You've got us into a right big hole here, lad," said Simlee, his tattooed forearm curling around the bars of his cell like a hungry snake.

"Something you're quite used to I'm sure," said Wettman from the cell beside him. "If anyone knows more about hitting rock bottom it's you."

Simlee let out a deep groan. He bumped his own forehead against the reinforced iron with a loud clunk.

"Gods above..." he muttered. "Tell me I'm not doomed to listen to your incessant whining for the rest of eternity. I'd rather suffer the death penalty."

"I'd say the death penalty is looking highly likely," said the captain. "Treason comes at a hefty price."

"Glad you're here to confirm all that for us," said Simlee. "Fingers crossed then."

The bickering continued long into the night. Both men were equally stubborn, and the sound of their voices gave Aran the last morsel of comfort he had left. These pirates had been closer to a family than his own relatives. He imagined his blood relatives feasting away in some great dining hall at that very same moment.

The back-and-forth arguments sent Aran into a deep sleep. When he next opened his eyes, he slammed himself back against the stone wall. The face now peering back at him through the rusted bars sent a violent jolt through the pit of his stomach.

"I'm pleased to see you haven't forgotten me," said the man outside his cell. "Because I have not forgotten *you*."

Standing before him, in his magnificent Brenin armour, was Sir Ruegon. He studied the boy's horrified face as though he had been waiting for this moment for quite some time.

"Don't look so surprised," the knight said. "It was only going to be a matter of time before we crossed paths again."

The cell door swung open. Two guardsmen stormed in and dragged Aran to his feet. His legs had turned to jelly, and it took both men to force him outside into the narrow hallway.

"Where are you taking me?" asked Aran, kicking out his legs as they gradually came to life.

"Somewhere with a little more privacy," said Ruegon. He looked around at the gawking pirates. "We have a lot to catch up on."

They headed down a series of long passageways. For Aran, it was the longest walk of his life. The hollow sound of Ruegon's heavy footsteps only increased his feeling of dread. Prisoners watched them pass by with lifeless expressions, as if they were witnessing someone on the morning of their execution. Time and place were both nonexistent within these damp walls.

Up ahead, at the end of the dingy hallway, was a metal door. Its hinges screamed out in protest, as a guard swung it open with all his strength. They were only a few cells back from the open doorway when one of the prisoners came charging against the bars. He appeared to be a man who had truly lost his mind after months of darkness and solitude. The impact of him hitting the iron cage caused Aran to step aside and look away.

"Aran!" cried the prisoner, his voice weak, yet full of emotion.

The boy was startled by the mention of his own name, and if it wasn't for the desperation in the man's cry, he would have ignored the stranger and continued moving forward. Instead, he turned his head to find a familiar pair of wide eyes staring back at him through the darkness. The overgrown hair and wild beard would have made the man impossible to recognise — but this was no ordinary man.

"Uncle Gwail?" The words came flying out from the boy's mouth. The sight of his uncle's malnourished face sent him running towards the cell, much to the protest of the accompanying guards.

Gwail grabbed Aran by the hands. His own were as rough as the boy had remembered. "*Did you find him*?!"

Aran stared back at him and nodded. The panic in Gwail's face completely melted away.

"I knew you would," Gwail said, with a nod. "You were always a good lad."

There was a warmth in the man's eyes that Aran had never seen before. It was a fatherly love, a love that might well have been there all along, even if it hadn't been very well expressed. Gwail's words almost choked him to tears.

Aran leaned in. "He told me everything," he whispered. Gwail squeezed both of his hands and pulled him in close.

"Don't be afraid, Aran," the man said. "Everything will be alright, I promise.

Sir Ruegon witnessed the entire scene with great amusement.

"What a lovely reunion," he said, and turned to his guards with a frown of contempt. "What are you waiting for? We need to keep moving."

Despite his resistance, Aran was dragged away from the cell bars and carried towards the end of the hallway.

"Let the boy go!" cried Gwail "He knows nothing!"

The Brenin paused to turn around.

"Really?" he said with a wry smile. "From what I just heard, he appears to know *everything*."

The enraged prisoner watched them continue towards the heavy door.

"Ruegon!" he roared. "Do what you want with me, but leave the boy out of it! He has done nothing wrong."

Sir Ruegon ignored the cries, which followed them out through the doorway. "There is nothing more I need from you, *Rider*," he muttered in disgust.

On the other side of the metal door were even more corridors. They eventually made their descent down a series of spiralling staircases, until the boy was certain he would never see the light of day again. Once they had completed this maze of underground passageways, they entered into a dimly lit room, a space much larger than any of the prison cells. Chains lined the rotting walls, and in the corner was a table of sharp objects and mysterious tools. There were no windows for prying eyes, and the minimal furniture offered little sign of comfort.

The stench of dampness crawled through Aran's nostrils, as his wrists were handcuffed to the dangling chains.

"Leave us," said Ruegon to his men. The guards nodded and made their way outside. The slamming of a heavy, iron door caused Aran to leap with dread. They were now alone.

Ruagon stepped into the centre of the room and looked around.

"There has been some terrible suffering in this room," said the Brenin. "But that needn't be the case today."

He reached into the small satchel on his lap and pulled out the emlon gauntlet. Aran tugged on his thick chains and felt his body begin to tremble. The instruments on the nearby table made him nauseous.

"You should feel proud," he continued. "There are not many people who have knocked me off my horse and lived to tell the tale."

"We have done nothing wrong!" Aran exploded. "That man out there is innocent!"

He yanked the chains with such force that their hollow crashes echoed around the room.

"No person is innocent," said Ruegon. "Anyone who aligns themselves with a known assassin is as guilty as anyone in this entire prison."

He walked towards him, his face in a dark shadow.

"It is not wise to get in my way, boy," he said. "And that night you did exactly that."

Aran could feel his piercing eyes studying his every reaction. There was a darkness in the man's face that he had not witnessed during their first encounter in Skelbrei Forest. The layers of the Brenin's true self were peeling away before his very eyes.

"I came to that farm of yours to do two things," he continued. "To arrest your uncle, and to retrieve that suit of armour. They were my orders from the queen herself. And because of you, Aran, I failed."

"The queen sent you?" asked Aran in surprise.

"The news of an Emlon Rider posing as a Brenin knight had not been received well. The lies... the deceit... We had been searching for those two assassins for years. Little did we know that one of them was right under our very own noses all along."

His hands clenched tightly around the gauntlet. The joints in his fingers turned white from the anger burning up inside him.

"My queen is a ruthless one. That woman and her family are capable of some terrible things. It's in their blood."

Aran swallowed the largest gulp to have ever slipped down his throat.

"You're lying," he said.

"I've seen everything that goes on behind those castle walls. I have been her trusted council from the moment she took the throne. It was no coincidence her beloved husband did not last long. The queen is a very shrewd woman. She has many secrets, ones that I keep very close to my chest, of course."

Once again, Aran grew tense.

"The queen is building an army. I have shown her what these Emlon Riders are capable of. Soon we will take our revenge. I have been searching long and hard for a way to rid this world of every last one of them. Now we have found a way..."

He slipped his hand into the inside of his cloak and pulled out a sword. It was green in colour, greener than any knife or sword that Aran had ever seen.

"This entire blade is pure emlon," Ruegon announced. "Soon we will have enough weapons to arm all of our Brenin knights."

His last sentence turned Aran cold. He no longer wanted to listen.

Ruegon slipped the gauntlet over his right hand and admired its beauty. He took the sword and carved a giant cross against its smooth surface.

"This sword is made from the very same emlon that Sir Vangarn himself brought back during his famous voyage — right before he was assassinated by the same people you are trying to protect."

He waited for the new revelation to sink in.

"There is still time for you to choose the right side." Sweat poured down Aran's face as Ruegon ran his fingers along the edge of the sharp weapon. "All you need to do is tell me where I can find the rest of that armour."

"The rest?"

"Don't play the fool with me, boy. We've all heard the stories. I'm sure you know exactly what that suit is capable of."

Aran yanked down on the chains.

"I can't!" he cried. "It was stolen from me!"

"You are an even worse liar than your precious uncle," said the knight. "But if you won't tell me willingly, we can always find another way. You will tell me everything I need to know. In this room, everyone always does."

Ruegon lifted up the emlon sword and hovered its sharp tip near the boy's face. The blade began to glow, and Aran could feel its power radiating against his hot cheeks. He pushed back against the wall and braced himself.

The knight took hold of his prisoner's small arm. Just as he was about to do something quite unpleasant, the heavy door on the other side of the room flew open. A flustered looking soldier hurried into the room, sweating and huffing, as he tried to catch his breath.

"Sorry to interrupt, Sir – but we have an emergency," said the guard.

Ruegon turned around with an irritable scowl.

"Can't it wait?" he growled.

The guard hesitated with his response, knowing full well that it would only anger his superior even more.

"I wish it could, Sir," he said. "But we have an intruder."

"An intruder?" asked the Brenin. "This is a *prison*! People are normally trying to escape – not break in!"

"He's already made it into the southern wing."

"Then deal with him!" shouted the Brenin. "There are more than enough men to neutralise a single intruder."

"This person is different, Sir," said the guard. "He's been slicing through guards as though they were loaves of bread. He doesn't fight like any man I've ever seen."

Aran felt a tingle of hope. He prayed that his own suspicions were true, as unlikely as they might have been.

"Please, Sir, we don't have much time. He'll be here any –"

Before the guard could even finish his last sentence, he was pulled back through the open doorway. A few crashes later, he came flying back into the room and dropped down into a sorry heap.

Aran's heart raced with excitement, as his chances of escape had dramatically increased. The man now standing in the open doorway was Wyn Drathion.

Sir Ruegon was far less pleased.

"You think you can just march straight in here and walk out alive?" he cried out.

The Emlon Rider merely shrugged. He was covered from head to foot in his green armour. Aran had seen the various pieces before, only this was the first time he had witnessed them covering an entire human body.

"At my age, staying alive is less of a priority," said Drathion. "Nothing is ever guaranteed."

He lifted up his steel sword and pointed it towards the Brenin's head.

"But I can guarantee one thing," he continued. "I will live longer than you will."

Ruegon seemed cautious. He took the emlon sword and

sliced it through his prisoner's chains. Aran's moment of freedom did not last long, as the Brenin grabbed him by the neck and held him in close.

"Don't you know who I am?!" Ruegon cried.

Drathion stepped towards him with a cold stare.

"I know exactly who you are," said the Rider. "Your father, Sir Vangarn, had that exact same temper when he was cornered."

Ruegon's bloodshot eyes widened. In a burst of rage, he lifted up the green sword and went charging towards him. Before he had even reached his target, the weapon charged itself up into a blinding glow, a burst of uncontrollable energy that surprised even its owner.

He struck his opponent in an almighty explosion of green light, sending both men hurling back towards opposite ends of the room. The sheer force of the hard impact had been enough to daze even the attacker, and the floored Brenin was now flat on his back in a confused state.

A wounded Drathion sat up to reveal a large, gaping hole in the middle of his breastplate. The emlon sword had broken through, cracking open what many had presumed to be an inde-structible wall of armour. He groaned in agony as the damage to his body began to take effect.

Aran looked over to see that the green sword was now lying in the middle of the room, still glowing from the surge of power. Sir Ruegon cried out in his groggy state, as he saw the boy go running to retrieve it. The knight stumbled to his feet to find his recently forged blade now pointing back towards him.

"Don't be such a fool, boy," he told him. "Do you really think some stableboy like you has what it takes to stop a Brenin?"

Aran clutched the sword with both hands. It trembled in front of his terrified face, lighting up the entire room with its green shine. He could feel the emlon's energy, as he had done with the gauntlet, only this new power felt beyond the realms of anything he had experienced before. He stood in front of Drathion, determined not to let the Brenin inflict any further damage on an already defeated opponent.

Sir Ruegon smiled. He could feel the boy's terror from the other side of the room and began walking towards him with confident strides.

"Stay back!" Aran cried.

The Brenin continued his march. "You don't have it in you, lad. This war is inevitable. Hand me the sword and let me finish what needs to be done."

In a flash of anger, the boy lifted up his sword and felt a burst of energy flowing through his entire body. The emlon lit up into a beacon of bright light. With one enormous swing, he sent a bolt of green lightning crashing down against the man's legs.

Aran slowly opened his eyes to see the knight rolling around on the floor in pain.

"My legs!" he cried. "I can't feel my legs!"

The boy remained frozen in position, still stunned by what had just happened, until a large hand clutched his shoulder.

"Come along," said Drathion's voice. "We need to leave."

Aran did not need telling twice. He had no desire to remain in that room any longer than he had to.

Although reluctant at first, the outlaw took hold of the sword and held it as if it were burning with a mysterious and evil power.

As they approached the doorway, Aran spotted the emlon gauntlet lying on the ground. He greeted it like an old friend and picked it up.

They both headed back up the spiralling staircase. Drathion kicked into action once again, swiping his new weapon towards a couple of oncoming guards. After both men were sent rolling down the stone steps, he took a moment to catch his breath. The man did not look well.

"Are you alright?" asked Aran.

Drathion shook away his pain and nodded.

"If I were a younger man, I'd be just fine," he said. "But alas, I am not."

He led the way through into the next passageway. More guards appeared and more guards were swiftly taken care of. Drathion was nowhere near his physical peak, but these common foot soldiers caused little obstruction. The real challenge would come once they had made it outside, which felt a very long way off from the gloomy bowels of the prison.

They burst through a metal door, before pausing at a familiar looking prison cell. Drathion lifted up the emlon sword and smashed it against the giant lock on the cell door. The blade cut through it with perfect ease, and the prisoner inside was soon free to escape.

"It appears that we are now even, brother," said a grateful Gwail.

The two men stared at each other for a moment, embracing the countless years since their last encounter. There was clearly a lot of history between these two brothers, and, for a split second, they almost looked pleased to see one another.

"You and I will never be even," replied Drathion.

Gwail gave his honesty a respectful nod, before continuing the great dash for the outside world.

Aran and his two Drathions hurried around the next corner. They were met with a choice of two separate passageways; one going left, and the other heading right.

"The way out is down here," said Gwail, who immediately headed right.

Aran paused. He had seen the left passage before.

"There's something I must do before we leave," he said.

Gwail turned around to see him scurrying away down the opposite path.

"Aran!" he called. "We don't have time!"

The two men looked at each other with disapproving frowns.

In his mad charge, Aran darted past a series of occupied cells. The prisoners inside called out with long, heavy groans and many reached out to grab him as he ran past. He weaved away from the lines of clawing hands, until he finally reached the cells he had been looking for.

"You must be joking..." said Simlee in disbelief, who was sitting back against his iron bars. "Why am I always the one stuck inside a cage whenever I'm with you?"

Aran squeezed the bars as if he wanted to rip them apart with his bare hands.

"I've come to get you all out of here," said Aran.

"Oh, aye?" asked Simlee. "And how do you plan on doing that? Got a set of keys on you?"

Aran hesitated. It suddenly occurred to him that he hadn't thought this part through. He tried desperately to think of a solution, until he was pushed aside by a man with an unusual sword.

A confused Wettman peered through the narrow gaps of the bars next door and gazed at the green armour. "Wait, isn't that – "

Wettman's words were drowned out by the sound of bashing metal. Sparks sprayed out into the air, as the lock on Simlee's door was pummelled by an emlon blade. The impact from Drathion and his reinforced sword dented the large hole until it was no longer recognisable. With a final smash, the door swung open.

"Now *that's* a sword!" cried Simlee, leaping out of his cell with a merry jiggle.

Drathion marched over to the other cells, and, one by one, he struck his new weapon against each of the giant locks. He swiped and cursed, like a child in an uncontrollable tantrum.

"We really don't have time for this," he grumbled.

Each pirate cheered with joy as his cell door was flung open.

They all poured out like a group of excitable birds. In all the commotion, they had barely noticed the arrival of another man. Gwail looked around at the group of merry pirates and shook his head.

"You have made some interesting friends, Aran."

"Wait, you idiots!" Drathion roared. Larson and Phen halted in mid-sprint and turned around. "The way out is *this* way."

Drathion pointed his sword towards the opposite side of the hallway, causing both men to immediately change direction.

The group stormed through the southern wing, up and down stairwells, in and around cell blocks, and straight into a series of incoming guards.

Drathion took these men down as if he were mowing through a line of grass. Soldiers went flying to their backs and their swords scattered across the floor. In a bid to provide their new guide with some much needed backup, each pirate picked up their own stray weapon.

The more corners they turned, the more it became clear that the two brothers were leading them deeper into the bloated belly of the great prison.

"Are you sure this is the right way?" asked Wettman, as he descended yet another flight of stairs.

"Trust me," said Gwail. "I know this place like the back of my hand."

"Well I'd rather trust *your* hand," said Larson. He pointed towards Drathion. "He's only got the one!"

After leaping down the final hurdle of stone steps, they came across a narrow river. Its murky waters flowed straight towards a curved tunnel up ahead, and the stench of rotting sewage could not be denied.

A line of boats, normally used for escorting prisoners to their new homes, were bobbing in the nearby docking area.

Drathion hopped straight into the first watercraft and looked up at a line of apprehensive faces.

"Why do you all look so worried?" he asked the crew. "You're all pirates, aren't you? They're just boats!"

He picked up a paddle and threw it towards Wettman.

The group took a reluctant look at each other and dived off the platform to join him.

"I've got no problem with a spot of rowing," said Simlee. "I just normally like to see where I'm going."

"Then you're not going to like this next bit," said Gwail, with a heave of his own paddle.

With at least two men in each boat, the seven of them rowed towards the great mouth up ahead. Within seconds they had entered into a wall of pitch blackness, swallowed whole by the tunnel's long throat. All they could do now was row.

Phen, the tallest of the group, cried out in a burst of pain as he bashed his head against the low ceiling. The loud shriek echoed throughout the cobbled walls. The sound of squeaking rats gave Aran a nasty shudder, knowing that they were probably only inches away from his own face. He could hear the commotion of their escape causing a stir in the levels above, as more guards charged down the passageways to the wailing of excited prisoners.

Just as it began to feel as though the tunnel would never end, a shred of light pierced through the darkness like a beacon of hope.

They all looked up. Coming towards them was another small docking area, only this time it featured a giant gate that loomed up ahead, burying itself in the turbulent water. On the other side was the teasing glow of a morning sun, which peeped through the small, rectangular holes like prying eyes.

Guards swarmed out onto the ledges of the docking area, waving their swords in an ensemble of angry cursing.

"The gate's closed," said Wettman. "*Now* what are we supposed to do?"

"We need two people to man those levers," said Gwail, pointing towards the giant handles on either side of the river.

Simlee and Wettman looked at each other and raised their swords.

"Ready then, sunshine?" asked Simlee. "I'll race you."

They both leapt out of their boat and climbed up onto their own separate banks. With a twirl of their weapons, both men began charging through a series of guards, whilst knocking most of them down into the water.

The others did their best to protect the three boats, as the floating soldiers surrounded them like a sea of hungry monsters.

Simlee reached his platform merely seconds before the exhausted captain. He threw up his arms in celebration.

"You're only as young as you feel, eh?" he called out. "You must be feeling like an old fool, lad!"

He had barely finished his heckle when an angry guard tackled him from behind. Simlee wrestled with his aggressor and bashed him in the head with the handle of his sword.

"You think this is a game?" asked Wettman, who sent two of his own attackers flying off the platform.

"Life is but a game, my dear!" said Simlee, swinging his sword towards a soldier's fortified head. "And that man just lost!"

Wettman ignored the cackles and began yanking at the lever in front of him in a frantic burst.

"Start turning!" he cried, thrusting his body up and down.

Simlee soon joined in, swinging his own lever like an overpowered mechanical toy.

Down below, Drathion and his pirates continued to fight off the onslaught of furious guards. Aran looked up to see the gate finally begin to rise. Its unauthorised operators tugged and pushed, putting everything they had left into this last hope of escape.

More guards pounded their way down the stairwells on either side of the river and surrounded the platforms with their armoured scalps and raised swords.

"That will have to do!" called Simlee.

Wettman let go of his lever and looked down at the line of soldiers heading towards him. They both dived towards the river in one, simultaneous leap and plummeted into Gwail's boat with a heavy crash. Their own boat had long capsized, and it was now being salvaged by the more accomplished swimmers among the prison guards.

The gate had been raised up a good eight feet above the water, however, it was now making its way straight back down again at an increasing rate.

"Close the gate!" shouted one of the guards.

The two boats began making their way towards the narrowing gap, all whilst the levers on either side were being pumped in a mad frenzy.

Every member of the escape party was now paddling for dear life, as the spiking edges of this solid structure came closer with every second. They all threw themselves flat against their stomachs, until their faces were squashed firmly against the limited deck space.

With only inches to spare, the boats snuck underneath the gate just in the nick of time.

When it came time for the men to stand up again, the small exit was nowhere to be seen. The pirates all let out an exhilarated howl, hugging each other like giddy school children. Even the frosty pairing of Simlee and Wettman had found themselves embraced in a brief display of physical affection.

As they drifted away from the lower regions of the great dungeon, Simlee cupped his mouth and called over to Aran's boat: "You know where we are now, boy?" He had a beaming smile on his face.

Aran looked around to see that they were cruising along a great river. The prison, it had turned out, was built upon a small island in the middle of its flowing centre. The morning sun gave the formidable structure a strange beauty. Even so, it was much easier to admire this impressive piece of architecture from the outside.

"We're on the *River Aran*!" cried Simlee.

The current was proving to be quite a force to be reckoned with, and it required every paddle they had left to steer themselves along.

"Is he going to chip in, or what?" asked Larson, slashing into the water like a madman. He pointed towards Drathion, who was now lying at the back of his boat with a sedated look on his face.

"I think he's done more than enough, don't you?" snapped Phen.

Aran sat himself down beside the exhausted looking Rider. He had known something wasn't right ever since the altercation with Sir Ruegon.

Drathion clutched the side of his torso. Beside his hand was the enormous hole in his pierced armour. The boy reached inside and let out a short gasp.

"You've been wounded!" Aran cried.

Drathion looked back at him in a sleepy daze.

"Looks like I'm not as quick as I used to be," he said.

"Why did you come to save us?" asked Aran.

Drathion did his best to hide the pain. "Because I always knew that the Brenin were looking for more than just the arrest of an old outlaw. I couldn't risk them finding the rest of that armour. Ruegon knew you had the knowledge and he would have sucked it out of you, one way or another."

He looked down at the emlon sword.

"Now I can see what they have been planning all along. The future of Emlon depends on you now, boy," he said. "I was there, in the Ogofinia. I watched you run into that pit to save a woman you had never even met, a woman whose death would make you the rightful successor to the crown of Morwallia. And yet, you rushed in to defend her. Such loyalty is rare in this world."

His expression grew dark.

"Miel had become like a daughter. I always knew, deep down, that she would betray me in the end. Just not so soon... She was clouded by her own motives. But you are different, Aran. I can see it in your eyes. You have the blood of two kingdoms coursing through your veins. You are both Morwallian royalty and the son of an Emlon Rider. There aren't many who can claim that."

Gwail stood tall in the boat up ahead. Although he was too far ahead to hear the conversation, he knew it was a meaningful one. He had seen the state of his brother during their final escape; the broken armour, the look on his face. He could sense that the end was near.

"If anyone can prevent this war, it is someone like you, Aran," Drathion croaked. His strength was waning with every sentence.

"How am I supposed to stop a *war*?" asked Aran.

Drathion took in a long breath and looked down at the emlon sword in his hand.

"You must go to Emlon," he said. "Both you and my brother. My armour will guide the way."

He lifted up the green sword that continued to trouble him.

"They need to know what's coming," he said. "Ruegon and his Brenin will find a way to get there. And when they do, the people of Emlon must be prepared."

Aran took hold of the weapon as if he had been handed a

scalding-hot poker tool. It was light in weight, just like the emlon armour.

Drathion sat back and looked up at the morning sky; a great weight had been lifted from his shoulders. The fate of his home-land was no longer in his own hands. There was nothing more he could do. He had committed his entire life to the service of his kingdom, and, now, his service had finally come to an end.

Aran watched as the Emlon Rider closed his eyes for the last time. His body loosened, and his face looked peaceful.

Aran looked down at the emlon gauntlet. The deep scratches that Ruegon had so easily carved out with the tip of his sword filled him with both sorrow and dread. When news of Drathion's death reached the second boat, none of them said a word for quite some time, which was a rare achievement for this group.

A silent Gwail sat in the corner of his boat, deep in his own thoughts. He had already mourned the loss of his brother many years ago, or, at least, the Wyn Drathion he had once known. This did not make his physical passing any easier, and he had been surprised by the level of emotion he was still carrying.

"We should bury him when we reach the coast," Aran announced, when the two boats were finally along side each other.

Gwail nodded in agreement. Wettman was a little more surprised.

"The coast?" asked the captain. "You have a destination in mind?"

Aran prepared himself for the answer.

"We shall head to the Kingdom of Emlon," the boy said.

Silence struck the two boats, once more. Wettman smiled.

"Well, we do have a crew," he said.

"And a captain," added Aran.

Simlee looked at them both with a heavy shrug.

"Very well," he said. "We might as well find out, once and for all, whether this Emlon place really does exist."

"It does exist," said Gwail. "I will show you myself."

"The more the merrier!" Simlee cried out, before turning to face the serious looking man beside him. "I hope you're more fun than you look."

"So you're definitely coming with us?" asked Aran, who had failed to hide his excitement.

"On one condition." Simlee said, and pointed to the gauntlet. "I want my own suit of invincible armour."

Aran smiled.

"I don't know about that," said Wettman. "You'll have a hard time finding a size that'll fit a waist like yours, old man."

He tapped Simlee on the belly. The others laughed at his furious expression.

The two boats continued their way down the river. Calon loomed behind them and eclipsed the morning sun. Aran turned around to see the city's sharp, pointed spires gradually shrinking away. He took one last look at the great capital, hoping that it would not be too long before he would get to see it again. For he knew that, someday, the stableboy from Galamere would make his return.

THANK YOU FOR READING

We hope you enjoyed this book. Make sure to head to the website link below to join the P. L. Handley author e-mailing list. This newsletter will give you all the latest updates on current and future releases.

www.plhandley.com

Finally, please feel free to leave a short review on either Amazon or Goodreads. Doing so will be a huge help in introducing other new readers to this book.

Printed in Great Britain
by Amazon

82762568R00181